Seaside Sweets

Seaside Sweets

Love Along Hwy 30A
Book One

Melissa Chambers

Perry Evans Press

ISBN: 978-1-7324156-0-7

Edited by Trish Milburn
Cover image from depositphotos
Formatting by Polgarus Studio

melissachambers.com

Also by Melissa Chambers

For all of those who love South Walton, and for those of you who've never been and just don't know you love it yet!

Chapter One

Seanna wasn't exactly running away, but the opportunity to hide at her favorite aunt's beachside bungalow was way more appealing than spending another second in the same house as her piece of crap ex-fiancé. When Seanna had rung Cassidy just yesterday, thankfully her aunt only focused on the logistics of getting Seanna from Nashville to the dream world of Seaside, Florida and not on asking why she needed to get away.

As she cruised through town on her way to Cassidy's place, the community around her popped in pastels, mod art galleries, and artisanal eateries with the Gulf of Mexico roaring to the shore in the background, causing her to question why she hadn't escaped from her ridiculous life sooner. Cassidy's street, Seagull Lane, showcased houses colored in mint green, lavender, and peach, all trimmed in white featuring picket fences and palm trees. As she connected Cassidy's street address with a baby blue cottage, she smiled as she wheeled into the drive. She popped the trunk to her Honda Civic, shouldered a couple of bags, and then headed up the cobblestone walk.

She needed a hug from Cassidy like a supermodel needed a hamburger. Seanna had yet to explain to her aunt or anyone else not only why her engagement was over, but that it had ended at all. She'd been holding this secret for nine months. The lie should have gotten easier by now, but it hadn't, and Cassidy was no fool.

Seanna rang the bell, and then held her arms out wide to give Cassidy a smile at first sight. But when the door opened, a man about a head taller than her stood there in a pair of shorts and no shirt, shaggy hair dripping wet. Mimicking her, he held his hands out to his sides. "I thought a handshake was more appropriate, but I'm good with a hug if you are."

Stupefied by his lean body with just enough muscle to make her sweat and crystal blue eyes that sucked her in like a tornado, she took a step backward almost teetering off the porch. Holy crap he was hot. Wait. She hated men now.

She righted herself and peered around him. "I'm sorry. I must have the wrong house. I'm looking for—"

"Cassidy Anderson?" he asked.

She lowered her chin. "Yeah."

"You're in the right place. Come in."

He reached for her bag and she retracted instinctively, causing a frown to form on his face. She had to remind herself that all men were not thieves and scoundrels.

"Sorry," he said. "I didn't mean to answer the door without a shirt. I was actually just getting ready to grab one, but I wasn't sure how long you'd been standing there. I just got out of the shower. That bell doesn't work."

She relaxed and relinquished the bag to him. "Thank you."

He pointed to a room. "This one's yours. Cassidy had me paint it a few months back. I hope you like blue." A phone buzzed in the man's pocket, and he pulled it out. "It's your aunt. She wants to know if you're here. Says she's been calling and texting but can't reach you."

Seanna had turned the stupid thing off. Jason had started texting her somewhere around Birmingham with his whiny crap. Could they talk? He needed to explain. He'd just slipped up this one time. It wasn't what she thought. Blah, blah, blah.

She pulled her phone out of her purse and powered it back on. She rolled her eyes as the notifications filled her screen. A few from Cassidy, but a million from Jason. She tossed the phone back down inside her purse with a little more gusto than she meant to.

He tilted his head to the side. "Should I ask?" His piercing blue eyes beamed through her, and a little spark ignited in her chest.

She blew it out, resting her hands on her hips. "Bad day. So who are you?"

He closed the distance between them, offering a hand. "Blake Evans. I'm a friend of your aunt."

The light bulb went off above Seanna's head. *Go, Aunt Cassidy.* She was turning forty-eight this year, and this guy was, what, thirty? Thirty-five, tops. Not that Cassidy wasn't gorgeous. Regal but rugged, she could have easily strutted down a runway in her day rather than volunteering in the Peace Corps. She'd never known Cassidy to date younger men. In fact, she'd usually liked them a little older. But geez, a guy who looked like that could change most girls' tastes.

Seanna shook his hand. "All right." She walked around,

taking in the shabby chic, beach decor. Cassidy had been renting a condo when Seanna had visited last. What was that, four years ago? It was before she'd gotten the job she'd just been booted from. She didn't realize it'd been that long since she'd been here for a visit. Cassidy usually came to Nashville for a little while in January when she closed the shop for the season.

"So did you two buy this place together?" she asked.

He gave her a quizzical glance. "No. It's all your aunt's."

"I take it I'll be seeing you quite a bit around here."

He walked into the bathroom and grabbed a shirt from a bag on the sink. "Actually, you will. I work for your aunt. Not full-time, but I'm in and out a lot."

An employee. How scandalous of her aunt. "At the bakery?" She could imagine him hauling around hundred-pound bags of flour, muscles bulging through his white T-shirt. There was something about a man in a plain, white T-shirt and jeans that made Seanna's insides turn into hot molten fudge sauce.

"Mostly. I'm a handyman," he said. "I work for a lot of businesses in the area." He pointed toward her car. "Do you have anything else out there?"

She had to look away. She couldn't believe how attractive this guy was, and he belonged to her aunt. Even if he didn't, it wasn't like she was in any sort of position to be dating. She didn't plan on doing that until sometime around mid-century, and even that timeline was iffy.

"No, I'm not staying long. But thanks for the help," she said.

"Sure." He walked through the doorway and down the steps toward a pickup truck parked on the street. He turned around. "I hope your bad day gets better."

She leaned against the doorframe. "It's actually more like a bad year."

"Well, in that case, I hope your year gets better. Anything I can do?" He slipped her a sideways smile that was likely to have caused a few thousand pairs of panties to drop to the ground.

"Oh, no. Let's just say I won't be dating another man until the cows come home."

He took a few steps backward. "The cows? Wow. That's pretty serious."

She rested a hand on her hip. "Men suck."

"Sometimes that's not a bad thing." He widened his smile as he turned around and headed for his truck.

Man alive. Seanna's luck with men may be sketchy, but her aunt was doing just fine.

Blake tossed his keys on the kitchen table as Sadie mowed him down. He really needed to train her not to jump on him, but he was a sucker for her hugs. He pulled a bottle of beer out of the refrigerator and peered around for something to eat. It wasn't like he was bound to find anything. He hadn't cooked in a week. He plopped down on the couch, and Sadie followed, resting her head in his lap as he stroked her fur. He started flipping channels, but he couldn't focus on television.

The picture Cassidy had shown him of her niece had not done her justice. Seanna was cute in the close-up shot—shoulder-length hair, a wavy mix of brunette and blond highlights, hazel eyes, no make-up…not that she needed it. But standing in front of Blake in Cassidy's house she had come to life.

Something else had been missing from the picture. He was trying not to stare, but holy shit. He was only a human man. She wore a V-neck T-shirt with the tip of her cleavage peeking out. Curves in all the right places, even in jeans and a T-shirt her body looked like it belonged to a sixties pinup model.

He snapped out of it, reality swarming in. This woman was off limits for more reasons than he could count. He'd known it before she arrived, and certainly nothing had changed. Apparently her engagement was off—not that a fiancé was the only reason he couldn't move in on this girl. Blake had happened to be there when Seanna made the call to Cassidy about coming to Seaside for an immediate visit. Cassidy had been confused and not just a little worried.

Blake walked over to his computer and checked his email—a message from Dr. Kevin Jacobs, the Emergency Department Director at the hospital in Atlanta. As much as he liked and appreciated Kevin, he couldn't help the churn in his gut at the sight of his name and of the reminder of the life Blake had worked so hard to put behind him the past three years. He double-clicked on it.

> *What's up, man? Been a few months since I've talked to you. It's been a year since I moved to Kansas City, but I swear it feels like a month.*
>
> *I assume you're still hammering nails and walking people's dogs down there at the beach, huh? I think it's time we changed that. Don't you?*
>
> *Let's talk. Call me when you get a minute. I'm off a full twenty-four hours on Sunday. Call me then.*

A change. That meant Kevin wanted to get Blake back to practicing medicine. He wasn't ready for that change...not now, and maybe not ever.

Chapter Two

Seanna had just finished unpacking when she heard the front door open. She peeked around the corner and smiled. Cassidy with her supermodel height and her out-of-control curls seemed an unlikely candidate for relation to Seanna's 5'4", fluffy frame. Seanna had to work for her waves, where Cassidy's curls refused to be tamed. Seanna took her favorite aunt into her arms and inhaled sweet cakes and sugary frosting.

Cassidy pulled away and looked her up and down. "Oh, my goodness. I can't tell you how wonderful it is to see you, sweetheart."

Seanna gave a relieved huff. "Oh my God, Cass. You have no idea."

Cassidy pulled Seanna down on the couch, eyeing her. "So, you know I'm not going to butt into your business, but I do need to know if you're okay."

Seanna nodded. "I'm fine. Really." Cassidy tilted her head to the side and lifted an eyebrow. The humiliation of all Seanna had been through the past year washed over her like a churning stomach virus. Her aunt was such a strong, independent woman. Seanna had always wanted to *be* her when she grew up. But even though Seanna was pushing thirty, right off a cliff, she felt like a silly sixteen-year-old. Make that six-year-old. Seanna actually made smarter decisions when she was sixteen than she was making now. Besides, she couldn't tell Cassidy yet…not until she got another payment under her belt. She didn't want her aunt trying to save the day with a loan.

"I'll tell you everything," Seanna said. "I promise. Right now, I just want to *not* think about it. Is that okay?"

Cassidy smiled, worry creasing her brow. "Okay. But when you're ready—"

"I'll be ready soon. I promise."

"So how long are you going to stay?" Cassidy asked.

Seanna squinted apologetically. "Until I get a job interview back home?"

"You quit your job? You love that job."

She'd worked her behind off at that job for four years. Her boss, Phillip, had brought her to job sites with him any chance he got, teaching her how to be a project manager, readying her for her career. And now, because of her piece of crap ex-fiancé, he thought she was a thief.

"Something like that. I'm hitting the online job sites in the morning."

"You're here. You might as well take a break. Lay on a blanket on the beach for a day."

Seanna couldn't afford to take a break. She was paying a hefty monthly rent for an apartment she had leased that her ex-fiancé refused to vacate. December. If she could just get to December, she would be rid of her apartment and of him for good.

Cassidy nudged her. "You stay here too long and you won't want to go back to Nashville. That's what happened to me."

The idea had definitely crossed Seanna's mind. But Jason had humiliated her professionally. She wasn't one to run from her problems...at least not in a permanent way. She would show her boss and everyone else that she was not going to tuck her tail between her legs and disappear. She wanted her life back. Through this hell she'd been in with Jason, she'd lost her friends, her financial stability, and even her job. She was not about to start over anywhere but where she belonged...in Nashville.

"I'm sure. But I've got to get back home...soon," Seanna said.

"Well, you're welcome here as long as you need or want to be here. You know that."

"I do. Thank you."

"So...the wedding?"

A fresh wash of humiliation flooded Seanna's chest. The wedding had been off for a good nine months now, but she hadn't been able to tell anyone. The circumstances were too complicated. But it was time to stop hiding, stop covering the boiling pot that was her relationship with her ex. She shook her head, eyes trained on her aunt.

Cassidy nodded understanding. "You haven't told your mom anything yet, have you?"

"No, why?"

"Because she called this afternoon wanting to know when we could talk about the wedding cake."

Seanna rested her head on the back of the couch. "I'm going to tell her."

"Sooner rather than later, I hope. You know I'm a terrible liar. And nobody knows that better than your mom."

"I know. I'll call her tomorrow," Seanna said.

"Thank you. So you met Blake earlier?"

Seanna sat up straight. "Oh, my gosh." She poked her aunt in her side. "You dawg."

Cassidy's eyebrows rose. "Excuse me?"

"Blake," Seanna said.

"What about him?" Cassidy asked, faking innocence. Nice try.

"What about him?" Seanna mocked. "He's gorgeous."

"Oh, well, I guess so. If you like that type."

"You mean if you like tall, broad-shouldered, blue-eyed, scruffy-jawed men who work with their hands?"

Cassidy narrowed her gaze. "I'm surprised you're ready to date again, but…"

"Me? What are you talking about?"

Cassidy looked at Seanna out of the corner of her eye. "What are you talking about?"

"Your boyfriend."

Cassidy's face broke wide into a smile, and she busted out in laughter.

"What?" Seanna asked.

"Blake is not my boyfriend."

Seanna couldn't help the jolt of excitement that shot through her belly. "He's not?"

"No. He's like fifteen years younger than me."

"So?"

"So, I usually go for guys older than me."

"I would think you'd make an exception for that guy," Seanna said. "Have you seen his ass?" Cassidy gave a guilty

11

roll of her eyes, and Seanna held out her hands. "Thank you. Have you slept with him?"

"Seanna!"

"I'm serious." She nudged Cassidy in the side with her elbow. "We're both grownups here. You can tell me."

"No, I haven't. He's my friend and co-worker."

Seanna lifted an eyebrow. "He answered the door shirtless and with wet hair. How do you explain that?"

Cassidy thought about it a second. "Oh, yeah, I told him he could shower here before he went home for the night. He re-grouted his own shower this morning. He lives right down the street in Grayton. Cute little house, but just one full bath." Seanna gave her a skeptical look, and Cassidy backhanded Seanna on the thigh. "Come on. Let's get something to eat."

"And drink. I haven't had a chance to properly drown my sorrows."

Cassidy stood up off the couch. "We'll do that, too. We'll figure out how to break the news to your mom that there's not going to be a wedding."

"I think I'm going to need pure grain alcohol for that."

Seanna rolled out of bed, her head surprisingly clear. She'd had three glasses of wine—more than usual but at least they hadn't made it all the way through that second bottle. Must have been the good kind—the hangover-free kind. Spending the past six months footing the bill for all the rent and utilities, she'd all but forgotten what good wine was like.

She opened the refrigerator and found a single bottle of Diet Coke with a red bow around the neck. A Post-It note was attached to the bottle that read, "Enjoy your wallowing."

Swigging the soda, she made her way to the front porch. She folded her legs into her lap and laid her head back on the rocking chair, letting the sun warm her chest while a cool breeze passed by, kissing her toes. She could get used to this life quickly. But this wasn't real. This was an escape, a temporary asylum from the mountain of worry that awaited her back home.

She was dreaming thinking she could take a day to relax. There was no resting when it came to her life. She had no money coming in but plenty going out. And it wasn't like Jason was going to be kicking in any cash. He was desperate, no doubt about it. Probably had thugs threatening to break his kneecaps or worse.

Now she felt guilty. The vicious cycle of living with a gambler was eating her alive. The constant guilt when she tried to stand her ground and exercise tough love always gave way to one last helping hand. There was no way to win…hell, there was no way to exit the game.

Her computer beckoned her. She needed to start applying for jobs. Asking her parents for money was not an option, because they'd help without question. She wasn't about to drag them down into this abyss with her. They lived modestly and were looking at retirement. She wouldn't take even a day of that from them.

She shouldn't have come here—she knew that. But after this last bit Jason pulled, she could not stay one more day in that apartment and there was nowhere else for her to go. She'd been putting on a façade for her family and friends for nine months now, and the pressure and lie of it all had finally taken her down.

She stood without even making the decision to do so. She took a shower, washing Nashville out of her hair, and then dressed in cut-off shorts and a halter top she'd found at a cute boutique in her neighborhood in Nashville back when things like boutique shopping weren't laughable for her.

Resettling herself in the rocking chair on the front porch, she placed her laptop on her legs and pulled up her old resume, the pathetic little thing. It wasn't often that her lack of a college degree got to her. She took a moment to seethe and blame Jason for her situation, but she'd have to quit that nonsense. It wasn't helping her move forward, and it certainly wasn't going to help her find a job.

Parking in front of Cassidy's house, Blake found Seanna sitting in a rocking chair glaring at a computer on her lap. He swallowed hard as he approached the porch, gripping the bag in his hand. Her large breasts were covered with a short, red shirt that tied behind her neck. She had her wavy hair pulled up on top of her head, a few stray strands falling down her cheeks and her neck. Damn, did he want to tug on that tie and see what was underneath that shirt.

She glanced up at him, and then back to her computer without changing her expression. "Did you go to college?" she asked. He stopped, not sure how to answer that question. She looked up from her computer, meeting his gaze. "Sorry. I didn't mean that as a trick question."

He shuffled a little. "Yeah, for a while." He'd been lying about his past for three years, but it never got easier. And now, somehow, lying to her was even harder.

"Did you graduate?" she asked, point-blank. He frowned and gave a weird sort of shake of his head. He should be a better liar by now. She pursed her lips. "Good. I don't feel so bad now."

"You didn't go?" he asked.

"For three years…until I got the brilliant notion to follow my boyfriend to Phoenix."

He hesitated. "Is this the guy that you…" He trailed off, not sure how to continue.

"Oh, God no. This guy was from when I was like twenty." She looked up in thought. "Twenty-one? Anyway, old news. I only think about him when I go to apply for a job and have to list 'some college' instead of 'degree'."

"He's to blame, huh?" he asked.

She chuckled. "No. Unfortunately that burden falls squarely on my shoulders. I'm the dummy who followed the penis, not him." She fingered the mouse pad, her expression impassive.

Blake couldn't help a chuckle. "The penis?"

She let out a frustrated sigh and rested her head on the back of the chair. "Certain silly, young girls follow penises across the country, leaving their banked college hours to wither up and die." She held up a hand like she was waiting to be called on. "Guilty."

He didn't know what to make of her candor. He wasn't used to people who laid all their cards on the table. "How long did you live there?"

"A year and a half. That was how long it took me to resent the heck out of him and my waitressing job at Chili's. It's amazing how quickly the puppy love fades when you're dropping trays of food and getting stiffed on tips by poor college kids. Are you going to sit down?"

He eyed the chair next to her. He could sit, but then he'd want to stay. And he'd be closer to that string that dangled on her neck. "No, I just came by to give you this." He handed her the bag Cassidy had given him.

She peeked inside. "Yum," she said with a waggle of her eyebrows. She pulled out the croissant and took a bite. "Oh, this is fantastic." She dropped the bag on the table next to her and then set her computer beside it. She stood and headed toward the door. "Sit and eat with me. I'm going to grab my Coke. What do you want to drink? I think she has iced tea."

He didn't need to stay. He needed to go for a dozen reasons, none that seemed strong enough to make him walk in the direction of his truck. "That sounds good, thanks."

As she headed into the house, his eyes were drawn to her ass in those jean shorts. She worked curves like no woman he'd ever seen. Her legs were stout but toned with just a touch of muscle working in her calves. Jesus Christ, he'd been way too long without a woman's touch. He was behaving like a horny fifteen-year-old.

He reluctantly sat down in the chair next to hers. What was he doing? Getting to know her? She wasn't here to stay. She'd already made that clear. He needed to drink his damned tea and leave.

She opened the screen door and handed him a glass of iced tea. The chair squeaked as she sat and tugged her bare foot under her leg, the other dangling off the rocker. Her purple-painted toes wiggled as a breeze hit. He hadn't been turned on like this for half a decade.

She handed him a croissant. "So, I've worked out you're not actually dating my aunt."

He pulled a piece off the bread. "You thought I was with your aunt?"

"Why wouldn't I think that? You answered her door with no shirt on."

He huffed a laugh at the idea of him and Cassidy. Not that Cassidy wasn't a beautiful woman, but he didn't see her like that. She was way too good of a friend. He nodded at Seanna's computer. "Are you applying to colleges?"

"No, jobs."

"Down here?" he asked.

"I wish. Back home in Nashville."

"What's wrong with here?" He looked down at his bread, wishing he could learn to keep his mouth shut. He wasn't typically a talker, probably because he forgot how to communicate properly three years ago when his life became a sham.

"Because I'm not willing to settle again. I've been settling since the Phoenix fiasco." She picked at her croissant. "I've worked hard these past four years, built something. I'm not stepping back...not this time." Her playful demeanor turned serious.

"What's your work?" he asked.

"Construction management."

He held back his smile. Why was he surprised? While she was female through and through on the outside, he could just as easily see her with a hardhat and a jackhammer. He let a smile slip through with that thought.

She poked his leg with her toe, which gave his midsection a wiggle. "What's so funny about that?"

He straightened up. "Nothing."

"God, all you penises are the same."

"Now I'm a penis?"

"You have one don't you?" She dropped her gaze to his lap, which gave him a twitch he hoped she didn't notice.

"Last I checked."

"What are they good for, anyway?" she asked. He raised his eyebrows, and she held up a hand. "Don't answer that." She finished off her croissant and drew both her legs up into her chair.

"So is that what you were in school for? Construction management?" he asked.

"Hardly. I was doing sociology. I didn't know what I wanted to do with my life."

"But you figured it out, right? You can go back. Get your degree."

She let out an exhaustive sigh. "I'm getting ready to be thirty."

"So?"

"So it's not that simple. I don't have—" She stopped herself. "Nothing. Sorry." She fidgeted in her seat.

"You don't have what?" he asked.

She held up both hands. "I'm over-sharing. It's not your problem."

He sat silent for a few minutes while he ate the rest of his croissant. She rocked and stared at the slit of ocean peeking through the houses on the cliff. He wanted to dig in, talk her through whatever was holding her back from finishing college. Time? Money? Interest? Age?

But digging into her life meant getting to know her, getting close to her. He was already painfully aware of his physical attraction to her. That was as far as this needed to go.

He stood and wiped his hands off on the back of his pants. "You don't strike me as someone who lets a little thing like a lack of a degree get in her way. I'm sure you'll figure it out." He nodded at the computer, and then met her gaze. "Good luck on your job applications."

She tilted her head to the side, her brow slightly furrowed, and then she smiled genuinely. "Thanks."

His heart clenched. With a smile like that, no, it wouldn't take long at all to get hooked.

Chapter Three

Something about Blake stuck with Seanna and wouldn't leave her. He was good-looking...okay, gorgeous. But that wasn't it. Sure, his full, kissable lips were part of it. She wasn't interested in dating at the moment, but she wasn't dead inside. She hadn't been kissed in nine months. If being kissed properly counted, it'd been way longer than that. She'd have to learn to ignore those lips. There was something mysterious about him that left her wanting to know more. He had this strong, silent type thing going on that made him not only sexy but interesting.

She ran her hand through her hair. She had to focus, get at least five resumes sent before lunch. That had been the goal she'd promised herself.

Six job applications later, her stomach begged for more food. The croissant had only gone so far, and Seanna was an eater. She found Cassidy's bike in the garage and hopped on, deciding to make her way to Cassidy's shop where she was certain to find food. Rounding the corner onto 30A, an aqua and pastel pink, retro-looking sign boasting the name of Cassidy's shop, Seaside Sweets, came into view. She chained her bike to the rack out front.

As she opened the door the aroma of fresh-baked cinnamon rolls wafted up to her like a hug from Grandma. She soaked in the smell as a thin man at the front counter whipped around. He turned to Cassidy with a grin. "This is her, isn't it?" Cassidy nodded confirmation with a smile. "She's beautiful." He backhanded Cassidy lightly on the arm. "You didn't tell me she was beautiful."

"Actually, yes I did."

"Okay, you did." He walked across the room, his fancy leather shoes that looked like they cost more than her car clacking on the aqua tiles, and he embraced Seanna in a hug. He pulled away from her, still grasping her shoulders. "For years I've been listening to your aunt drone on about this fantastic niece of hers, and I'm always like, 'Make her come visit,' and she's always like, 'I know, I know,' and then all of the sudden, you're here. Poof." He made a hand gesture in front of her face, causing her to flinch.

He walked toward the counter and picked up a bag. "We've got lots to discuss, but I've got an appointment. I'll pick you up at six." He shuffled toward the door, his pale pink Ralph Lauren button-down blending with the walls of the same color. "Welcome to 30A!" The door shut behind him, the bell ringing in his absence.

Cassidy smiled at Seanna, who was standing speechless. "Meet Sebastian Peyton."

"The fabulous guy you're always mentioning. Who is he picking up at six, you?" Seanna asked.

"Afraid not."

"He's picking *me* up at six?" Seanna asked.

"Mmm hmm."

"For what?"

"Music on the Lawn at the Seaside pavilion. You should go. You'll get a chance to meet some of our friends." She waved a dismissive hand. "You'll love them."

Seanna approached the counter, getting a peek at the variety of sweet treats in the case by the register—black and white cookies, whoopie pies with strawberries protruding, key lime squares dipped halfway in white chocolate, raspberry cake swirls, and a blondie with big chocolate chunks. Seanna's mouth watered as she selected her lunch. But she wasn't sure if she could have any of this. Inventory was running low on all the selections.

She pointed at the case. "You did all this?"

Cassidy wiped her forehead with the back of her hand. "I did." Her eyebrows went up as the bell dinged on the door. "Excuse me." She readied herself with a genuine smile behind the counter as two families with more kids than Seanna could count came bouncing in.

Kids bounded up to the case pointing and picking favorites. Cassidy only had one blondie left, so naturally that became the star of the show, the kids battling for possession.

"I think I have another tray in the back," Cassidy said as another child screeched for a whoopie pie, the parents too engrossed in the choices to call the kids down. Cassidy gave Seanna a look that sprung her into action. She pushed through the teal swinging half-doors to find the baking portion of this bakery. Sure enough, a pan of blondies sat stacked in a rack among several other empty pans and half a pan of whoopie pies.

Cassidy appeared at the door. "Grab the whoopie pies, too. Second to bottom shelf."

Seanna did as told, mesmerized at this world of sweets and

wondering how her aunt managed all of this. By the time Seanna made it out front, a line had formed, the shop alive with chatter and kids. Where were these kids coming from, anyway? Didn't they have school? It was the start of October after all.

Seanna fell into a groove, handing pastries to patrons, Cassidy manning the register. By the time the place cleared out, the Felix the Cat clock on the wall struck three o'clock.

Seanna collapsed onto a stool behind the counter. "Geez. Is that normal?"

Cassidy shrugged as she leaned on the countertop. "Pretty much. I swear, it used to be like that just in the summer months, but the more people that discover it down here, the more I find myself baking extra pans."

"Where are all these kids coming from? Don't they have school?" Seanna asked.

Cassidy shrugged. "Fall break, I guess."

"Do you not have help?" Seanna glanced around the shop like an apron-donned co-worker was going to magically materialize.

"I did. They left for college a month ago. I hired one girl to replace the two who left, but that didn't work out."

"And you've been carrying on like this?" Seanna asked.

Cassidy nodded, glancing around the shop, napkins and crumbs covering the tables. "Pretty much."

"Hire yourself somebody else," Seanna ordered.

"I will. I just have to find someone I trust. The girl I just let go stole from me. She was so sweet, too. I didn't want to believe it about her. I kept making excuses for her until one day I left her here to watch the shop. Blake used his key to come in the back door and caught her shoving a stack of bills into her purse."

A strange disturbance occurred in her belly at the sound of his name. "You trust him though, don't you?"

Cassidy furrowed her brow. "Oh yeah. Without question."

Seanna fingered a stray chocolate chip on the countertop. "Thanks, by the way, for sending him over this morning with that croissant."

"Sure enough," Cassidy said. "Those were the last two."

"It was incredible. How do you get those so light and flaky?"

Cassidy winced, glancing at the door. "Place and bake. Don't tell." She winked. "So did you share those croissants with Blake?" she asked, all casual-like.

Seanna pursed her lips, narrowing her gaze. "Mmm hmm."

Cassidy grabbed the spray cleaner and a roll of paper towels and headed into the dining area. "That's nice."

Seanna scooted out from behind the counter. "What do you think you're up to?"

She held up her spray bottle. "Cleaning tables." She sprayed a shot in the general direction of Seanna for effect.

"I call horseshit," Seanna said.

Cassidy rolled her eyes as she wiped a table. "I'm not trying to set you up on a date. Don't be ridiculous. Blake's a good listener. Sometimes it helps to talk to someone who doesn't know you from Adam's housecat."

Seanna pursed her lips. "Thanks, but the last thing I need is…" She trailed off as she caught sight of a guy very much matching Blake's description at the building next door to Cassidy's dipping a roller into a bucket and then pressing it onto a parking lot. She walked to the door and got a better look as he stopped and used the sleeve of his T-shirt to wipe sweat from his forehead, his hands covered in dirty work gloves. The muscles in his tanned calves rippled as he put his whole body into his manual labor.

Cassidy appeared by her side, resting an arm on her shoulder. "You were saying?"

Seanna sucked up the drool and then cut her eyes at her aunt. "That is the very last thing I need right now."

Cassidy looked down at Seanna, her eyes a question. "When is the last time you and Jason...you know..."

Seanna bumped her. "Cassidy!"

Cassidy held up both hands in surrender. "You said we could talk about these things now. I'm just sayin'." Cassidy turned and went back to the business of cleaning tables. A customer came in, and she abandoned her cleaning to get behind the counter. Seanna took over where Cassidy left off, catching glimpses of Blake as she could. Seanna and Jason hadn't shared a bed in nine months, and it'd been even longer than that since they'd...

As the customer exited, Seanna followed her aunt into the back room. "So he's not coupled-up with someone?"

"I don't think he's the coupled-up type."

Seanna leaned against the counter next to her aunt. "Wonder why not."

Cassidy shrugged, pulling a bowl down from the shelf. "He doesn't talk a lot about his past. He's a fantastic guy though. I don't think he dates a lot, if at all, and I think you could use a distraction right about now...something to loosen you up...knock the water out of your ears." Cassidy bumped her hip against Seanna's with a grin, which was as contagious as a yawn.

Seanna guessed that Cassidy didn't like Jason. She was probably thrilled to hear they weren't getting married. Cassidy had spent a couple of nights at Seanna's place last January after she closed the shop for the season. It had been right after Seanna had discovered Jason's gambling addiction and things were bad between them, to say the least. They'd both put on a show for the sake of hiding what was going on between them, but Cassidy wasn't stupid.

Seanna focused on a stray pile of flour on the countertop as she imagined running her hands over Blake's biceps, damp with sweat.

"Make yourself useful and start on the brownies," Cassidy said, waking Seanna up. Cassidy pointed at a recipe taped to the wall in front of her alongside ones for chocolate cookies, key lime squares, cheese puffs, eclairs, and more. She got to work. One night with Blake before she headed back. Now that was something yummy.

Chapter Four

Blake stood next to his buddy Bo in the big, open grassy area in front of the pavilion at Seaside listening to a funk-jazz fusion band. Bo took a drink of his beer. "You busy day after tomorrow?"

That was Sunday, the day Blake was supposed to call Kevin. "Not at all. You got something in mind?"

Bo shrugged. "You want to come with me on some jobs? I'll take you to Layla's for lunch after if you do."

Blake gave him a look. "Not many people work for food, my friend."

"You do."

Blake shrugged. "True. Sounds good."

The two stood in companionable silence. That was probably the best thing about his friendship with Bo—they didn't waste words. They were just as fine standing in silence as they were yappin' away…or fighting. That was what they did best. One of them would pick a fight with the other one just so they could go at it like brothers then go for a beer. Their version of therapy.

Bo whistled. "Hot damn. Who's that with Sebastian and them?"

Blake followed Bo's gaze across the horseshoe-shaped lawn to find Sebastian sitting on a blanket with Desiree, Ashe...and there she was. Hot damn was right. Seanna was all done up with her hair hanging in loose curls, a tight-fitting black shirt with a scoop neck presenting her cleavage.

Blake's chest burned with what seemed like a hint of jealousy. "That's Seanna, Cassidy's niece." He didn't intend it, but the words came out possessive.

Bo picked up on it right away, turning toward him dramatically. "Is that so? What do you know about her?"

Blake shrugged, now on the defense. "I don't know anything about her."

"You know she's Cassidy's niece. You met her?"

"Yeah, I met her," Blake said.

"When was this?"

"Yesterday. Cassidy had me let her in the house. She had to finish up an order."

"Did you ask her out?" Bo asked.

"No." His answer came out way too fast and definite. He added a shrug for damage control.

"She married?"

"No."

"Boyfriend?" Bo asked.

"Doesn't look like it."

Bo nudged him. "Well, what the hell?" Blake let out a huff of air as he shifted irritably. "Whatever, man. More for me," Bo said, lifting the bottle to his lips. A hot sensation moved up Blake's spine. Bo looked him up and down. "Or not."

"What? I didn't say anything."

"You didn't have to. If you like this girl, take her on a date."

"Don't be stupid. She's Cassidy's niece."

Bo craned his neck. "Can't see her up close from here, but she damn sure doesn't look like a kid to me."

"She's not. She's a woman."

Bo chuckled.

"Fuck you."

Desiree spotted them and waved. Sebastian pointed and crooked a finger, summoning them over. Bo gave a finger wave right at Seanna and then looked at Blake, obviously to see if he'd sufficiently aggravated him. Seanna gave a shy smile, and then picked at the grass. "Aww, damn," Bo said. "She's cute as hell."

Cute? Cute didn't do her justice. "She's all right," Blake said.

"All right, huh? Then I suppose you don't mind if I ask her out."

An unexplained flame licked Blake's throat. "Knock yourself out." Bo stared at him, waiting him out. "We both know how you got off with Cassidy the one night you tried with her," Blake said.

Bo chuckled. "I knew you'd bring that up."

"Hell yeah, and you can count on me bringing it up many more times, my friend. Any time I can talk about the time you got your nose bloodied by a woman is a good time far as I'm concerned."

Bo slid a hand in his pocket. "I was drunk. I didn't even know what the hell I was doing."

"Screw you. You'd kiss her today if you thought she wouldn't punch you again."

Bo laughed again. "Hell yeah, I would. She's damn sexy."

Bo was right. Despite the fact that Cassidy and Blake

were too good of friends to ruin their relationship with sex, Blake didn't deserve a woman like Cassidy. He was just to the point that he could stand to look at himself in the mirror, and much of that progress was thanks to Bo.

When Blake had gotten to this town three years ago, he wasn't sure how he was going to recover from his deadly mistake. And then he met Bo, and Bo brought Blake back into the light. Funny thing was Bo didn't even know he was doing it. But he knew when to talk, when to shut up, when to ask questions, and when to accept silence for an answer. They did nothing but constantly give each other shit, but Blake didn't know how he could live without the stability and camaraderie he'd found in Bo. That was one reason Bo could never find out what Blake had done three years ago.

"Cassidy 2.0, huh?" Bo said, breaking Blake from his thoughts.

Blake shifted his weight. "She isn't anything like Cassidy."

"What is she like?"

"Sweet. Funny, kind of like she doesn't give a damn what anyone thinks."

Bo turned to Blake, his eyebrows furrowed. "Damn, you've got it bad."

Blake's chest burned. "I do not. You asked me what she was like." They both nodded as a couple of girls, way too young for them, shuffled by, giggling.

"I just needed to know what pickup line to use," Bo said.

Blake rolled his eyes. "Your tired-ass, cheesy pickup lines aren't gonna work on her."

"My tasteful, well-crafted pickup lines have always worked," Bo said.

"Bullshit."

Bo chuckled it off, but he was right. Blake had never seen Bo attempt to pick up a woman and fail. He was just a hair shorter than Blake, and he worked out like a madman. He lived at the gym and it showed. Bo held a rugged charm of the redneck variety that women flocked to. But Bo also had a huge heart. He'd take the shirt off his back if he thought Blake needed it, and he'd go hungry for a week before he'd let any one of his friends or family miss a meal.

Sebastian made a big production of waving them over.

"Looks like we're being summoned," Bo said.

"Yep," Blake said.

Bo nudged him. "Come on, mister personality. Your public awaits."

Blake followed Bo to the blanket filled with the people who'd become his friends. They were an oddball configuration, but somehow their dynamic worked. They'd come together through Cassidy and Sebastian…and he guessed himself. Sebastian was always stopping by the shop, and Blake would be in there too. They just sort of became a funny little threesome, doing this and that together, and Cassidy cooking for them on Thanksgiving. Sebastian wasn't close with his family, and he talked to Blake about that some, which gave Blake a different perspective on family…something he'd never known much about.

Sebastian started inviting Ashe and Desiree to come along, and Blake invited Bo and their other friend Chase, and here they were. Then there was Marigold, who just sort of appeared somehow, keeping them all on their toes.

None of them knew the real him though. If they ever found out about his past, they wouldn't have a thing to do with him. He knew it was wrong to keep them in the dark about him, but right now these people were one of the things keeping him going every day.

Sebastian shifted a flirty gaze between Blake and Bo. "Boys."

"Sebastian," Bo said, mimicking him.

Sebastian's face colored. He flirted shamelessly with Blake and Bo, but he turned shy as a church mouse when one of them gave it back to him even the slightest bit.

Desiree stood and wrapped her arms around Bo first, and then Blake. He was always careful when he hugged her because he didn't want to mess up her hair, but when he fessed up to that once, she swore he wouldn't. Tonight, she had it intricately woven into braids that weaved and curved around her head.

"As it turns out," Sebastian said, "Seanna has not met our resident pool boy. I thought we needed to remedy that, pronto."

Bo stepped forward and held a hand out to Seanna, who was sitting with her legs tucked behind her on the blanket. "Bo Harrison." A smile slid across Bo's face as he turned on his so-called charm for Cassidy's niece.

"Seanna," she said.

"Cassidy's niece, huh?" Bo asked.

"Ah, so the boys do gossip," Sebastian said.

Seanna lifted her eyebrows. "Pool boy?"

"I have a pool cleaning and supply company in Panama City Beach," Bo said.

"He does me," Sebastian said.

Ashe picked a piece of grass off his hand and flicked it at Sebastian. "You wish."

"My pool, of course," Sebastian said.

Bo squatted next to Seanna, and she scooted over on her blanket to make a place for him to sit. Son of a bitch. Blake had been sure Bo was just aggravating him with this flirtation bit. But he was laying it on fairly thick—thicker than Blake was comfortable with.

"How long are you here?" Bo asked.

Seanna shrugged as she gazed into Bo's eyes. "We'll see." Blake's nose curled upward, taking his top lip with it.

Bo glanced at Blake, eyeing him, and Blake gave a slight shrug. Bo lowered his eyelids in a way that indicated he didn't buy Blake's indifference in the least. This was so typical of Bo—his way of drawing Blake out and forcing him to step in and go for what he wanted. Blake wouldn't do it. Bo could take her home and screw her for a nonstop week as far as Blake cared. A sizzle burned his chest at the thought.

"Have you been to the beach yet?" Blake blurted out.

She looked up at him, a hint of surprise in her eyes. "Actually, no, not yet."

"Want to go?"

"Sure."

Holding his hand out to help her up, he glared Bo down, and Bo gave a satisfied grin in return.

Chapter Five

Now that Blake had Seanna alone, he grossly regretted his decision to one-up Bo. It made Blake look like he was desperate. He'd put her on the spot. She pretty much had to say yes.

He frowned as they walked along the outer perimeter of the lawn toward the street. Cars stopped on either side of the crosswalk, so they made their way across 30A and past the restaurants to the beach walkway.

The ocean opened up to them, and Seanna stopped, gazing at the view. "Man, I always forget how white these beaches are."

"Some of the whitest in the world, supposedly," Blake said.

They walked down the stairs and kicked off their shoes at the bottom. She pulled ahead of him and went straight for the water. The waves washed up on her legs, wetting the bottom of her rolled-up pants, but she didn't seem to care. "Why did I wait so long to come here?" she asked, still facing the ocean.

"You tell me."

She turned to face him as if she almost forgot he was there. She walked down the beach, and he followed her, the ocean lapping at their feet. "What's your story?" she asked.

He lifted his eyebrows in a delay tactic. He had a standardized story he gave people, but she wasn't *people*. Something tugged at his heart, warning him not to lie to her. "My story?"

"Yeah, how long have you been here? Are you from here?"

"No. I'm from Atlanta."

"Mmm," she groaned.

He considered her. "Not a fan?"

"No, there's not anything wrong with Atlanta…just someone I know who's from there."

"Would this be the same person who made you say you wouldn't date again until the cows came home?"

She pointed at Blake without looking at him. "That's the one."

"You want to tell me what happened there?"

She stopped and planted her feet in the waves, gazing out into the dark night ocean. "He lied to me," she said, venom dripping off her tongue.

A pang of guilt irritated his chest. He cleared his throat. "That's not good."

She rolled her eyes and shook her head. "I was such an idiot." She turned to him suddenly. "Did I tell you I'm going to be thirty soon?"

"Yeah. Happy birthday?"

She glared at him, and then broke out in a smile. "That's not what I meant."

That smile of hers was poised to do him in if he let it. "What did you mean?" he asked.

"I mean I'm not a kid anymore. I'm supposed to be entering the next phase in my life. A thirty-year-old woman should be able to detect a load of crap when she hears it."

"And your crap detector was broken?" he asked.

She ran her toe through the wet sand. "I didn't want to admit it, but I knew something was wrong." She shook her head. "Anyway, how long have you been here?"

That was a simple enough question he could answer, he supposed. "Three years."

"What brought you here?"

His mind fumbled for a logical excuse. "The beach."

She nodded. "I guess that's as good a reason as any. So you've always done handyman work?"

The pit of his stomach churned. He hated these questions, but he knew she wasn't prying, just making conversation, getting to know him. He had to get better at this somehow…better at the lie. "For a while."

"So what's up with your friend?" she asked.

"Bo? Ignore him."

"Sort of hard to."

His chest heated at the thought. "His mission in life is to irritate me."

She grinned up at him. "Is yours to irritate him?"

"Pretty much."

"You're both single?" she asked.

He cut his eyes at her as a wave crashed into his legs. "Yeah."

She gave him a wry smile. "I bet the two of you do pretty well down here in the bars."

"I'm getting too old for the bar scene."

"How old's that?" she asked, lifting her chin.

He raised an eyebrow in consideration, and then conceded. "Thirty-four."

"Oh, so you know all about your thirties. Tell me about them."

"What do you need to know?"

"Is there some beacon of knowledge waiting for me on my birthday?" she asked. "Will I suddenly have all the answers and quit doing stupid stuff?"

He gave a humorless chuckle. "Certainly didn't work that way for me."

She turned to him, squaring herself in front of him. "Tell me one really dumb thing you've done since you've been in your thirties. And I don't mean wore two different shoes out of the house or drank a few too many and had to deal with a hangover. I mean something that changed your life and put you on the wrong course."

He gazed into her eyes, his insides rolling over. Did she know about him? How was that possible?

She stabbed a finger at him. "See? You can't come up with anything. Actually, I don't feel so bad now. I did my stupid stuff in my twenties. My thirties should be smooth sailing."

She turned to walk away, and he took her arm. He wasn't sure he'd ever felt so natural around someone he'd just met. She turned back toward him. "What happened?" he asked. She gazed at him, searching his eyes. He squeezed her arm and then let go. "You can trust me."

She squinted at him. "How do I know that?" He froze, afraid she could somehow see inside his convoluted brain. She closed her eyes and shook her head. "I'm so sorry. Here you are just trying to be a nice guy, and I'm being all paranoid."

"It's okay," he said. "I get it." More than she could know.

"It's just been a weird year. Ever had one of those?"

He gazed into her eyes, the ocean air breezing through her hair. "Yeah," he admitted. More than he'd ever admitted to anyone in Seaside.

She narrowed her gaze at him. "Really? You want to listen to my drama?"

"Why not?"

"But you don't even know me."

He shrugged. "Sometimes people who don't know you are the best ones to tell your problems to." She looked down at the ground, her brow worried. He nudged her arm. "What happens at the shore stays at the shore."

Her lip went up just a little in a smile, and she looked heavenward, shaking her head slightly. Her gaze fell on his, and she studied him hard. "I haven't told anyone about this. Not even Cassidy."

He stared at her, hoping to convey trust. The last thing he ever wanted was to be involved in drama. He ran from drama like a kid confronted by a skunk with its tail lifted. But for whatever reason, he wanted to know whatever she was willing to tell. "I'm here. Nobody else is around...nobody on earth."

She considered him. "Right now, you think I'm just a regular girl, but after we're done here, you'll think I'm an idiot."

"I can assure you, I won't think that about you."

She took a step toward him across the invisible line of personal space, holding up one finger in between them. "Ten bucks says you'll think I'm an idiot."

If he were the kind of guy who flirted, he'd grab her finger. He drew his bottom lip in between his teeth and then released it to say, "You're on."

She dropped to sit, leaning back, placing her hands down in the sand on either side of her. She cut her eyes at him. "I just met you. I'm not trying to scare you away."

"I don't scare easily. Try me."

She inhaled a breath like she was getting ready to go diving without a mask. "I've gotten myself into a tricky situation with my ex." She glanced over at him to get his reaction, but he kept his expression impassive. "I've been paying all the rent and bills since last January, and I'm going to keep doing this until December when our lease is up."

"Why can't he pay his part?"

"Because he's sick." She put the word in air quotes, and then dragged her gaze to meet his. "He's got a gambling problem."

Blake nodded, remembering an acquaintance of his in med school who went down a rabbit hole with gambling. It was tough to watch. He'd had to quit school. Last Blake heard he was tending bar somewhere. Who was Blake to judge, though? He was a handyman.

"I just love how people treat gambling like it's a sickness," she said, "like it's something that's not the fault of the gambler. You should hear some of the things his sponsor has said to me. I need to be supportive and sensitive to his illness. Like he's got cancer or something."

"How long have you two been together?"

She held up a finger. "We're not together. We haven't been together since last Christmas."

He hated to admit that he didn't mind hearing that. "How long has he been…sick?"

She let out a breath as if trying to blow out the frustration. "He's gambled since I met him a few years ago.

It was always on football or basketball games. Simple stuff…or so it seemed. But it got worse. Last Christmas, I went to swipe my credit card at Macy's, and it was declined. I was over my limit, which was really strange. I only use that card at Christmas, because I've always been able to pay it off with my year-end bonus." She huffed a laugh. "What's so ridiculous was I was trying to buy him this outrageously expensive watch he'd had his eye on for months."

"So you were spending your year-end bonus on him?"

She lifted one eyebrow. "Ready to pay up yet?"

He smiled at her. "No. Did you report it stolen?"

She shut her eyes tightly. "It's not as cut-and-dried as it sounds. I loved him. It's so weird to say it now, because the last thing I feel when I look at him or think about him is love, but I did love him." She shook her head, staring out at the dark ocean, seeming to look for answers there. "I thought I could help him…make him better." The last part of her sentence came out in the form of a laugh, as if the idea were preposterous.

He understood more than she would ever know…more than he'd let her know. He drew his knees up closer to his chest. "Is that the worst of it…the credit card?"

She huffed a laugh, shaking her head. "He was so deep into my accounts in such a short amount of time. It was like a tornado hit my finances. I didn't have much to begin with, but he drove up a lot of debt."

"Are you suing him?"

"Have you ever tried to sue a gambler? I'd have to get in line behind the guys who bust knees."

He nodded, realizing it was a naïve question to ask. This was her battle to fight. She was a smart woman. No doubt she'd thought through the ins and outs of it all and was doing what she needed to do to get through this. "So I take it you can't break your lease."

"It's worded in such a way that you can break it any time you want, but you have to keep paying on your apartment until it's rented, and there's been five to ten units sitting empty all year. They keep multiplying."

A thought occurred to him…one that made him a little uneasy. "So, have you been living there with him?"

She gritted her teeth like she was in physical pain. "Yeah."

All sorts of thoughts about sleeping arrangements and shared showers invaded his brain. "It's a two-bedroom?" he asked hopefully.

"Oh, God yes. If it wasn't his ass would be on the couch, trust me."

He nodded, ridiculously relieved, as he watched her pick up a handful of sand and let it flow through her fingers. "Have you been dating other people?"

"I can't even think about opening up to another guy like that."

That was precisely the reason this walk with her was a bad idea. It was too goddamned romantic. The moonlit ocean, the deserted beach. The intimacy between them, her sharing so personally with him at his request. He should have stayed up on solid ground with her where it was safe. This was Bo's fault for prodding him, poking him to make a move.

She swiped the sand off her hands. "At this point, I'm just trying to make it to December 1 with my sanity."

"What happens then?"

"That's when my last payment is due."

He liked the sound of that. "Until then?"

"Until then I continue to pay for my ex to live in my apartment."

He couldn't fathom the loser who would allow a woman to pay his way without contributing something.

She looked at him curiously. "Hey, are you okay?"

"What?" he asked.

"You look really agitated," she said.

"Sorry, I just...I'm not trying to get in your business."

"Seriously? I just laid all that on you, and you think I don't expect you to have a reaction?"

He clenched his fists, letting the frustration out. "I can't understand this guy. He just lets you pay, no questions asked?"

"I know it's all so stupid. This is why I haven't told anyone. This is why I didn't want to tell you."

Even in the moonlight he could see her cheeks turning pink. "Hey," he said nudging her leg with the back of his hand. "I'm sorry. It's not my problem to fix. I'm sure you've covered all angles. You're doing the right thing, whatever it is, I'm sure."

She met his gaze, her eyes hopeful. "Thank you...for saying that."

He narrowed his gaze. "Do you want Bo and me to go up there and kick his ass out of your space?"

She chuckled. "I would pay you so much money. Of course, I don't have that money, which is part of the problem of all this, but it's a lovely thought."

"Where is your apartment? We'll pay him a visit."

"12 South neighborhood. Ooh, but go kick his ass at his

job so he's humiliated in front of lots of people."

He blinked, shocked to hear the loser worked. "He has a job? What does he do?"

"He's in medical equipment sales."

Blake couldn't help making the immediate connection… medical equipment sales rep who used to live in Atlanta. That was way too close for comfort for him. Those guys were in and out of his hospital daily, and he'd been to lunch with a few of them. He had to know if he knew him. "He did that in Atlanta?" he asked.

"Yeah, that's where he got started."

"What's his name?" Blake asked, knowing he was on shaky ground.

Seanna frowned. "Jason Monahan. Did you know him…back in Atlanta?"

The name wasn't familiar. That didn't mean anything. It wasn't like Blake remembered all their names. "No, I just was thinking, those guys make decent money. He should be able to pay his half of the rent."

"That's true, but it all goes to his gambling problem." She air quoted. "'The disease.' Anyway, if you want to kick his ass, you'll probably have an opportunity without going anywhere. I imagine he'll show up here when he gets desperate enough…or gets enough money to travel down here, whichever comes first."

That wasn't a pleasant thought. Not only did he not want this guy anywhere near Seanna, he didn't want to take the chance that the guy would recognize him. He'd look him up when he got home and see if he was a regular at his hospital in Atlanta. Blake needed to be prepared for anything.

"So why are you here?" he asked, wanting to get away from this subject quickly.

"I had nowhere else to go. I couldn't be around him anymore after this last bit he pulled. None of my family or friends know about any of this, and I want to keep it that way…at least until December. I can't have my mom and dad swooping in and saving me, because they absolutely would and they can't afford it. And if I ask to stay with one of my friends, they'll want to know what's going on and why I haven't kicked him out and it'll be a whole thing. Besides that, I've been retracting from all of them this past year. It's much easier than explaining all this to someone and waiting for the judgment. Not that they'd be wrong." She drew in the sand with a stick, aimlessly.

He knew exactly what she meant. He'd done the same thing three years ago. Kevin was the only person he'd allowed to stay in touch with him. Everyone else went. It was too difficult to be around them knowing they probably blamed or judged him for what he did.

He wanted to pull her in close to him, easing her stress just for a minute. With every word she spoke he was clear on two things: he was the last thing she needed, and he was growing closer to her by the second.

He let silence sit between them for a bit and then asked, "What happened? What was this last bit that broke your limit?"

She stared solemnly at the ocean. "He stole money from the firm where I work and made it look like I did it."

He winced, thinking of the humiliation she must be going through. "How did he…" Blake wasn't sure how to finish that sentence.

"He hacked into my company's system using my credentials." She shook her head, a humorless smile on her lips. "He's done some low stuff before, but I never dreamed he'd go that far."

She stared off into the dark ocean distance, worry etched on her features. He wanted to reach for her hand or some similar gesture that showed he cared. But the moment already seemed intimate enough, the two of them alone in the dark, lit slightly by the activity of 30A behind them. He didn't want to seem like he was coming on strong, but more importantly, he wasn't sure he could trust himself to keep from getting even more intimate with her if she let him.

He cleared his throat as he adjusted himself on the sand. "So what's going on now…at your company? Are they pressing charges or…"

She closed her eyes and dropped her head. "No. My boss Phillip went to bat for me. He was able to stop them from pressing charges, but he wasn't able to keep my job." She looked up at the sky, shaking her head. "He's done so much for me these past four years. He sort of took me under his wing and helped me learn the ropes of the business."

"Construction, right?"

She sort of rolled her eyes. "Yeah."

He considered her. "That's what you love to do?"

She blinked, staring at him hard. "Yeah," she said, after a long moment's hesitation. "I guess."

"How's the job search coming?" he asked.

She pursed her lips "I don't know. I've sent out about twenty-five resumes between yesterday and today, but my resume's weak since I hadn't been promoted from assistant yet. I need a resume builder…a project to work on…something that's mine." She leaned forward, pulling her knees to her chin, wrapping her arms around her folded legs.

He wanted to help her, to be the one to make everything okay for her. "What about a kitchen remodel?"

She separated her chest from her thighs. "Hmm?"

"I have a friend who's looking for a kitchen remodel. Would you be up for quoting it?"

She turned her whole body toward him, a sparkle in her eye. "Are you serious?"

He swallowed. "Sure. Can you handle a quote like that?"

She closed her eyes quickly, and then reopened them with a nod. "Of course. I'll just need to do a little research on local prices, but yes, I can handle it."

He nodded, feeling proud and guilty all at the same time. He loved the fact that he could help turn her mood from solemn to hopeful in a snap. But he also knew he was full of shit. Chase was going to kill him. He'd get over it.

He hauled himself up off the sand, and then held out his hand to help her up. After he stood her upright, he held her hand a second longer than he should have. He couldn't help it. He wasn't ready to let her go just yet, even though the touch of her hand would be as far as he'd ever let himself get with her.

She turned away from him, a hint of a smile tugging at her lips. She wiped the sand off her pants, and they headed back down the beach. When they got to the bottom of the stairs, they put on their shoes and started to head up, but he took her arm and she turned toward him. With her on the step and him still on the beach, they were face to face.

He held out his hand. "Where's my ten bucks?"

She smiled. "I'll do better than that. I'll take you out to lunch to thank you."

"I'm just making the connection for you. There's no guarantee—"

"An introduction is all I can ask for. Thank you."

Staring into her hazel eyes, an ocean breeze blew over them. Her face opened in a wide smile as she turned her back to him and walked up the stairs.

As he watched her rejoin the group, he held back, pulling his phone out of his pocket. He pulled up his buddy Chase's name and hit send.

"Yo," Chase answered.

"You know that piece of crap kitchen you've been talking about remodeling for like two years now?" Blake asked.

"I know the one," Chase said.

"You're getting a quote on it."

"I am?" Chase said, not missing a beat. Chase had more money than he knew what to do with. He always talked about fixing up his house, but he was just too damn busy to do anything about it.

"Yep," Blake said.

"Hmm," Chase muttered, and then sat silent for a minute.

"What?" Blake asked.

"Nothing," Chase said. "I'm just trying to figure out if you're hard up for money or if this has something to do with a girl. Maybe both. You getting engaged or something? Need a loan for a ring?"

Blake shifted, pocketing his hand. "Just make yourself scarce around eleven o'clock tomorrow morning, okay? I've got my key."

"Ah, so it *is* about a girl."

"It's about your kitchen," Blake lied.

"We'll see about that."

Blake rolled his eyes as he ended the call. Seanna sat on the blanket as Sebastian handed her a cup of wine. She shifted her gaze to Blake and held up her drink with a nod.

"Definitely about a girl," Blake said under his breath.

When he got home, he opened his laptop and pulled up a search engine. He typed *Jason Monahan medical sales Atlanta* and the results populated, pictures of Jason Monahans flooding his screen. One face took up more real estate on the page than the others, a decent looking, clean-cut guy in his late twenties or so.

Enlarging one of the pictures, he searched the man's face, looking for some sort of recognition. He clicked the source of the picture and found it connected with an industry newsletter featuring some accolades. This guy had been awarded rep of the month in this particular issue, and the article bragged about Jason's uncanny sales abilities. He was described as a force to be reckoned with.

No wonder Seanna had been taken in by him. This guy's job was to convince people to do things. She was an honest, caring person, and he'd seen that as a weakness and exploited it. He was less worried about Jason showing up in Seaside and exposing him, and more concerned about going to jail after he beat the hell out of the guy if he did show his face.

He shut his computer and ran his hand through his hair. He could feel his heart swelling as he thought about Seanna. His emotions were on high alert...more so than usual. He needed to be friendly and kind, and that was it. Keep this girl and this situation at a distance…that's what he'd do. As he lay in bed later than night, images of her rushing his brain, he begged the universe to help him figure out a way how to do that.

Chapter Six

Seanna cracked eggs into a cup while turkey bacon sizzled in the skillet. Cassidy stirred from somewhere down the hall. Nothing like the smell of bacon to wake up one of her family members. She plated their breakfast and poured orange juice.

"I love you," Cassidy said.

"Because I'm your favorite niece, or because I made you bacon?"

"What do you think?"

"I think I probably shouldn't push my luck," Seanna said, pouring Cassidy a cup of coffee.

"To what do I owe this pleasure?"

"Just thought you'd want a carb-free breakfast at least one day of the week."

Cassidy took a seat. "My body will probably reject it, wondering where the gluten is."

As they ate, Seanna gauged her aunt's mood. It was time to spill the beans. Telling Blake the whole story had helped tremendously. She'd broken the seal with him, and the world hadn't ended. He'd just listened and hadn't chastised her for any of it…hadn't questioned her actions. He had no idea how much that had meant to her. She'd wanted to tell him that but didn't want to get weird on him. She knew her story was strange enough on its own.

Cassidy would keep her opinions to herself, but that was almost worse. Knowing Cassidy was disappointed in her would be tougher to take than anything she could actually say. What Seanna could dredge up in her head was far harsher than Cassidy had the heart to actually feel. But none of that mattered. Seanna knew that she had to do this before she moved forward a minute longer living with Cassidy.

Seanna finished her eggs and took a deep breath. "So, do you want to hear the story?"

Cassidy wiped her mouth and then picked up her coffee cup. "Lay it on me."

Seanna told her the whole shebang, from the moment she first suspected the gambling had gotten out of hand, up till she walked out the door to head to Seaside.

"You know I would have loaned you the money," Cassidy said.

"That's exactly why I didn't say anything until now."

Cassidy eyed her. "Your parents would have—"

"Exactly."

Cassidy nodded, getting it, of course. "So just two more payments?"

"That's right. Then my money is mine again."

"What kind of man lets a woman pay his bills for a year?" Cassidy asked while Seanna fidgeted with her napkin, her face warming. Cassidy gripped Seanna's arm. "I'm sorry, sweetie."

"No, I deserve it. I picked a man who would let a woman

pay his bills for a year. Don't think I haven't beat myself up for that."

"Does he have any sort of excuse?"

"To be honest, we don't even discuss it anymore. I shut him up a long time ago. I'm just so sick of hearing the lies. The promises I know won't be kept."

"Well, you are welcome to stay here as long as you need. In fact, you've got a job at the bakery if you want it. God knows I need the help."

Seanna released a sigh at the idea of how heavenly that sounded. For half a second, she let herself imagine a life where she lived there in that house with Cassidy and worked in the bakery right down the road in this beachside paradise with her. But that wasn't real life. That was escapism. And Cassidy would want her life back eventually. What was the saying about houseguests? Three days and they started to stink.

She had to stay focused on the plan. "You have no idea how wonderful that sounds. But I need to stay on track. I think I've got a job opportunity. Just a kitchen remodel, but it's a resume builder."

"Oh yeah? How'd you come upon that?"

"Blake," Seanna said, trying to sound nonchalant.

"Mmm," Cassidy said.

"Friend of his, actually."

"Sounds like a good start."

"If I can get the job," Seanna said.

Cassidy squinted at her. "Something makes me think you've got a good shot at this one."

Cassidy kneaded cinnamon roll dough while Seanna surfed through local builders' websites trying to glean as much information as she could about kitchen rebuilds. She had never quoted out a residential job based on retail prices. They got their materials for far less at the firm, but of course they jacked up their prices in their quotes. She just had to figure out a way to balance it all out.

Cassidy blew a stray curl out of her eye as she pulled a piece of dough off of the ball. "How was Jazz on the Lawn?"

Seanna closed the browser and sat back in her chair, thinking about sitting on the beach in the dark next to Blake. She tried not to grin. "It was good."

"You met Desiree?" Cassidy asked.

Seanna looked up at her aunt. "Her hair is like a work of art."

"Did she have it in the braids?"

"Yes, but they were like these intricately woven rows that sort of…" Seanna made a swooping motion to her own hair, not really knowing how to explain it.

"I love it when she wears it like that. Did you meet Ashe?"

"So sweet," Seanna said. "All of them. Ashe and Sebastian were hilarious together."

"Oh yeah. They feed off each other. Don't be fooled though. They love one another."

"Oh really?" Seanna asked. She hadn't pegged them for partners.

"Not like that. They're just friends. Good friends. Rumor has it they were a couple when they first met but have long since been just friends."

Seanna thought about the group of friends she'd met last night and the family dynamic between them. She'd had plenty of groups of close-knit friends in high school and college, but there was something utterly unique about this group and their way with one another that made her heart ping.

She thought about that guy Bo, probably the hottest guy she'd laid her eyes on in years. Blake was far more her style, but Bo had a way about him that would be easy to get caught up in if a girl allowed herself. "I met someone named Bo last night." Cassidy huffed a laugh and rolled her eyes. Seanna twirled her chair around to face Cassidy. "Oh, so you know him."

"Not like you're thinking."

"Well, he seemed to know you. Smiled a mile wide when he said your name."

Cassidy shook her head and then rubbed her forehead with the sleeve on her upper arm. "He's a mess. Huge flirt. Charms pants directly off any woman in his path."

"Except you."

"Of course."

Seanna lowered her chin. "Mmm hmm."

Cassidy pointed at her. "Don't date him. He's a heartbreaker."

"I'm not dating anybody." It was true. She had no intention of dating anyone right now. She was a mess. Unloading the story on Blake last night really made her realize how much.

She'd instantly felt close to him, and she had no idea why. He wasn't an open book—that was for sure. He seemed guarded when it came to talking about himself, but open with listening to her. She couldn't deny an attraction to him. He was a beautiful man. Tall, gorgeous blue eyes. His nose was a hair too big for his face, but the more she noticed it, the hotter it made him.

But his looks were only part of what drew her to him. He had an easiness about him—a calming air so opposite from the situation she'd been in for the last nine months. She'd lived in a constant state of panic and unease. Being around Blake was like standing on solid ground after an earthquake.

The phone rang and Cassidy answered it. "Seaside Sweets." She snapped at Seanna. "Hang on, Jason, I've got a customer." Cassidy put the phone on hold and set it on the cradle. "Do you want to talk to him?"

"God no," she said, a darkness the size of the plague moving over her head.

"What should I tell him?"

"If you don't mind, tell him I'm here and I'm fine, and that I'll call him soon."

"You sure?"

"Yeah, I don't want him bothering Mom and Dad and everyone on Earth."

The bell on the front door rang, and Seanna went after it. She pushed through the double half-doors to find an attractive, blond woman sauntering through the dining area, inspecting the store with interest. "Welcome to Seaside Sweets," Seanna said.

The cat-eyed girl looked up at Seanna, searching her face. "Brianna, right?"

Had Seanna met this girl last night and forgotten? How else would she know her name? "Seanna," she corrected.

The girl nodded with a dismissive wave of her hand. "I'm Marigold, a friend of the boys." The girl stared her down, almost daring.

Seanna rose an inch or two taller. "Nice to meet you. So you're a local?"

"Oh yeah. I've got a gift shop down the road." She handed her a business card. "You're here visiting your aunt?"

"Yep."

"For how long?"

"I'm not really sure. A while." Seanna flicked the card against her other hand. "Can I get you anything?" she asked, motioning at the sweets inside the case.

"Oh, yes, hmm, let's see. Gosh, all of this stuff does look wonderful doesn't it? I just can't decide."

Seanna pulled out a waxed paper tissue, ready for Marigold to make her selection and then skedaddle. She didn't catch the best vibe off her.

"Goodness, you know, I think I'll just take a bottle of water, please. I can't wreck my diet with a goodie right now." Seanna turned around to pull a bottle out of the refrigerator. "You're lucky," Marigold said. "You look like you don't really worry about that sort of thing much."

Seanna paused, heat rushing up through her chest. This girl was calling her fat. She *was* fat compared to this waif, but still. She turned around and met Marigold's cat eyes. The girl was just begging Seanna to say something...start a fight.

Seanna looked down at the case and searched for the most decadent treat she could find. She zoned in on something dark and rich oozing with caramel. She put it on a napkin, setting it on the counter. "Have you tried our turtle pecan brownies?" She eased the gooey creation closer to Marigold. "They're made with rich, dark chocolate, toasted pecans, and buttery caramel."

Marigold's eyes glued themselves to the brownie, just inches from her, waiting to be bitten into. She tugged at her throat. "No, I couldn't. I can't."

Seanna took another one out of the case and put it up to her nose. "Mmm, you can smell the rich chocolate, and what is that, amaretto?"

Marigold watched the brownie at Seanna's mouth, swallowing hard, her nose twitching.

Seanna bit into it and drew her eyebrows together. "Oh, God," she said through a mouthful of chocolatey goodness. "This is her best batch yet. That caramel is so buttery." She chewed some more, closing her eyes. "Does she put toffee pieces in these?"

She opened her eyes to find Marigold's mouth open, her shoulders swaying back and forth like she was physically trying to restrain herself from the brownie on the counter.

Seanna inched it closer to her. "Go ahead. It's on me."

Marigold straightened up and cleared her throat. "Well, I am headed to a friend's house who has a little girl. I'm sure she would love for me to bring her a treat."

Seanna held back her grin. "Oh, well, if she's small then we have these ballerina cupcakes in the back she might like."

Marigold snatched the brownie. "No, this is good. She loves chocolate."

Seanna smiled. "All right then. Can I get you anything else?"

Marigold backed up. "No. I've got to run."

Seanna held up the bottle as Marigold pushed through the front door. "You forgot your water." But the girl was out of there and into her car in seconds flat.

Seanna took another bite of the brownie as the bell dinged on the door, and Sebastian came in. He pointed to the street. "Was that Marigold I just saw chowing down on something as she pulled out of the parking lot?"

"Yep."

He searched the case. "You aren't serving kale here now, are you? Because I'm sure she didn't get a sweet from in here. She doesn't eat."

Seanna winked at him. "I have my powers of persuasion."

He dipped his chin. "So, did you have fun last night?"

"Oh, yes. So much. Everyone was so precious."

"It's a fun group, I have to admit." He leaned in conspiratorially. "So what'd you think about Bo?" He bit his fist with a pained expression.

"Not as much as you do, obviously."

"Oh, girl," he said. "He's like my ultimate fantasy."

She shrugged. "He was all right."

"Oh, okay. I get it. Blake's more your type?"

"He's a nice guy."

"Mmm hmm."

"He showed me the beach."

He rested his forearms on the counter. "How thoughtful of him."

She met his knowing gaze and couldn't help a giggle. He was so cute and fun.

He tapped the counter lightly. "So, real talk. I know you've got Cassidy, but I am here for whatever you need—tour guide, restaurant recommendation…listening ear." His eyebrows went up. She blinked, not sure how to respond. He lifted both hands. "I'm not being nosey, but I know you were engaged and now it doesn't seem like you are. Cassidy is wonderful, but she's family. And sometimes it's hard to talk to family. So if you need a neutral, nonjudgmental ear, I'm good for that." He zipped his lip. "And I don't gossip, I promise. It's bad form."

She was truly touched by this guy's generosity. "That's very kind of you. Thank you."

"I adore your aunt, and you by association."

Seanna was amazed how much clout these people down here tossed her way just because of her relation to Cassidy.

"Bring it in, sweetheart." He walked around to the side of the counter and wrapped around her in a skinny bear hug. He broke their embrace. "All right, give me five cinnamon rolls." She eyed him. "What?" he asked. "I'm hungry."

She gazed at his zero-fat physique. He couldn't be actually eating these sweets she'd seen him purchase these past couple of days. "Do you always buy pastries in bulk here?"

"And? So what if I do?"

She blatantly perused his body and bobbed her head. "Well, you're clearly not eating them."

He held out his credit card to her. "Are you going to sell me some damned cinnamon rolls or do I have to go to Publix?"

She boxed the pastries and handed them over. "Nope. They are on me today."

"Why?"

She hesitated then gave him her most sincere gaze. "Thank you…for taking me in."

He gave a single nod, and then turned and walked toward the door. "I'll be back tomorrow morning. Be thinking of what you're going to be Saturday."

"Saturday?"

"For the party. I'm picking you up at 7:30." He opened the door.

"Picking me up for what?"

"Gwendolen and Rob's Halloween bash!" he shouted through the glass.

"A costume party?" she asked the empty room. "But I don't dress up."

Cassidy came through the double doors. "You do now."

She gauged her aunt. "What did Jason say?"

"He said okay. He said to tell you he loved you." Cassidy looked as enthused about that idea as she might be for dental surgery.

"Thank you," Seanna said, and Cassidy nodded. Seanna pointed toward Sebastian backing out of the parking lot. "Are you going to this thing?"

"Nah," Cassidy said, "My cul-de-sac is doing our annual Fall Fest. We hang out at the end of the street drinking spiked cider and the kids carve their pumpkins. But I'll help you get dressed for it."

"Dressed in what?"

"What do you want to be?" Cassidy asked.

"Geez, I don't know, something that doesn't stand out, I guess."

Cassidy sized up Seanna. "I think I might have the perfect character for you."

"Should I be afraid?"

Cassidy squinted one eye. "Maybe just a little."

Chapter Seven

Seanna scribbled down the last of her notes and leaned back against the countertop to re-read them. She wanted to make sure she got this right the first time. She had something to prove with this quote…not necessarily to Blake or the client, but to herself.

Blake had told her this client wanted a new, modern kitchen, and it was simple as that. This was a single guy in his thirties with very little interest in the specifics of the buildout or the interior design. Maybe he was planning on selling. Who knew. All she cared about was presenting a plan and a quote and gathering a crew to get the job done. She had no idea where to find workers or what the local workforce was like for jobs like this, but she felt confident she could figure it out. At least that was the mantra she kept repeating to herself.

She looked up as the sound of the back door opening got her attention. Blake had made himself scarce after he explained the client's wishes. She hadn't even noticed he'd left until she was already into the job for a few minutes. It had felt absolutely incredible taking charge of this job, pulling out her tape measure and assessing the area. She probably needed an interior designer on hand, but she'd worked so closely with so many of them these past four years that she was certain she could pull this whole thing off on her own. She was biting off more than she could chew, but she really felt confident that she could do this. She needed to, if not for the client, for her own sanity.

Blake raised his eyebrows as he pocketed his phone. "Well…"

She looked around the room. "It's a great space, and you've given me carte blanche." She looked at him for a final confirmation.

He nodded. "Absolutely. Chase isn't picky. He just wants his kitchen to look nice when you're done."

She dropped her hands down to her sides. "Well, that's why I'm here." It felt so good to say that with authority. She was there, ready to unburden this client from dealing with the stresses of a buildout and the irritation of choices. The whole thing made her want to squeal like a twelve-year-old girl who just learned her latest crush said he liked her.

"Very good," Blake said easily…like he had every confidence in the world that she could pull this trick off without a hitch. Now it was up to her to prove him right.

Blake dragged a net through a Panama City Beach condominium complex pool alongside Bo, who yapped away like a seventh-grade girl on the telephone with her best friend. Blake's phone vibrated in his pocket, and he pulled it out. The caller ID revealed Kevin's name.

Blake wasn't sure he wanted to take the call, but he respected Kevin enough to hear him out. Blake's life was working here in South Walton. He liked his job and the people he called his clients. The beach didn't suck, and the work he did was brainless. The problem was medicine lived in his veins. He sat up at night thinking of the people who came into the emergency department when he was a resident there—those he helped, those he couldn't save. But none stuck out more than the one who ended his medical career.

He stepped away from the still-talking Bo and walked toward Bo's work truck as he answered. He inhaled a deep breath and took the call. "Hey, man."

"Thanks for answering. I was afraid I was going to have to hunt you down."

"What's up?" Blake asked.

"A job. Here in Kansas City, working with me. There's a doctor who's pregnant and due in January. We'd need you here early December to get acclimated and in case she delivers earlier than expected."

"Interim work?" Blake asked.

"She's not coming back. Her husband's a cardiologist. She wants to stay home with the baby." Blake nodded, even though Kevin couldn't see him. "Look, man. It's time," Kevin said. "It's been three years."

Blake knew how long it'd been. It didn't mean it was time to do anything different. "I don't know."

"I do know. You are a doctor. You're not a maintenance man."

Blake's chest heated up. "It's a respectable job."

"I'm not saying it isn't. But you're a talented doctor. You are needed elsewhere."

"I'm needed here." The words sounded weak.

"The only way you're going to get right about this is if

you jump back in. It's the reason you haven't gotten over what happened yet."

His chest was being torn apart with conflicting emotions. He hated Kevin right now as much as he appreciated what he was trying to do for him. Kevin cared about him. He was only trying to help. But need it or not, Blake didn't want it.

"How long do I have to decide?"

"I'd love to know as soon as possible."

"If I have to tell you now, the answer's no," Blake said.

"I figured as much. Give me an idea of how you're leaning by the middle of next month. I'll need to know for sure before Thanksgiving."

"Thanks. I'll think about it."

"Think long and hard, man. This is a chance for you to jump back into what you were made for. And I'll be here with you. Once you've gotten through the first month or two, you won't even remember why you were holding off."

Blake's chest burned, and he let out a frustrated sigh.

"Sorry, man. I didn't mean it like that. I know you'll never forget what happened, but you've got to get to the point of self-forgiveness. You think I haven't had to forgive myself for letting someone die on my watch?"

Blake checked to make sure Bo wasn't looking at him or within earshot. "Was it your goddamned fiancée?" Blake asked.

Kevin let a moment sit between them, likely for Blake to calm down. "Yes, you should have stepped back and let me handle it, but I'm telling you I've been over that autopsy report a hundred times. She would have died no matter who was treating her."

"You don't know that."

"I do. And I take just as much responsibility for that night as you do."

"Because you didn't fight me to get me out of the room?"

"Damn straight. I should have done whatever it took."

Blake's gut churned, and he thought he might throw up, reliving the night.

"I take responsibility. I was the one who let you stay," Kevin said.

"You didn't *let* me do anything," Blake said.

"I know. You're the most headstrong asshole I've ever had the privilege to work with."

"I don't need your charity."

"My getting you to come here to work isn't charity. You're the best doctor I know, and we work well together. You don't have an ego, and you care more about patients than anyone I've ever worked with. I want you here because you're the best at what you do, and that's not an easy thing to find. For you to quit medicine for the rest of your life would be like Eddie Van Halen refusing to play guitar." Blake had to admit he didn't mind the comparison. "You are needed here. I'll talk to you mid-October, but call or email me as you think of questions."

They disconnected their call. Working under Kevin's supervision couldn't be a more ideal situation for getting Blake back into medicine. Kevin understood the gravity of Blake's mental state. He would ease him into the job rather than any other hospital which would cut him no slack. And he liked Kevin. He was the only person from his old life who regularly reached out to him and tried to bring him back among the living. It wasn't as if anyone else knew where he was though.

He pocketed his phone and made his way back to the pool. Bo was crouched by the water with a testing strip. He looked up at Blake. "Next time I'd appreciate a head's-up that you're walking away. I sat here and told the goddamned water all about my sister's promotion."

"Shayla got a promotion?" Blake asked.

Bo glared him down. "Yeah. What's with you today, anyway?"

Blake's head had been screwed on sideways since Seanna had come to town. Just the half hour he'd spent with her the other day when he met her at Chase's house to quote on the kitchen remodel had messed him up for the rest of the day. He'd been nervous around her like when he was fourteen and a pretty girl at school said hello to him in the hallway. But just like back then, he knew that was as far as it could ever go.

She made him smile wider by the minute when they were together. He liked her mix of humor and realism. He liked that she cared deeply and how she seemed to feel comfortable enough to talk to him. And he liked most that she trusted him. He was honored to be the one she'd chosen to talk to.

"Earth to Blake?" Bo waved his hands elaborately.

"What?"

Bo tapped his finger against his chin, squinting. Blake rolled his eyes, knowing what was coming next. Bo stood and approached his friend, still squinting. He pointed at Blake. "I know that faraway gaze."

"Shut the hell up."

"I know it well. I haven't seen it from you before, which is why it took me a while to catch on. You like a girl."

Blake busied himself with picking up a net. "Jesus Christ. Get a freaking life."

Bo's smile widened even farther if that was possible. "It's Cassidy's niece, isn't it? Susan."

"Seanna."

"I knew it!"

"You're so full of shit we're gonna have to drain this pool," Blake said.

"You never did tell me what happened when you disappeared on me the other night at Jazz on the Lawn. Where'd you take her?"

Blake shrugged as he picked up the rest of the equipment. "The beach."

"Sex on the beach, huh? You still finding grains of sand in your ass?"

Blake headed toward the truck with the equipment. "I don't have to screw every girl I meet."

"Ah. Deciding to wait. Must be someone special."

"She's nobody to me but Cassidy's niece."

Bo rested his arm on the side of the truck bed. "What would be so terrible about taking this girl on a date?"

"You're one to talk. I haven't seen you take a girl on a date in months."

Bo dumped the remainder of the equipment in the truck bed. "I don't keep you abreast of all my female situations."

"You mean your late nights spent with Skinamax and a jar of petroleum jelly."

Bo shoved him, Blake shoved back, and before he knew it they were knocking each other around like brothers. Nothing helped release stress like a brawl with his best friend. When they finished, Blake dusted himself off and took a look around. "You're gonna get yourself fired from this job site."

"I'll just explain I had to put up with your bullshit, and they'll pay me double."

Blake rolled his eyes and got in the truck. "That the last job? You owe me lunch."

"Just get yourself buckled in there, Romeo. Wouldn't want anything to damage that pretty face of yours."

Blake pulled the visor down and assessed the damage. "I think I'm gonna have a bruise on the left side of my chin."

"Want me to kiss it and make it all better?"

Blake punched Bo in the arm and they headed down the road.

The thing was, Bo wasn't completely off base. Not only did he like her personality, but he turned into a protective warrior when anyone even mentioned her name. He didn't know how to explain it. He just wanted her to be his.

But he couldn't even ask her out on a date. He wasn't worthy of any woman after what he did, especially not her. She'd had a tough go of it, dealing with this asshole who lied to her and stripped her life from her dollar by dollar. That was what she needed—another boyfriend who kept secrets from her. She'd run like the wind if she had a clue about him.

He needed to keep his distance as much as was possible, as much as he could force himself to. Maybe heading to Kansas City wasn't a terrible idea.

Chapter Eight

Seanna rubbed her temple as the nice woman on the other end of the line let her down easy. "No, I understand completely," Seanna said. "I hope you'll keep me in mind if anything else opens up."

"Oh yes, of course," the lady said, but Seanna knew that was code for *delete resume.*

It'd only been a week since she submitted the resumes, but she'd sent out more than fifty, and the only ones that had responded were low-level assistant positions. She'd rather work at the bakery with Cassidy for that kind of money.

Her stomach rumbled as she sat in the car at the client's house waiting for Blake to meet her there. He had texted her that he was running late. He'd insisted on being there to make the introduction between her and the client. She could certainly handle introducing herself to a client, but since he was the one making this connection, she was happy to follow his rules.

If she could just land this kitchen remodel, she'd have it as a resume builder. She could prove that she was capable of handling a project all on her own, start to finish. This job could help her build her career. It could open doors that were shutting hard in her face.

The front door to the house opened and out walked a dark-haired guy who practically had to duck coming through the doorway. This was the guy she'd been waiting for all week. He'd been out of town, and Friday was the earliest he could meet with them.

He walked toward her, bare-footed, with a smile on his face like he was up to something. The closer he got to her, the cuter he got. He had a deep, rich tan...or possibly that was his natural skin color. Either way, he was easy on the eyes from head to toe. She got out of the car, leaving the proposal on the passenger seat.

"So you're Cassidy's niece," he said. "I haven't heard so much gossip slung around this town since that guy on the city council mowed down his neighbor's palm tree."

Seanna couldn't help a grin. Not only was this guy cute, but he had an easy way about him. She was suddenly not nearly as nervous about presenting her quote. She held out her hand. "Seanna Perry."

"Chase O'Neil. Pleasure." He grinned so kindly she actually felt her heart warm.

She looked down at the proposal in her car. "I know Blake wanted to be here to connect us. We can wait for him to go over the proposal or..."

"Oh, yeah. He's been texting. Wants to be here for the whole production." He motioned to her as he turned back toward the house. "Come on. Let's have a beer while we wait for him to get here."

"Okay," she said and grabbed the proposal from the front seat of her car.

He held the screen door open for her, and she walked into his house. Before, when she'd been in there without him, she'd had a sense of empowerment. The space had felt like hers. Now, it was clear this was his domain, and she was an employee…if she was lucky enough to get the job.

"Have a seat," he said, nodding at the kitchen chair she was standing next to. "Do you like a hoppy beer or something lighter?"

"Whatever you have is fine."

He eyed her. "You like Blue Moon?"

Relieved, she said, "Perfect." She hated hoppy beer, but she loved a good wheat beer.

He closed the refrigerator door. "I knew it. Girls love Blue Moon."

She frowned, seeing he had an Abita. Rather than seeming like a girl to him, she wanted to seem like a capable, hoppy-beer-drinking woman. "Thanks," she said, taking the bottle.

"You want a glass?" he asked.

"No. This is fine just like this."

He was easy and kind, but her nerves were kicking in. She just wanted to get this quote presented. Where was Blake? Chase pulled out a chair and sat. "So Blake said you're just here visiting,"

"That's right, but if you select me for this job, I'll see it through. It will take about two to three weeks, and I can get started immediately."

He picked up the quote and perused it. She glanced at the door. Blake had wanted to be here for this, but she couldn't grab it out of Chase's hands. He frowned and then eyed her. She swallowed, not liking the look on his face.

He set the quote down and relaxed back in his chair, studying her. "How long have you been doing this?"

"Four years," she answered. It was true, she had been working in this business being prepped and trained for four years. Did she need to disclose this was her first job on her own?

He narrowed his gaze. "Commercial?"

"Yes."

He gave a knowing nod, like it all suddenly made sense. "Did Blake mention I have a property management company?"

"No, actually he didn't."

Chase rolled his eyes. "Of course he didn't, mister tight lips. I've been in this business for over a decade, and I've looked at about a hundred quotes for kitchen remodels."

She swallowed, hard, realizing she'd screwed up. She was too high.

"Look, with you being Cassidy's niece and a friend of Blake's, before you got here I had every intention of accepting this quote unless you were more than double what I knew it should be." He tapped the quote. "I can't in good conscience let you take this job at this price. You'd lose your shirt."

She blinked, realizing she had it backwards.

"You're used to quoting out commercial jobs," he said. "Residential is a whole different ball of wax."

She nodded, trying to keep her emotions in check. She'd screwed up, and he was letting her know, likely keeping her from getting herself further in debt. She needed to be thankful, not humiliated.

He walked over to a drawer and pulled out a red pen. He

came back to the table and started marking up the quote, and the paper began to bleed. She refrained from shaking her head at her own idiocy. She'd wanted so bad to impress this client, to impress herself, to prove she was ready for this step in her career.

He slid the quote back to her. "This is what this job should cost. And it's going to take a month if it takes a day."

She remained stoic, reviewing his changes. He'd initialed beside all of them and signed on the dotted line. He was giving her this job. Holy crap. She nodded. "Got it."

He sat back in his chair. "So why are you doing this if you're down here on vacation?"

She fiddled with the pen, looking at the quote. "Well, it was an opportunity. I wanted to take it."

"But you live in Nashville?" he asked.

"Mmm hmm."

"Are you on a leave of absence or between jobs?"

She pulled together her pride. "Between jobs."

"You looking for work?"

"Yes, actually," she said.

He narrowed his gaze at her again, thinking. "Look, I've got a property under contract set to close in a few weeks—gut-job, whole house. I want someone who will redo it top to bottom and get it ready to rent. If you want to put your hat in the ring, you're welcome to."

"You'd be willing to give me a shot?"

He shrugged. "We'll see how you do on this buildout. Are you in a place where you could stick around here a while? I assume you're staying with Cassidy."

She'd been so determined not to let Jason kick her out of Nashville, but she was getting nowhere with the fifty plus jobs she had applied for. And going back to Nashville meant living in the same space with Jason, at least until December. As much as she wanted to stake her territory back home and show him he could not send her scurrying from her own town—her own apartment—this was an opportunity she could not pass up.

She could stay here a while. If she was able to score this job he was talking about, then that would certainly be enough to keep her busy until she was through with her lease in December. She could continue looking for a job back in Nashville and be building her resume while she was at it.

"Yes, Cassidy's already told me I can stay with her as long as I need to."

"You got some workers lined up for this job?" he asked.

"Yes." That wasn't the whole truth, but she knew she could find workers. That was part of what she did at the firm.

"I know some guys who do good work if you wouldn't mind using them. I'm usually not that controlling, but since this is my own house…"

"Of course," she said, a tad relieved. She knew she could find workers, but it certainly helped that he already had some in mind.

He pulled a card out of his wallet and handed it to her. "My assistant's information is on there. Call her, and she'll get you names and phone numbers. If you'll bring her a copy of that contract, she'll get a check cut for the cost of materials and half the labor."

Seanna tapped the card twice against her palm. As much as this guy had put her in her place, he was also being generous to a fault. She met his gaze. "I screwed this up. We both know I did. Do you mind if I ask you why you're willing to give me such a big opportunity…not just on your kitchen but possibly this gut-job?"

He let out a deep breath. "Because I think a lot of your aunt and of Blake. If you've got their stamps of approval, then that's all I need to know."

Her heart swelled with appreciation, but the pit of her stomach rolled with the sense of responsibility. "Thank you, seriously."

He shrugged. "It's just a kitchen." To him, sure. The front door opened and Chase yelled, "There he is."

He gave Seanna a comforting smile and then went over to his refrigerator. Blake rounded the corner and met her gaze, his face flushed red, hair wet, but looking as fine as ever. She swore every time she saw him he got yummier.

"Sorry, I'm late," Blake said. "I see you two met one another."

Chase handed him a beer. "We're old friends now."

Blake gave him a look, and Chase returned it with a smile. Blake glanced at the marked-up quote. Seanna quickly folded the papers over and slid them into her bag. She'd had enough embarrassment for the day.

"Did you already go over the quote?" Blake asked.

Chase took his seat. "She came in a little high. But you know me and my master negotiating skills. We were able to meet in the middle."

She was really starting to like this guy. She shouldered her bag, and then held her hand out to Chase. "Thank you for the opportunity. I'll be in touch with your assistant."

"You're leaving?" Blake asked.

"Bo's coming over," Chase said. "We're gonna play cards. We could use a fourth."

A card game with three gorgeous guys. That was tempting. But she knew when to make an exit. "No, thanks. I need to get going. It was nice to meet you, Chase."

"Let me walk you to your car," Blake said.

Seanna headed toward the front door, her heels clacking on Chase's hardwood floor. She'd come dressed to impress but couldn't wait to get back to Cassidy's, get into her comfies, and dive into this project.

She started to open her car door but Blake put a hand on her arm. "Wait. How did it go? Did he cut you down too low? He's a pussycat. It wouldn't take much to get him to come back up to where you need him to be."

She held back a laugh but couldn't restrain her smile. "No, he's fine. We're all good here." She started to open the door again.

"Wait," Blake said, moving to stand between her and the car. He peered at her, narrowing his eyes. "Are you sure?"

She rested her weight on her right hip. "Positive. I'm just eager to get started."

Blake searched her eyes. "So you two hit it off?"

Was that jealousy she sensed in his demeanor? "Yeah, we did," she said, liking this a little bit—especially since she was still dragging her pride up off the ground.

"Did he…ask you out or something?"

She cocked her head to the side, widening her eyes. "What kind of a project manager do you take me for, Blake?"

He dropped the tension in his shoulders and shook his head. "Sorry. So when will you start the job?"

"Soon, I think. I'll coordinate all that with his assistant." She let out a deep breath, pulling herself together. "Thank you for setting this up. You have no idea how much I appreciate this opportunity. Seriously."

She wrapped her arms around him and held him tightly to her. Inhaling his clean and freshly-shaven scent, she let her mind roam as she imagined him all soaped up and dripping wet in the shower. Damn it was getting hot out there, and it was probably only about seventy-five degrees outside.

When she pulled away from him, she could swear his cheeks were pinker than they were before she went in for the hug. She pointed to the house. "He's giving me the opportunity to quote on another remodel, a whole house."

His eyebrows went up. "That's great. So does that mean you're staying here for a while?"

"If I get that job, I don't see how I could pass up the opportunity. I'm not working, and I need this money. Now I've just got to make sure I don't screw up this kitchen job. I think I'm being graded."

His smile sent a shiver up her spine. "You're gonna do great."

"Thanks." She smiled at him, and for a moment she thought he might go in for a kiss. She stared at his lips, her mouth watering with anticipation.

Now that she was staying for a while, sleeping with him for a quick one-night stand was off the table. She was too interested in him. He was too good of a guy. Once she slept with him, she'd want more, and she wasn't ready for more…not at this point. Her life was too much in disarray. She needed to work on herself right now. Get her life in order. Get invested in her work. Get back to Nashville…eventually. She took a step backward.

"All right then. I'll see you." He went to walk away, but

then turned back around. "By any chance is Cassidy bringing you to Rob and Gwendolen's Halloween party tomorrow?"

She held back a grin. "Sebastian is."

He nodded understanding, all aloof. "What are you dressing up as?"

"You'll find out tomorrow," she said.

He gave her a grin that made her sway a little. "Looking forward to it."

He turned to walk away and she got into her car, admiring his ass as he went. It was a great ass, a superb one as a matter of fact. One she could really...the job. She would focus on the job. He turned to her with a smile before he headed inside, catching her staring.

Good lord.

Chapter Nine

"Umm…Cassidy. I'm not so sure about this." Seanna surveyed herself in the mirror. She was either going to come off looking like the sexiest woman on throwback television or like a dowdy librarian.

"Come on out. Let me see you." Seanna scrunched up her face and opened the closet door to reveal herself. Cassidy put her hand to her chest. "You look fantastic. You look just like her."

Seanna touched her hair. "Are you sure about the hair? You promise it will wash out?"

"In three shampoos. I used it once for a girls' night out."

"You went red?"

"I didn't say it looked good on me. I said it would wash out."

Seanna took one last self-conscious glance at herself in the mirror. "Are you sure everyone else is going to be dressed up?"

"Trust me. You'll be the most underdressed person there. People go all out for this bash."

Seanna turned around to check out her backside in the skin-tight dress. "*Mad Men* isn't even on anymore. Will people get it?"

"Sweetheart, you've got the bod to pull off Joan. You have to go as her at least one Halloween in your lifetime. Wish I could."

Seanna pursed her lips at her aunt. "Just go as Giselle Bunhchen instead. That's your bod." Cassidy gave a dismissive wave as the doorbell rang, and she followed Seanna to the front door.

"Did someone call 911?" Sebastian stood at the door donning a quite authentic policeman's uniform, twirling a whistle around his finger. He stopped and covered his mouth dramatically. He pointed at Seanna. "Joan Holloway. My God. You are her!"

Seanna fondled her gold pen necklace. "You think? I was afraid people would think I was a dowdy librarian."

He dropped his hands to his legs. "You should have told me. I'd have gone as Don Draper." Cassidy giggled, and Sebastian's eyes widened. "What? I can do Don."

She put an arm on his shoulder. "Of course you can, sweetie."

Sebastian snapped at her hand, and she retracted with a smile. He turned to Seanna and touched her hair. "Is this a wig?"

"It's a rinse out. Three shampoos," Cassidy said.

He shrugged. "That's a shame. I kind of like it."

A horn sounded from outside. Sebastian rolled his eyes. "Come on before Zorro out there lays an egg." Cassidy waved out the screen door to Ashe, who blew her a kiss from under his Zorro mask.

"Are you sure you won't come?" Seanna asked.

"Oh, yes, sweetie. These days an evening on the couch is hard to compete with. You all go. Have fun."

Seanna kissed Cassidy goodbye, and they were off. Sebastian drove them to a community called Alys Beach, which boasted palm trees on either side of the road Beverly Hills-style. He turned onto a street that led to the beach, and they made their way toward a large, Mediterranean-style house dressed in purple and orange lights with its back seaward at the end of the cul-de-sac.

"Wow," Seanna said. "I want to live here when I grow up."

"Wait till you see the inside," Ashe said.

Just after stepping through the foyer they were greeted by a couple dressed as Morticia and Gomez Addams. Sebastian hugged Morticia, and then motioned to Seanna. "Gwendolen, Rob, I want to introduce you to a new friend of mine, Joan Holloway." Sebastian waved in Seanna's direction like Vanna White.

Seanna offered a hand. "Hi, I'm Seanna."

"Oh, I loved *Mad Men*," Gwendolen said. "You make the perfect Joan."

"You make the perfect Morticia," Seanna said. "I always loved Angelica Huston."

"Oh, I know. Me too," Gwendolen said.

"Seanna is Cassidy Anderson's niece," Sebastian said.

"No kidding? I adore your aunt. Tell her we missed her like crazy tonight."

Seanna smiled. "Will do." Gwendolen excused herself graciously as another group of party guests behind them grabbed her attention.

They walked through the foyer and past the front rooms

to an open living room with the back wall comprised entirely of glass showing off an unbelievable view of an infinity pool with the Gulf of Mexico acting as a backdrop. People were sprinkled all around the pool socializing, and "The Time Warp" spilled from the sound system. Seanna spotted Desiree by the pool sporting a perfectly rounded Diana Ross 'do straight out of the seventies.

She pointed at Desiree's hair. "Your hair could have its own reality show."

"I'd watch that," Ashe said.

Desiree patted it. "I do love my Miss Ross look. What about you? Not many people can pull off Joan, but you, my dear, have." Sebastian cleared his throat, and she held her hands out palms up in question. "Why aren't you her Don Draper?"

Sebastian gave Seanna a playful shove. "What did I tell you?"

"Have you been here long?" Ashe asked Desiree.

"I came early to help them set up some of the décor." She motioned to the patio covered in lanterns, lights, and Halloween decorations that looked like they'd leapt out of a high-end architecture magazine feature.

A voice barged in. "Seaside Sweets." Seanna turned to find the source, which was a customer she'd served a few times this past week. She'd been helping her aunt out most the week since Chase couldn't meet until Friday.

"Oh, hello…"

"Vivian." The lady offered her hand to Seanna.

"Seanna."

"Tell me, when will Cassidy have that pumpkin praline cheesecake out? It is fall you know?" the lady asked.

"Oh, I'm sorry. Looks like we're slacking a bit on the job." Seanna smiled. Vivian didn't. Seanna cleared her throat. "I'll let Cassidy know of the request."

"Thank you." The woman turned and walked away.

Seanna felt like she'd just been called down for talking in class. She regained her composure and turned to rejoin the group to find it had dispersed. Ashe and Desiree were dancing to the "Monster Mash" while Sebastian stood talking to a tall, thin man dressed as Priscilla Queen of the Desert. Beside them was a couple who were contestants on *Dancing with the Stars* talking to a lunatic butcher with a bloody meat clever sticking out of the pocket of his smock. R2D2 and C3PO casually sipped cocktails with John Lennon and Yoko Ono.

Cassidy wasn't kidding about Seanna being underdressed. She walked around taking in the house and the people. There was more money in this room than she'd see in a dozen lifetimes. She wondered how many of these ladies were footing their ex's bills and chuckled at her own situation by comparison.

As Seanna stepped out onto the patio, the ocean air permeated into her skin, making her feel like she was a million miles away from the mess back home. She rested a hand against the back of an empty chaise lounge and drew her drink to her lips. That was when she found two guys standing together on the other side of the pool, one in a toga and one in a forties gangster outfit. She practically had to catch her breath. Blake and Bo. She wasn't sure there were two more appealing guys in the state of Florida, and these two stood right there mere steps away from her. Her lips parted in a smile without her control or permission. Bo smiled back with a wave. Blake's smile was far less genuine though, sending a wave of unease through her chest.

Seanna dropped her gaze and walked down the steps toward the beach. "What the hell's wrong with you?" Bo asked.

"What?" Blake asked, but he knew exactly what his friend was talking about.

"Seanna just smiled at you, and you barely even acknowledged her."

"I smiled back," Blake said weakly.

"Bullshit. I smiled at her. You turned your head."

Blake wanted to smile at her. He wanted to take her hand and lead her down that beach walkway and not come back until tomorrow. But the more he thought about her, the more he wanted to see her...to touch her...to know more about her. And all of that was a huge problem.

"It's just that I don't see any sense in it," Blake said.

Bo raised his eyebrows. "In what? Being a nice person?"

Blake dug his hand into the pocket of his pants. "In starting something with her."

"How come?" Bo asked.

Blake grimaced at his friend. "She's Cassidy's niece. We've been over this."

"Let's talk worst-case scenario," Bo said. "You take her out. There's nothing there, so you remain friends."

"That's not worst case."

"Then what is?"

"I don't know. We date for a while and it ends ugly, and then I have to answer to Cassidy."

Bo turned toward him. "What are we, in seventh grade? How's it gonna end ugly?"

Blake shrugged with pursed lips, Bo's persistence starting to get to him. Bo ran a hand over his crew cut and looked around conspiratorially. "All right, look. I've spent three years keeping my mouth shut when it came to asking about your past or anything too personal. But you know I know something's going on there."

Blake shifted uncomfortably. Bo was no idiot. But Blake had preferred living under the pretense that Bo didn't even think about his past or try to excuse his odd behavior when it came to certain things, mainly women. But of course he did. He'd just been giving Blake space and time. Blake had always wondered when the day would come that Bo would finally want answers. He guessed three years was long enough to keep his questions to himself.

Blake lifted his beer bottle to his lips. "What do you mean?"

Bo stared him down, not buying Blake's bullshit act for a second. "I mean I'm starting to get offended here. How long do we have to be friends before you figure out you can trust me?"

That one hit Blake in the chest. He loved Bo like a brother. Bo helped him keep sane a lot of days. Blake didn't want Bo to think he was holding out on him, but of course he was. Blake couldn't tell him about his past. Not now. He would…eventually. He just wasn't ready yet. But he could see now that he needed to give him something. "I wouldn't make a good partner for someone right now," Blake said.

"I don't know if that's true or not, but I'll tell you what I know to be a fact. You make a damn good friend."

Blake glanced at Bo, who was looking at him with utter sincerity. Blake's throat tightened at Bo's words. He straightened it, looking at his beer bottle, furrowing his brow. "You do too, man."

They'd never exchanged any sort of words like those. Their relationship was built on giving each other a hard time. Knowing Bo cared in no uncertain words meant more to Blake than he could ever let Bo know.

Bo chuckled. "If it isn't the devil herself."

Blake followed Bo's gaze to Marigold in a devil costume headed their way.

Bo laughed. "Look at her craning her neck around looking for you."

"You don't know she's looking for me."

Marigold caught sight of him and perked up. She scooted around people, moving in a beeline toward them.

Bo nudged Blake. "Seanna's on the beach by herself. Go down there and say hello."

Blake looked in that direction, and then back at his beer bottle. "I can't."

Someone grabbed Marigold in a hug. She kept eyeing Blake like she was itching to get out there to him while some woman held her hostage with conversation.

"Why? Something wrong with the stairs?" Bo asked. "Get your ass down there. I'm not saying you should elope. I'm saying have a conversation with her."

"I can't go there," Blake said. "I've got...shit going on."

"Yeah, yeah. I know all about your shit." Blake cut his eyes at him. He couldn't possibly know. Bo held up a hand. "I mean I know you've got it. I don't know what it is. But what I know is that girl down there on the beach has got something. You know what I'm talking about."

Blake knew exactly what Bo was talking about. It wasn't

something he could put his finger on, but she was sweet, and real, and honest…and sexier than anything he'd ever seen. He couldn't be the only one who noticed it.

"She's not the kind of girl who stays single for long," Bo said. "I can guarantee you that." Marigold broke free from the woman and was scooting past more people. Bo gave Blake another nudge. "Go. I'll take care of Marigold."

Blake considered him. "You will?"

"I can play wingman." He motioned with his head. "Get."

Blake smiled, and then turned sincere. "Thanks…for…"

Bo gave a nod. "Yeah."

Blake headed for the steps.

Seanna sat in the middle of the long swing, pushing off with her bare feet. Blake's chilly reception hadn't been her favorite thing about the day, but oh well. It wasn't like she needed to be dating right now. She hadn't planned to tell him all about her mess, but there was something about him, about his demeanor and the look in his eyes, that told her she could and that she wouldn't be judged. But maybe she was wrong. God knew she had been before. Still, it stung.

Someone walked down the steps. As the black pinstripe gangster pants came into view, her heart couldn't help a hint of relief. He peered at the ocean, scanning the beach…for her? She whistled. When he turned toward her, his face lit up, and her heart melted into her chest.

She scooted over as he walked toward her. He sat next to her, causing all kinds of imbalance, not only in the swing but inside her.

He set his toy gun between them. "The party's up there, you know."

"Are you kidding? These crabs and I are getting ready to do the Electric Slide."

"Do people do that anymore?"

"My friend got married about a year ago. We did all the group dances. My favorite is the Chicken Dance, of course."

"The Chicken Dance?"

She slid him a look. "You do know the Chicken Dance, don't you?"

"I've seen it, sure."

"Yes, but have you ever done it?" He lifted his eyebrows in concession, and she put her hand to her forehead in dramatic fashion. "Oh, my God. You haven't lived until you've done the Chicken Dance."

"I'll be sure to get myself invited to a wedding soon."

"It's a necessity."

He shifted in his seat, opening himself a little to her. "So, how's everything going?"

"Great. I'm starting the job with Chase Monday…thanks to you."

"I meant with everything else? Have you heard anything from your ex?"

She rolled her eyes. "He called the shop so Cassidy was stuck talking to him."

"So he knows you're here," he said.

"That part isn't rocket science. He knows none of my family or friends know we've broken up. And he also knows I trust Cassidy with my life. So where else would I go? It's not like I can afford to go anywhere else."

"What did Cassidy tell him?"

"I let her spill the beans that I was here and okay. That should hold him off for a hot minute." She turned to him.

"You know, I've done nothing but talk about myself since we've met. Tell me something about you, something I could never guess."

He shrugged, but his face turned red. She was starting to learn his tells. "There's not much to talk about."

"What about your family? Where do they live? Do you have brothers and sisters?"

He squirmed in his seat a little. "Sort of."

She studied him. "You sort of have brothers and sisters?"

He scratched his neck under the collar of his shirt. "I'm burning this cheap Halloween costume when I get home."

She wondered what he meant by *sort of*, but she was afraid to push. Maybe he had a sibling who'd passed away…or maybe he had step siblings or half siblings he didn't know very well. Suddenly, she was plagued with a ridiculous desire to know the full story. "Are your parents still together?"

He gnawed on his bottom lip. "How are you doing on that drink?"

"Full up." She turned her body to face him, zipping her lip. As much as she wanted to prod this forward, she wondered if the best tactic here might be silence.

He pointed at the ocean. "Have you seen a dolphin yet? They poke their heads up sometimes at night when they think nobody's watching."

She considered him. "I have an older brother. We're not very close. There's a bit of an age difference, and I don't know, we just never really clicked." She slid her hand over to his forearm. "I'd like to know about your family."

He met her gaze, his brow worried. "I don't really talk about it much."

She squeezed his arm. "Could you tell me?"

His forehead creased in consideration as he searched her eyes. Finally, he scooted over to his side of the swing, holding onto the chain. "I'm an orphan."

If someone would have offered her a million dollars to guess what he was going to say, she still wouldn't have thought of that. "Oh, wow. I'm so sorry."

He shrugged. "Nothing to be sorry about. I never knew my parents. I always wondered, of course. When I was eighteen, I got my birth mother's information and researched her. I found out she was fifty-three years old then."

Seanna's heart constricted. "So that would have made her…"

"Thirty-five when she had me."

Seanna let that sink in for a moment. "Did you go talk to her?"

Blake kept his expression even. "I spent a lot of time mulling over the reasons a thirty-five-year-old woman would give up a baby for adoption. I finally figured whatever the reason was, it didn't involve her wanting to see me again. Honestly, I didn't think she should have to see me." Seanna opened her mouth to respond but didn't know how to. He shrugged. "She stuck it out for nine months so I could be born. I figured I owed her the courtesy of being left alone."

Sliding her hand across the swing cushion, she found his and squeezed it. He smiled down at his lap.

"So your mother gave you up as a baby, but you were never adopted?"

"I was set to be, apparently, but I developed GBS." Seanna knitted her eyebrows together. He shook his head quickly. "Group B Strep, which eventually resulted in bacterial meningitis."

Her hand drew to her lips. "Oh my gosh."

He smiled and pointed at her. "I think that was the exact reaction of a dozen other potential adoptive families."

"I'm so sorry," she said, her heart aching for him.

"Don't be. Meningitis is a scary word."

"But you obviously got better from that," she said, still wondering how he didn't get adopted.

"One of the long-term effects of GBS meningitis is developmental delay. I didn't hit the milestones when I should have. Walking, talking. I didn't say a word until I was four. I didn't make for the most adoptable kid."

Seanna's heart hurt as she thought about a little Blake, sitting in the corner, coloring outside the lines, not able to speak with potential parents who came to adopt him. Her nephew was autistic and delayed developmentally. He didn't talk until he was three and a half. Seanna had seen the frustration in his features and what a completely different kid he was when he was finally able to use his words.

"So where did you grow up?" she asked.

"Partially at a Presbyterian children's home in a suburb of Atlanta. It was a series of houses on a two-hundred-acre property. We had cows and horses, chickens. It was a beautiful place."

"So you grew up on a working farm?"

"Somewhat of one. I got to ride the horses, milk the cows, collect the eggs from the chickens. I saw the birth of a baby llama once."

She laughed. "That's the coolest thing ever."

He nodded in memory. "It was. Kids from other schools would come to the farm for field trips. One of the local stations did a special interest story on us. We kids were like rock stars."

"Seriously?"

He chuckled. "Yeah."

"Are you close with the couples who raised you?"

"No. They raised a lot of kids. I stayed out of trouble, kept to myself. A couple would come and care for my house for a while. Some would find it wasn't for them, move on to another place in their life. I learned not to get too attached to any of my house parents."

Seanna tried to imagine what life would be like without permanent parents. Her own parents meant the world to her. It'd been hard calling her mother earlier this week and telling her the wedding was off, but she couldn't imagine not having her mom, or her aunt for that matter, to confide in. No wonder he was so shut off.

"What about the other kids in the house?" she asked.

"I stayed in touch with some of them for a while. I think they mostly keep in touch on Facebook. That's not my thing."

She couldn't imagine Blake taking a selfie or posting a status update on any social media site. She considered him...so many questions. She wanted to choose wisely. "So where do you go for the holidays?"

"Bo's family has me for Christmas. Your aunt has Sebastian and me over for Thanksgiving every year."

Seanna took note that this covered the past few years, but what about his time in Atlanta? Where had he gone then? She knew better than to ask that.

"Is Sebastian an orphan, too?" she asked.

He frowned. "No, his dad is still living. I'll let him tell you the rest of that story."

She had a feeling she wouldn't like it. She considered

Blake. "You know, he comes in the shop every day and buys five cinnamon rolls, and he's very hush-mouthed about who eats them. It's clearly not him. Who are those for?"

Blake smiled. "I guess I can reveal that secret. He visits a nursing home every day. He has this group of women whose hair he does. He invited me along one day because one of them wanted a shelf built. You should have seen the way those women doted over him."

Seanna could only imagine. "He's a pretty special guy, huh?"

"Yeah. Definitely."

"What does he do for a living that he has time to go to the nursing home every day?" she asked.

"He's a financial consultant. Really smart guy. I think he's made a mint in the stock market, but he still works when he wants to."

"Wow. Must be nice. I guess if all goes well with this kitchen remodel, and I get that gut-job of Chase's, we'll be spending Thanksgiving together this year."

"If that's okay," he said. "Now that your aunt has actual family here, I'd understand if I needed to find somewhere else."

"Are you kidding? Looks like I'm the one intruding."

He shook his head with a smile. She was starting to notice that one eye closed a little more than the other when he smiled genuinely. God, he was handsome with those clear, blue eyes with the little laugh lines around the edges, that crooked nose that she wouldn't want fixed for anything in the world, and those stupid, perfect kissable lips…the lower one a little bigger than the upper one except for when he smiled, and then they evened out into perfect symmetry. Damn. She was so screwed.

She wiggled in her seat. "So how do you know the Baldwins? Do all the locals in this town know each other or something?"

"Actually, I know them through Bo. His company handles their pool. He recommended me to do some work for them a while back. This is the first year I got a direct invite." He stuck out his chest in a show of pride.

She smiled. "Climbing up the social ladder, huh?"

"Not bad for a blue-collar guy." He gave her a lazy grin and then set his gaze on the rolling surf in front of them.

She walked her fingers toward his hand. He caught the movement out of the corner of his eye and glanced down. She made a show of fisting her fingers, like she wasn't up to anything. He smiled. She loved how she could make him do that.

She shifted on the bench so she had her back against the arm, facing him. She smoothed her knee-length pencil skirt against her thighs and rested her knees against the back of the bench. She cursed her aunt for outfitting her in this confining sixties librarian getup. "Tell me something else about you."

"I told you I was an orphan. That wasn't enough?"

"Tell me something you like."

He peered at her, narrowing his gaze. "I like Batman."

She attempted to hold back her smile but failed miserably. "Batman? He does it for you?"

"I respect him."

"Oh, okay. I get that. He's got superpowers."

He frowned. "No he doesn't."

"He's a superhero, isn't he?"

"Well, yeah, but that's what's so cool about him. He

doesn't have superhuman strength or the ability to fly on his own, so he's got to come up with creative ways to fight the villains."

She nodded, holding back a grin. "Interesting."

"Of course he is. He's Batman."

"No, not him...you. I hadn't pegged you as a comic book geek."

He huffed a laugh with a shrug, seeming about as un-geeky as possible. "I actually never had any of the comic books. I like the movies, though." She nodded, trying to seem neutral, but the way he was looking at her, she suspected she was busted. "You've seen the movies, right?"

She scratched her chin. "Umm..."

"You're kidding. Not even the Christian Bale ones?"

"What other ones are there?"

"Well, there's the original ones from the forties and sixties, then the first Tim Burton one came out in 1989."

"Which ones are better?"

He considered her. "Want to put it to the test?"

She looked him up and down like he'd laid a challenge before her. "Okay."

"We'll watch the first Michael Keaton one and the first Christian Bale one back-to-back."

"It's a d..." she said, stopping herself just in time, "plan."

"Cool." He furrowed his brow and looked her up and down, sending shivers up her spine. "That's a good look for you, you know."

She held up her pen necklace and stuck out her chest. "Would you like me to take a memo?"

He grinned and slid his gaze to her mouth, waking up her bottom half. The sound of what was certainly a herd of elephants on the wooden stairs had them both turning their heads. Desiree led the pack, flinging off her sandals when she reached the sand. She held out the skirt of her flowing stage dress and twirled around in circles until she dizzied herself, stumbling and laughing.

Sebastian came next. "Don't ralph up your cocktails, Diana."

Ashe held his Zorro mask over his eyes and ran headlong toward the ocean.

The blond, cat-eyed girl from the bakery the other day was next, dressed in a skin-tight sexy devil costume. She was so skinny Seanna thought she might lift right up off the ground with the next ocean breeze. As she spotted Blake and Seanna, her expression tightened. Seanna dropped her feet to the ground, feeling a little exposed.

She sleeked their way. "Hey Blake, Brianna."

Bo stepped off the stairs and followed behind her, wearing a weary expression. "Seanna."

The girl tossed a hand up in irritation as she narrowed her gaze on Seanna. "What are you, a librarian?" Seanna knew it. She should have gone with a black cat. But then it wasn't like she wanted to stand next to this girl in anything figure hugging.

"She's Joan, from *Mad Men*." Blake turned to Seanna. "Right?"

She nodded, glad someone got it.

"Oh," the girl said, her nose scrunching up on the side. "How cute. Wasn't she like a secretary or something on that show?"

Bo pulled the tail on her devil outfit. "We can't all have such a fitting costume."

She glared at him in the way only a tween girl with a huge crush on a boy could. Seanna figured out quickly that she was on this girl's territory, or what she perceived to be her territory. The girl—*Marigold was it?*—turned to Seanna. "So Sebastian's bringing you everywhere, isn't he? I assume you came with him."

"I did," Seanna said.

"That's…great." she said, practically clenching her teeth.

Sebastian approached them and tugged at Bo's toga. "Let me get a good look at your costume." Sebastian pursed his lips in disappointment. "I see you've got it tightly fastened. Good for you." He shrugged and mouthed the words *I tried* to Seanna.

Zorro ran up behind Marigold and wrapped her in his cape. He dipped her, leaning in like he was going to kiss her. Her eyes bulging, he pulled her upright. "Sorry, can't do it."

Sebastian grabbed the chain of the swing next to Seanna. "Even that costume can't turn him straight."

Desiree floated over to them. "I want to dance. We should go to Wooley's."

Ashe pulled the mask from his face and widened his eyes, jumping up and down. "Ooh, yes! The ghouls and goblins will be out in full force."

"Try the drag queens and shirtless boys," Sebastian said.

"Even better." Marigold took Blake's hand, tugging at him. "Come on. I'll ride with you."

Sebastian pulled out his phone. "We'll get a ride. Everyone's been drinking."

"That won't be cheap all the way to PCB," Desiree said.

Sebastian waved her off. Seanna wondered what it'd be like for just one day to have his kind of money. She had no idea how much he had, but by the look of his clothes and car, he didn't want for much. "Come on," Sebastian ordered, and took off for the stairs, punching into his phone as he walked.

Marigold pulled Blake up and pushed him, drumming on his shoulders, claiming back her rights to him. Bo held out his hand to Seanna. "Need help up?"

"I was thinking of taking up residence here."

Bo glanced up at Gwendolen and Rob's Mediterranean mansion. "I'll let you take the master if you let me have one of the spare bedrooms."

She took his hand and let him haul her big behind out of the swing. "I meant right here on this beach. Does it ever get old?"

He shrugged and walked toward the stairs. "I don't know. I've never lived anywhere else, except for Tallahassee for college."

"Florida State?" she asked.

"Yep," he said.

"I went to UT. Our real rivalry is with the Gators, so you're forgiven."

He grinned at her. "That's a relief."

He offered her the staircase first, either because he was a gentleman or he wanted to check out her ass. "I tried to keep Marigold at bay as long as I could, but once the others came around, there was no holding back."

"She's…" She wasn't sure how to finish that sentence, so she didn't.

"She's got her moments. Unfortunately, they're few and far between. I'll warn you though, if you get close to Blake, she's liable to strike."

"I'm not getting close to anyone right now," she said.

"Why's that?" he asked, showing her the way to the side gate. "There's a spigot around the corner."

"Thanks," she said. "I'm still dealing with my last breakup."

"How long ago did you break up?"

He turned the handle on the faucet, and she put her foot under the cold water. "Nine months ago."

He whistled. "That's a long time to be dealing with a breakup."

"What's your excuse?" she asked, shoving her wet foot into a pump.

"For being single?" He turned off the faucet, his eyebrows narrowing. "Call it a hazard of living in a tourist town. I've already dated everyone who's from here, and anyone new I meet is only here for a week."

"So what you're saying is I've stepped into a tourist trap. If I stay here, I can expect to be single until I'm dead?"

He shrugged. "Pretty much."

"Good. Let's go dancing."

Chapter Ten

Seanna had thought the costumes at Gwendolen and Rob's were some of the most elaborate she'd seen at a Halloween party...until they arrived at Wooley's. Drag queens of all shapes and sizes were decked out in everything from a regal Queen Elizabeth to an early two thousands Britney complete with a faux python. Young, shirtless, barely legal boys danced on speakers with wet heads and glistening chests. Seanna hadn't enjoyed a scene this much since the last Channing Tatum movie.

Desiree pulled Seanna out onto the dance floor, and she opened up like she'd just arrived from ten years in lockup in the state penitentiary. A drag queen dressed as Cher, and looking about as good, took her hand and twirled her in circles. Seanna let her body unwind from a year's worth of misery. She'd hidden from all her friends for so long, she guessed she'd all but forgotten how to have fun. But now, she remembered. This was who she was. Not the miserable mess who spent every night huddled in her bed with a hand on her wallet and an eye on the calendar.

After a zillion songs, her feet needed a break, so she

scooted off the floor. On her way back to her seat, she passed Marigold dragging Bo onto the dance floor. He rolled his eyes at Seanna, but she could tell he wasn't completely annoyed. She found Blake on a barstool solo. "I can't believe you're not being hit on." She glanced around the place. "What's the matter with these guys?"

"I know. I think I'm too old. What do you want to drink?"

"I'll take a bottle of water." He got her one from the bar and handed it to her. "Thanks. So I take it you don't dance?"

"Not if I can help it."

She considered him and got a really bright idea. "Will you excuse me?" She didn't wait for an answer. She pulled a bill out of her purse and made her way to the deejay stand. The deejay's booming voice came over the speakers before she even made it back to her seat. "How is everyone tonight on this All Hallow's Eve?" The room erupted in a shout. "Okay, all you ghosts and goblins, I've had a strange request, but since it's a strange evening, I'm feeling generous…and so was the lovely lady who made the request." The deejay grinned at her across the bar, and she held up her water bottle in response. "Turns out we've got a virgin in the house." The crowd cheered even louder. "Don't get excited, you perves. I'm talking about another sort of virgin…a dance virgin."

Blake raised his eyebrow. "Am I getting ready to really hate you?"

"Probably so."

The deejay fanned himself. "Oh, goodness, he's a hot one, too." Seanna waggled her eyebrows, and Blake's face filled with color. "Who wants to pop a cherry?" the deejay asked. Hands went up all around. "Then everyone, let's circle 'round and welcome Blake to the sacrificial center." A spotlight searched the room and landed on Blake. Seanna cracked up, knowing she was so going to get it for this. "No hiding now," the deejay said. "Come on, and make your way to the center of the dance floor."

The people on the floor formed a circle, leaving space for Blake to come through. They all yelled and motioned him over. There was no getting out of this scene. He tried to glare at her, but his smile poked through. "You're doing this with me."

"Wouldn't have it any other way. I've never popped a cherry before."

He took her hand, holding onto it for dear life. Desiree and Sebastian motioned them their way, giddiness in droves. They broke through the circle and Seanna and Blake were center-stage, surrounded by a room full gay men and straight women decked out in Halloween garb. The music faded, and in came the tune of the Chicken Dance.

Seanna went through the motions, showing him the hand moves, then flapping her arms, then the shaking of her tail feathers, then the clapping, over and over. He tried so hard to get it, but he was having trouble keeping up. She realized now why he didn't dance.

When the part came to go arm and arm in sort of a figure eight, she took him by the arm, but had to let go when a line of smartly-costumed gay men took their turns dancing like they were Chicken Dance instructors. A particularly kind one dropped him off back in front of her where they went for round two.

When the music sped up, Seanna wasn't sure she'd ever

laughed so hard in her life watching Blake try to do this dance that he was terrible at faster and faster. When the whole debacle was finally over, and the room exploded with applause, Blake's face opened with a smile so wide he could swallow the entire place whole.

He started to walk off the floor, but the deejay's voice came back over the loud speaker. "Hold on, hold on. Don't go anywhere little virgin-no-more. You were an excellent sport this evening, and your Joan Holloway companion is so hot in that red dress with the plunging neckline that I'm going to reward you with something we never do at this club…a slow dance."

An M83 song came over the speakers, electronic dance music's answer to the slow dance. She tilted her head to the side, lifting an eyebrow. "After that Chicken Dance, you got this one in the bag."

He huffed a laugh, trying to hold back his grin, but not doing a good job of it. She hadn't seen him smile this much the whole time she knew him. He pulled her to him, resting his hands on her hips. She eased her hands up to his shoulders, her stomach alive with a nervous flutter. She had always been fairly confident around men. It had been the rare bird who could put her insides into a tizzy. But there was something about Blake's quiet cool, the fact that he seemed to listen when she talked and actually care about what she said. He wasn't one of those straight guys where she felt she had a good thirty seconds then needed to wrap it up.

But more than anything, it was the way he looked at her—his blue eyes boring into hers like he knew her…like he was curious about her. And she wanted to know more about him—

anything he'd be willing to share. He lifted his chin, seeming ten feet tall so close to her, sending her heartbeat up a step. She looked away, breaking under his gaze.

She glanced around the dance floor at the paired-up drag queens, a handful of lesbians, a couple of guys dressed as tech nerds…or maybe they weren't dressed up? "I think we're the most unlikely couple here." She cringed at her misspeak. "Dancing couple, of course."

"Yeah, we're definitely the minority. Sebastian calls us breeders."

"He better not call me that. I'm nowhere near ready for kids." He nodded, looking almost a little disappointed. She considered him. "Are you ready for kids?"

"No," he said. "I'm not even ready for a wife."

"Oh yeah? Guys your age are usually married by now. You better be careful. People may start to talk. You have been seen walking into a gay bar tonight, you know."

"I'm no stranger to people talking."

She raised an eyebrow, but he didn't expound on the subject. She clasped her hands behind his neck. "There's a theory that if someone makes a fool of you, it doesn't count if you don't care."

He nodded. "That's very true."

She gazed up into his blue eyes, her heart thumping away. "Thanks for being a good sport tonight."

"Did I have a choice?" he asked, but not without a hint of a smile.

She leaned into his chest, as he pulled her there. She wasn't sure who had made the move—maybe both of them at the same time. She breathed in the scent of his skin and lifted her chin to get a good whiff of his neck. The subtlest hint of his body wash lingered, causing her to close her eyes and drink him in.

She would be stupid to jump into another relationship so soon. Sure, she and Jason had been broken up for nine months. But she'd been living there with him all this time. And there'd been a handful of good moments during that time. Few and far between as they were, they had existed. Of course, she hadn't been intimate with him for probably a year—and not for lack of his trying. Refusing him hadn't been exactly easy. Seanna loved sex. But more than she liked the act, she craved the closeness it provided between her and her partner. And this past year had been about moving on from him, not getting closer.

Her hands wanted to wander down Blake's back toward his ass—his perfectly proportioned, round ass. Tonight, it was covered by his blazer, but Halloween costume material was thin and cheap. If she could get her hands down there tonight, she could get a good squeeze in. He pulled back from her. "What are you smiling about?"

She woke up, glancing around, realizing the song was over, and a fast one had intruded. "Oh, nothing." She couldn't keep the smile off her face now. She touched her lips and walked off the floor toward her crew, who were all taking seats at a table near the bar.

As they approached, the same drag queen dressed as Cher who had twirled her on the dance floor earlier walked up to Bo, who was sitting on a barstool at the end of the table. "I was going to ask you to dance before, but she beat me to it." Cher nodded at Marigold, who stood at the other side of the table with Ashe.

Bo shrugged. "Maybe next time."

"How about now?"

"I'm no good at that kind of dancing," he said, nodding at people on the floor who were dancing to an EDM song.

"Have another drink, then maybe you'll be ready later." She brushed her fingers against his forearm and then sauntered off, displaying her heart-shaped ass for the table to admire.

When she got out of earshot, he looked around the table. "Anybody ready to go?"

Sebastian rolled his eyes. "Oh, come on you homophobe. Will it kill you to dance with a drag queen for one song?"

Bo's cheeks colored. "You know I'm not a homophobe, Sebastian."

Sebastian lifted his chin in defiance. "I know nothing of the sort."

"I'm here aren't I?" Bo motioned around the room.

Sebastian shrugged. "Big whoop. You came to a gay bar. You want a cookie?"

Bo put his hands on his thighs, his muscled up arms on display. "I'm a homophobe because I don't want to dance with a drag queen?"

"How would it hurt you?" Sebastian asked.

Bo pointed at Sebastian. "You're starting to piss me off." Sebastian gave him a look so snotty it would have pissed Seanna off if it didn't make her laugh. Bo sat up. "You know what? Fuck it." He stood up off of his stool and walked over to where Sebastian was sitting. Sebastian tried to remain cool, but his quivering body gave him away. Seanna needed popcorn.

Bo put his hands on Sebastian's cheeks and then planted a big kiss on his lips, making their whole group double over in laughter. When Bo pulled away, Sebastian looked rattled for the first time since Seanna had known him. He smoothed his hair back and touched his lips, his hand shaking. Bo picked up his beer bottle. "Convinced?"

Sebastian grabbed the beer from him and took a big swig, swallowing hard. "Yep."

As the van pulled up to Gwendolen and Rob's house, Sebastian said, "I'm hanging tight. I'm still not sober enough to drive, thanks to Bo's kiss."

Ashe rolled his eyes. "We're never going to hear the end of that kiss, are we?"

Sebastian waggled his eyebrows. "Not if I can help it."

Blake opened the car door and got out. "I can take you all home."

"And cheat this poor guy out of a fare?" Sebastian said. "Desiree can take Ashe home, and Marigold and I will hang with our driver. You can take Seanna though. She's on your way, isn't she?" He gave Blake a significant look.

"I'm on Blake's way," Marigold chimed in from the way back of the van.

Sebastian held out his arm like he was playing a game of Red Rover. "Stay put, Goldie."

Seanna looked at Blake. "Is that okay?"

"Of course," he said. "Come on."

Blake helped Seanna out of the van and was tempted to continue holding her hand until they got to his truck, but he abstained somehow. He closed the door behind her and made his way around the truck, both desperately wanting to be alone with her and knowing he needed to bear down, keeping his eyes on the road, and drop her safely home. Nothing else.

"That was fun tonight," she said as they made their way down 30A back toward Seaside.

"Which part?" he asked.

"All of it. But my favorite part was—"

He slid her a look, and she just broke out in the giggles in return. If making a fool of himself in front of a bar full of people made her that happy, he'd sign up for that gig every night of his life.

"I was going to say watching the Bo/Sebastian make-out session."

That gave him a chuckle. "Please call it that next time you see Bo. I'm begging you."

"Will definitely do." She wiggled a little in her seat and cleared her throat. "I'm not that tired, oddly. How about you?"

A heat wave jogged through his midsection and up to his stomach. "No. What time is it?" he asked, looking at the clock on his radio.

She checked her phone. "It's only eleven-ten? Ooh, it's eleven-eleven. Make a wish."

"You can do that?"

"Of course you can. Any time you like, actually," she said, smiling away at him. Resisting her was getting damn-near impossible. "So were you serious about that Batman viewing?"

He had been at the time. Deadly serious. And there was nothing on the planet he'd rather do than sit on the couch with her at his place and watch one of those movies...or nothing. But as the seconds ticked away toward midnight, his stomach knotted harder. Tomorrow was a significant day...the three year anniversary. If he woke up with Seanna in his arms on that day, he'd never be able to forgive himself.

"I am."

"How about," she looked at her wrist like she was checking a watch, "now?"

He scratched his jawline, squirming in his seat, ordering his middle to calm the fuck down. He could take her back to his place and just watch the damn movie. Then he'd take her home when it was over. Plain and simple.

"Yeah," he said after too much silence lay between them.

"Or, we could wait until another time. It is getting late."

"No...I mean...yes. Tonight." He rubbed his forehead, a headache starting to form.

"Nice. Now, where's the place to start? Is there any weird order like with *Star Wars* where you think you're watching from the beginning because it's old and filmed in the seventies, but you're really watching episode four or anything like that?"

"No, yeah, kind of, but...no."

Scenes from that night in Atlanta flashed in his head. Tara's green shirt covered in blood like some sort of bizarre Christmas decoration. Her wrists torn open, exposing a deep, dark, bloody gore.

"I'm open for either era, but if you're going to have me choose between Michael Keaton and Christian Bale...well..."

Blake whipped the truck onto Seagull Lane, the tires squealing from his last-minute decision. Seanna grasped the oh-shit handle, her words matching the handle's name.

"Blake?" she asked, leaving out the *what the fuck*.

He screeched to a stop in front of Cassidy's house on the cul-de-sac and put the truck in park. He met her gaze, still not knowing if he was going to take her in his arms, tell her everything, or kick her out of the truck.

Her hazel eyes stared back at him wide as white wall tires. He wanted her more than he'd ever wanted a woman in his life. She made him want to do stupid stuff like learn the Chicken Dance in front of a bar full of people and laugh with her till they were both in tears from it. She made him want to fall in love but for real this time and do dumb stuff like make dinner together and hold hands in a movie theater. She made him want to lie with her on a blanket on the beach with nothing between them and make love for hours and then count the stars and wish on one like it mattered. She made him want to live again.

"I'm moving to Kansas City," he said.

She blinked. "Oh. Wow."

"It's a good opportunity. More money, steady insurance, and I wouldn't have to run my own business anymore. I hate all that paperwork." Paperwork. He was telling the woman he was falling hard for that the absence of paperwork was more important to him than her.

"Sure, well, I can see that. Sounds like a good opportunity." She smiled at him, her eyebrows raised, nodding, like she was putting all she had into that smile to make it seem real. "When do you leave?"

He rubbed his forehead, eyes closed. "December 1 is when I need to be there. I need to wrap everything up here with my business...work out some commitments. I'll probably leave right after Thanksgiving."

"Okay, well. Thanks for letting me know."

He stared at her, the want inside of him hitting a crescendo like never before. "Rain check on that Batman night?"

"Oh, yes. Of course." She held up her hand in a wave. "Thanks for the ride."

He didn't answer…just watched her get out of the truck and walk up to Cassidy's door. She waved one last time before closing the door behind her and turning off the porch light.

He dropped his head to the steering wheel. He was doing the right thing. He had to keep repeating that to himself. She couldn't know what happened. He wouldn't put her through that. He wouldn't put himself through that.

Chapter Eleven

Blake loaded his dog Sadie into the cab of his truck, and they headed for Bo's house in Panama City Beach with plans to watch Sunday football. Blake hated to ruin the day, but now that Seanna knew about Kansas City, it was official. He needed to tell Bo.

Sadie hopped out of the cab and ran toward the front door, bullying her way inside as soon as Bo opened the door. Blake handed Bo a twelve-pack and set a bag of Fritos on the kitchen table. "It's not like you to take a day off," Blake said.

Bo put the twelve-pack in the fridge and pulled out two longnecks, handing one to Blake. "Who says I wasn't up at 6 a.m. hitting it hard?"

"Only thing you're hitting hard at that hour is your pillow."

Bo smiled in response and walked to the sliding glass door in his living room. "Jake! Come on." His black and tan mutt raced Sadie for the door, and they ran free in the fenced back yard. Blake followed Bo outside to the patio, and they sat in Bo's Adirondack chairs.

"I should have put one of these up for Sadie," Blake said,

glancing around at Bo's work on his privacy fence.

"Still can. I'll help you. Won't take us but a few days."

Blake frowned, peeling the label off his longneck. "I'm moving, actually."

"Oh yeah? Please tell me you've finally decided to come over to the dark side with me here in PCB. You're not quite redneck, but I'll teach you."

"No, I'm moving away…to Kansas City." Blake hesitated before meeting Bo's confused gaze.

"Are you serious?" Bo asked, like Blake had just gut-punched him.

"Yeah, I've got a buddy there. He's offered me a job."

Bo sat back in his seat, setting his forearms on the armrests. "Doing what?"

Blake thought hard about how to answer that question. "Public service."

"Public service?" Bo asked like he was drinking pickle juice. "What does that mean?"

Blake squirmed in his chair. "Just…you know…working with the public."

Bo narrowed his gaze. "Look, I've never thought of you as being naïve, but forgive me if I've got some questions."

Blake rubbed his hand over the top of his head, wishing like hell he would have just lied through his teeth, but Bo made that damn near impossible to do. "It's legit. I've known him a long time."

"Okay." Bo stared at him, his gaze probing, and Blake knew this wasn't going to end well. "Let me ask you something," Bo said. "Do you trust me?"

Blake met his gaze, heat starting to make its way up through his neck. "Of course."

"Then do you want to tell me what the fuck's going on here?"

Blake's gut churned, the few swallows of beer he'd taken about to make their way back up his throat. "It's nothing. I just got a good opportunity."

"To move from Grayton Beach, Florida to Kansas City? Something's not right with you."

"Maybe I'm sick of the ocean."

"And maybe I'm going celibate. You've drug me to the beach more times in the past three years than I've been in a lifetime of living here."

"Maybe that's why I'm sick of it," Blake said, realizing he was starting to sound like a twelve-year-old.

Bo considered Blake for a long moment. "Are you in the Witness Protection Program?"

Blake couldn't help a laugh. "No, dude."

Bo inhaled a deep breath and shot it out through his nose glancing around his yard, lips tight. "All right. If this is how you want this to go down, then fine, but I just want to say this to you. For three years I've been happy to rattle on about my family and exes, and my childhood memories while you sat tight-lipped in return. That was fine. I figured you had something to hide, and you'd tell me all about it someday. So I'll be damned if I'm going to invest three goddamned years of my life in this friendship and have you walk away without telling me what the hell is wrong with you."

Blake turned his head, not able to look at Bo. He was right. He'd told Blake everything about himself. Blake had lived vicariously through Bo for years. Bo's family had become his own in a small way. Blake watched Bo with his sister, who he loved more than anyone on earth...their easy dynamic with one another, and Blake had realized that the hole in his chest where family was concerned, that he'd seen as being the size of a penny, was more like the Grand Canyon. Shayla had become like his own sister in a lot of ways. And Bo's mom like the mother he never had. Bo had become his brother, and sitting here with him now, he couldn't imagine the day he would walk away from him. But he knew he had to.

Bo stood up from his chair, forcing it to slide back a foot. "You call me your brother. I'm not your goddamned brother. I'm as good as a stranger." The door slid back, causing a loud whoosh.

A storm brewed inside Blake's head as his stomach swirled with a nest of spiders crawling around and taking bites out of his gut. He gritted his teeth, fist clenched so hard his knuckles went white. The door swooshed back, and before it could close Blake shouted, "Okay!"

A beat or two sat between them before the door opened back up. Bo had the good sense to walk slowly back to his chair, wordlessly.

Blake rubbed his forehead, his whole body turned away from Bo. He wasn't ready to talk. He hadn't planned for Bo to know about any of this. He'd convinced himself that he was going to Kansas City and would leave Bo and everyone else here blissfully in the dark about him, but he understood now that he couldn't do that...not with Bo.

Blake took a long drink of his beer, looking for a little liquid courage. He peeled at the label as he swallowed. "I'm sorry I've been so secretive for so long. This is just...it's not easy for me to talk about."

"It's okay. Whatever it is, you can tell me." Bo's voice

was gentle, like he was helping a dog who'd gotten hit by a car.

Blake swallowed hard. He couldn't imagine how the retelling of this story would go. He'd never talked to anyone about it, not since it happened. He searched deep inside himself for the strength, remembering how easily Seanna told him about her ordeal from this last year. He'd been the only one she'd told, and he'd appreciated that fact—felt honored by it. Bo deserved that same courtesy, but Bo would probably not want to have anything to do with him after this conversation. That was a risk Blake had to take for the sake of the authenticity of their friendship.

"I haven't always been a handyman." There it was. No turning back now.

"Okay."

"I'm a doctor. I was a doctor." The words laid heavy in Blake's throat. Bo blinked in confusion, and Blake gave him a second to let the information settle.

"What kind of doctor?"

"Emergency care. ER doctor."

Bo furrowed his brow. "Okay. What changed for you? Didn't like the money?"

"The money was good, but I wasn't in it for that."

"I'm teasing. I wouldn't think you would have been."

Blake nodded, knowing how he was sounding. He just had to get through the next few minutes somehow. "I was engaged, back in Atlanta."

"Oh," Bo said, his shocked tone turning Blake's stomach over.

Blake closed his eyes, remembering Tara and that night. This was the part he had to get through. He'd come this far.

He just had to figure a way forward. "She was involved in an accident." Blake shook his head, realizing his words were a lie. "Not an accident, exactly." Bo just stared at him, waiting for him to get the courage to finish. Blake swallowed down some bile in his throat. "She cut her wrists open. The ambulance brought her to my hospital."

Bo narrowed his gaze, confusion…or maybe horror… etched in his expression. "Wow. Had she been dealing with depression, or…" He trailed off.

"Tara had bipolar disorder. I knew that going in. I was up for handling everything that came with it. I was a doctor. I was qualified…prepared. I was the right person for her."

"Are you describing your role as her caregiver or your role as her partner in life?"

Blake glanced at Bo's concerned face and then put his gaze back on his beer bottle. Sadie and Jake scrapped out by the edge of the fence, then two seconds later were off again chasing a squirrel.

"As her husband."

"Did you love her?"

"Of course," Blake said, his chest heating up like it did when he told a lie. Bo nodded as if he believed him, but Blake could see the doubt in his eyes.

"So, did she make it or…"

Blake shook his head and then ran his hand through his hair, his lip curled with disgust. "I tried to save her but…" His voice broke. Bo inhaled a sharp breath, and Blake clenched his eyes shut.

"Blake, man, this wasn't your—"

"That's the thing," Blake said, stabbing a finger at Bo. "It *was* my fault. I insisted on being the one to treat her. Kevin tried to get me to leave, but I shoved him. I had to save her. She couldn't die. I couldn't stand back and watch her die." Blake was mildly aware of his face being wet, but he plowed forward. "She was my responsibility. Mine. Not Kevin's or any other doctor's, and I failed her."

Silence sat between the two of them for minutes, hours for all Blake knew as he sobbed into his hand like a baby. He hadn't cried about Tara…not once. He hadn't cried in his adult life that he could recall. And here he was carrying on, and Bo just let him.

When Blake finally pulled his head from his hand, he found an old-fashioned, red handkerchief on the armrest of his chair. He took it, wordlessly, without looking at Bo, and cleaned himself up.

"You can keep that, by the way," Bo said, sporting a small smile.

Blake couldn't return the expression. Suddenly he felt guilty for smiling last night…for laughing and dancing like a fool. He had no right to do that.

"Can I tell you something?" Bo asked, but Blake didn't answer. "It's not your responsibility to fix everyone on this earth."

"You don't understand," Blake said, his voice coming out hoarse.

"No, I think I do. Look at me." Blake couldn't, so Bo rattled his chair. Blake whipped his head around, glaring at Bo. His friend glared right back at him. "It wasn't your responsibility to fix her."

Blake dug the tips of his fingers into his forehead. Bo didn't get it. He'd never get it. "Yes, it was."

"Why?"

"It just was," Blake said through gritted teeth.

"No it wasn't."

"Yes it—"

"No…it wasn't."

Blake stood up out of his chair. "Yes, it was!" he shouted, his heartbeat racing like a Kentucky Derby champion.

Bo stood up, too. "Why?"

"Because I'd…" he took a moment to breathe and lower his voice, "because I'd just told her I didn't want to get married. I'd told her I was leaving her."

Bo stared back at him, his expression etched with sympathy, which Blake despised. He didn't need sympathy. He needed judgment. He needed Bo to hate him for the sort of person he was. He needed Bo to hit him, hard in the face…right in the nose where he'd feel it the most. He needed to be punched in the gut where his guilt spent all its days and nights festering and climbing around. He needed to feel the pain that Tara felt that night.

Blake shoved Bo with both hands, and he stumbled backward, unprepared. When he found his balance, he just stared at Blake, bemused. Blake went for him again, but Bo was ready this time and stood steady after the next shove.

"Hit me," Blake ordered.

"Fuck you."

Blake went for Bo's shoulders again to push, but Bo deflected him. Bo was stronger than Blake, there was no question about that. Blake's workout was what he did for a living. Working with his hands and hauling things around. Bo's regime consisted of daily gym visits and weekly half marathons. When they fought for fun, Bo was like a kind Rottweiler who knew to take it easy on his Border collie best friend. But Bo lived a happy life with an adoring family surrounding him. Blake had years of aggression in his corner and a life of solitude, shame, and guilt to back him up. He'd take on Bo any day of the week.

Blake harnessed every bit of anger, frustration, and madness that swirled around in his head on a daily basis, ready to take Bo down, but Bo brought Blake to him in a bear hug, and held him there while Blake bawled. He hadn't even known that he knew how to cry before today. Bo didn't say anything, didn't move a muscle, just held Blake in his arms, and Blake wondered if this was what it would have felt like to have a hug from a dad.

Blake finally pulled away and walked aimlessly in the direction of the swing set in Bo's back yard. He wiped off his face, trying to return to some sort of normalcy, whatever that was. "Why haven't you ever hauled this off?"

Bo shrugged, walking up next to him. "I don't know. I guess I thought I'd be married by now with some little bastards who'd want to use it."

Blake turned to Bo. "If that's what you want, why don't you make it happen?"

"I don't know. Today's your day to be fucked up. We'll deal with me tomorrow." Bo grinned at Blake, and Blake wanted to smile back, but he wasn't sure he knew how anymore. "You're not God," Bo said.

"I know I'm not God." Blake hated it when doctors talked about God complexes. He'd never considered what he did God-like...quite the opposite. It was his job to save, and if he didn't do his job right, he failed. It was that simple.

"Then quit thinking you've got to take on that kind of responsibility. You're a human person. I didn't know Tara or anything about what happened that night. But what I do know is that you did everything you could to save her."

"You don't know that."

"I don't? You think I don't know you and the level of caring you have for people? That's your whole goddamned business. Helping people. Fixing things." He let silence sit between them for a moment before saying, "What's this job in Kansas?"

Blake rested against the wood panel of the play set. "I'd be working for a hospital under Kevin, my old emergency department boss in Atlanta."

"As an ER doctor?"

Blake nodded, his chest tightening around him.

"Is this what you want?"

He met Bo's gaze. "It's what I need to do."

"But is it what you want to do?"

He looked away from Bo, finding Sadie wiggling around on her back while Jake chewed on something underneath the bird feeder. "I think Jake caught a bird."

"He didn't catch jack shit. They die and fall from the feeder. At least I won't have to give him dinner tonight. And you didn't answer my question."

"It's just time to move on."

"Oh, I'm sorry. I didn't know there weren't any doctor jobs in the Florida panhandle. We must be a super healthy bunch here. No rednecks at all pulling idiotic stunts in need of having a thumb sewn back on or anything like that."

"I can't practice here," Blake said.

"Why can you practice in Kansas but not here?"

"I mean, I'm…eligible, but I can't."

"How come?"

"That would make a lot of sense," Blake said. "I'd just tell my patients, 'I know I've been scooping up your dog's shit for the past three years, but I'm totally qualified to reattach your thumb.'"

"Oh, I doubt any of your clients mess with fireworks. They've got people for that."

"You know what the fuck I'm talking about."

"No, I don't," Bo said.

"I came here to hide, to start a new life. But I'm a doctor, and I need to practice."

"So get a job in Pensacola."

"You aren't getting it. I can't hide who I am anymore, and I can't explain to a town full of people who've gotten to know me as their handyman or dog walker that I'm their doctor. So I've got to leave…now."

Bo narrowed his gaze, pocketing his hands. "Does this have anything to do with Seanna?"

Heat rushed through Blake's core. "Why would you ask that?"

"Because I saw the two of you on the dance floor last night."

Blake rolled his eyes. "Along with all of Panama City's LGBT population."

"I'm not talking about the Chicken Dance. The way the two of you were swaying together to that slow song, I thought I was going to have to come out there with a bucket of ice."

Blake crossed his foot over his ankle, gripping a pole on the swing set. "I can't be with her…not that way." A thought crossed his mind, and he looked up at Bo. "She can't know about any of this."

"Don't insult me. Is that why you're running away? So you don't have to deal with your feelings for her?"

"I'm not running away. I'm accepting an opportunity. I've got a three-year gap in my resume. I'm not going to be an easy hire. Besides, what happened that night at the hospital became sort of a…scandal."

"A scandal? How so?"

A rope cinched around Blake's heart. "Tara had written a note and made some accusations against me."

"What kind of accusations?"

He inhaled a deep breath, not sure he was ready to keep going, but he knew he had to. He wasn't dredging any of this stuff up ever again, and if Bo had questions, he wanted them all answered now. "She said I'd abandoned her, and I'd encouraged her to kill herself so I wouldn't have to be with her anymore."

"Fuck," Bo said.

Blake glared Bo down. "It wasn't true."

"Well of course it wasn't true. Who the fuck do you think you're talking to?"

Blake closed his eyes, his head stuffed full, his stomach sick from talking openly about this for the first time in years.

"So how did it all end at the hospital?" Bo asked.

"There was an investigation based on the note and my insistence to treat her. Everyone we knew was interviewed. Her parents, her friends, everyone at the hospital."

"And?" Bo asked.

"And I was cleared of any wrongdoing. That's what the official results of the investigation stated."

"But not what you feel in your heart," Bo supplied.

"So do you see now why I can't talk to Seanna about all

of this? I can't tell someone who I can see a real future with that I've been under investigation for my ex's murder, basically. Besides, she deserves better than someone who carries around this kind of baggage."

"Why don't you let her make her own decisions about what she wants?"

Blake looked at the play set and then back at Bo. Here was a guy who deserved someone like Seanna. He had a happy family, a nice house, dreams of his own family…even let a swing set sit out in his bachelor pad back yard in hopes of having his own children play on it someday. He knew right then exactly what needed to be done.

"Why don't you take Seanna out?"

Bo laughed. "Me? Are you kidding?"

"What's so funny about that?"

"Oh, I don't know. She's crazy about you for starters."

"She's not. Whatever she is, she'll get over it. Especially if she's got a good guy in the wings."

"So you're seriously asking me to ask out the girl you just said you could see a future with."

"I can see that. I can't have that. Have you not heard a word I've said this whole time?"

"Oh, I've heard you. And I think you're nuts," Bo said.

"Well, good then. It's settled."

"Ain't nothing settled, you idiot. I'm not asking out Seanna."

Blake eyed him. "What? Don't have the game for it?"

Bo waved him off and headed back toward the house. "Your stupid little Jedi mind tricks aren't gonna work on me."

Blake followed him inside, meeting him at the refrigerator. "Just think about it, okay?"

"It's time for kickoff," Bo said. He set two beers down on the coffee table. "Bring over that bag of fine hors d'oeuvres you brought."

Blake grabbed the bag of Fritos and handed them to Bo. They watched the game for a few minutes and then in between plays, Bo narrowed his gaze at Blake. "Say, now that I know you're a doctor, I was wondering if you could check out this bump on my ass."

Blake smiled for the first time all day. "Fuck you."

"What?" he asked with a laugh. "I'm on an HMO. You're the best I can afford."

They went back to the game and the beers, but Blake could think of nothing more than how lucky he was to have Bo in his life and how hard it was going to be to say goodbye.

Chapter Twelve

Seanna had learned more lessons in the first week and a half in Chase's kitchen than she had in four years at the firm. First of all, the pace moved way slower with a single residential kitchen than it did with a building full of kitchens. One set of custom-made cabinets took four months to be ready to install. And everything hinged on the cabinets.

She and the crew had emptied Chase's existing cabinets and stored all his dishes and things neatly in his dining room, which made her feel like she was packing to move apartments. Then they'd demolished the existing cabinets and measured for a set of ready-mades that she hoped would pass for just as nice. And they did…sort of. She had some adjustments and add-ons in mind that she hoped would help.

The countertops had been cut to the wrong size, and the backsplash didn't compliment the paint color like she'd hoped. The newly installed faucet was leaking, and the ice maker on the refrigerator wasn't working.

None of this would be nearly as irritating if she wasn't dealing with heartbreak on top of it all. She knew how silly that sounded, especially since she'd never even kissed Blake. But she had fallen for him. She hadn't realized how hard until that night on the dance floor at the bar in Panama City. She'd fallen fast and had been ready to hand over her heart and every inch of her body to him until he'd wheeled down Cassidy's street like the reincarnation of Dale Earnhardt.

Chase was out of town for a couple of days, and he'd agreed to let her stay as late as she wanted to work. She had to get this paint right. That was one thing she could easily control. She'd tried a lighter paint, but with the darker paint behind it, she was just digging herself a bigger hole, so she'd gotten a couple of gallons of primer to give her a blank canvas.

Her phone rang, and since she was ready for a break anyway she pulled it out of her pocket to see who was calling. Jason. How fitting for her week. She was all alone in this house, nobody to hear her conversation. She figured this was as good a time as any to take his call, and she did need to check in.

"Hey, Jason."

"Hello?" he asked. She hesitated, waiting for him to let it sink in. "Oh, wow. I didn't expect you to…never mind. So, how are you?"

"I'm fine. What do you need?"

"Well, I need my fiancée back is what I need."

"Jason."

"This is hard for me. You just left. You didn't give me a chance to explain anything. I didn't know where you were. I've been worried sick."

"I know you called the shop and talked to Cassidy, so don't try to act like you didn't know I was here."

"Well, yeah, but I thought you'd just be there a few days…a week tops, and then you'd be back. I've been watching the door every night, waiting for you to come through it."

He'd be waiting a long damn time. "I'll be back in December when it's time to move out."

"Move out? Of this condo?"

Just the idea of his acting like this news was a shocking revelation was about to send her over the edge. "Yes. We're moving out in December when our lease is up. You know this. You've known it since last January when I found out you'd run up my credit card and cleared the accounts."

"You never said—"

"Jason!" she shouted, not proud of the way she handled herself around him, but he knew how to push her buttons better than anyone on earth. "Did you think I was going to sign on for another year of paying a hundred percent of the rent for me and my ex-fiancé who has piled up my credit card debt, cleared my bank accounts, and gotten me fired from my job? Have you lost your mind?"

"All right. You just need to calm down."

"I am not calming down!" Why did she let him reduce her to a horrible, screaming, senseless mess? She forced herself to calm down despite what she'd said. "Why are calling? What do you need? Let's just get this out of the way right now."

"A letter has come in from our landlord. Your last check bounced, and he's requiring cash—"

"Jason, my god. I know you're lying."

"I've got the letter right here. I can scan it to you."

"You can skywrite it above the Gulf of Mexico if you want. I know it's a fake."

"It's notarized."

"Why the hell would it be notarized?"

He hesitated just a moment before saying, "I don't know. I'm not a lawyer."

Man, he was slipping, bad. Six months ago he'd have had this explanation all sewn up, iron-clad.

"Listen to me, Jason. I make my last payment on that place on December 1, and we have to be vacated and have it swept clean and empty by December 31. I will be there the day after Christmas to move all my stuff out and clean the place. You have until that day to clear out. If you have any stuff left there on the twenty-sixth, I'm going to clear it out for you. Do you understand what I'm saying to you?"

It was so hard to imagine a time when she was this man's girl, a time when she willingly had sex with him, when he took her out on dates, selecting a wine for the two of them to try. What a world away those times were.

"I understand. I just…I need help." There was that strangle in his voice that used to bring her down every single time. That desperation that would gut her to her core. Not anymore.

She rubbed her temple. "I am helping you. I'm paying your rent and your electric bills."

"You do know they cut off the cable, don't you?"

"I'm no longer there to watch it, so why should I pay for it? You're lucky I haven't cut off the electricity."

"I can't watch anything."

"I'm sure you've worked that out. Do you still have your job?"

"Yeah, I'm still working."

"That's great," she said, encouraged just slightly, but ready for the catch.

"I'm not at the same place though."

She didn't want to know anything more. The more she knew, the more she got sucked in, and being so far away from him was helping her cut the cord between them.

"I'm going to hang up now."

"I love you," he said.

"Bye, Jason."

"Wait," he said.

She held the phone away from her, finger hovering over the red button. She let out a big sigh and then put the phone back up to her ear. "What is it?"

"All bullshit aside, I really miss you. I can't believe how badly I've taken you for granted. I know we're done, and I'm accepting that. I just want you to know that there's no doubt in my mind that you are the love of my life, and—"

She ended the call and rested against the cabinets, sans the countertop. Nothing in the world mentally exhausted her like a conversation with that man. She couldn't take it anymore. She'd been taking it for way too long. He'd said a million sweet things to her just like that on so many occasions, then the next day she'd find her credit card missing or herself sitting in her boss's office with the pit of her stomach a mess.

Her belly told her it was way past her dinnertime, but she had to put that call behind her and get the base coat done before she left. That way, she could start on the new paint in the morning. She blew a stray wave out of her face and wiped her forehead with the back of her arm, getting a stinky whiff of herself while she was at it. She needed a bath and a glass of wine. Hell, she might even be too tired for the wine.

The drip, drip, drip of the sink echoed in her brain with each drop of water. The guy who had installed it earlier that day said he was coming back but he'd lied to her...just like Jason. Why did she believe anyone anymore?

She didn't need a man to fix a dripping sink. She had YouTube. She watched a video, finding it was easier than she'd even expected. She had the tools, and she had the brainpower. This was something she could take charge of and fix right this minute...and then she would finish rolling the wall, and then head home to eat or pass out, whichever came first.

She started going through the steps that she'd committed to her memory—remove the faucet handle, remove the nut that holds the stem in, pull the stem out with plyers...when she was met with a geyser of water to her face.

She stumbled backward from the shock of it, and then scrambled back over to the gushing water, idiotically trying to stop it with her bare hands. She'd failed to turn off the water, of course. Why had she not quit while she was behind?

She found the shut-off valves below. She got the hot one turned off, but when she grabbed the cold water cutoff, the handle was stripped, and it just spun nonstop like a merry-go-round.

"Fuck!" she screamed at the top of her lungs, because if ever there was a time to use that word it was now. She was backing away, pulling the hair that had fallen out of her ponytail back off her face when she stepped on the side of the aluminum paint tray, catapulting white paint all over her leg and shoe. "Seriously?" she shouted.

She flung off the shoe covered in paint and ran outside to get the water turned off, leaving the gushing geyser behind to demolish Chase's kitchen. Realizing she had to have a flashlight, she ran back inside the house, searching desperately for one and coming up empty. She picked up a bucket with some tile scraps in it, emptied it, and held it in front of the spray to collect the water. Was she going to sit here all night doing this until Jorge arrived the next day? That sounded like a super intelligent way to handle this.

She remembered her phone had a flashlight on it...duh...and she ran back outside to find that cutoff, hobbling with one shoe on and the other off. She flung off the other shoe out of frustration, but it certainly didn't give her clarity on how to find the cutoff to the water. Was she looking for something attached to the house? Or was it something for the whole street that was in a box somewhere that a few houses shared? She was infuriatingly clueless.

She ran back inside and grabbed the bucket again, trying to think. She'd remembered unpacking a platter last week when they'd taken the cabinets down. Where had she stored that? She found it in a box in the dining room, and then ran back into the kitchen. Holding it up against the spraying water like Wonder Woman with a shield, redirecting the water back into the sink, she turned to her best friend Google with the other hand and tried to figure out the most common place to find a water shut-off. But she discovered quickly that she needed a tool called a curb key to accomplish this task.

She needed help...desperately. Cassidy knew even less about plumbing than she did, and she couldn't call Jorge this late. Besides, she didn't want him to see what an epic failure his boss was.

However, she knew someone in Grayton Beach who was five, maybe ten minutes away, who had tools and very likely knew something about plumbing. He might not want to date her, but he could damn sure get his butt out of his house and help her.

Chapter Thirteen

Blake found Seanna in Chase's kitchen looking like a drowned rat. She was soaked from head to toe, her pale pink T-shirt clinging to her chest. He was trying not to look since she hadn't voluntarily entered this wet T-shirt contest, but forcing his eyes upward was like trying to get a dog to go out in the rain.

"I assume you are responsible for getting the water cut off," she said.

"Yeah."

"I could kiss you right now."

Jesus Christ, she didn't need to be saying stuff like that looking the way she did. He was doing his best to do the right thing with regard to her, but he was only human.

He held up the curb key. "You have to have one of these."

She motioned to it. "Of course you do. Out of curiosity, where exactly is the water cutoff for the house?"

"Down near the ditch by the street."

"Naturally." She let out a huge sigh, pulling her hair back out of her face, looking around the kitchen at the puddles of water sludgy with paint. "So, you think Chase is going to give me that gut-job?"

He set the tool down on the table. "I'll go get the mop."

"I'll just stand here dripping and try not to destroy any more of my client's house."

Blake found the mop in the garage and brought it to her. "I'll go find some dry clothes."

She took the mop, looking at him like she was so defeated. "Thank you, so much."

He wanted to pull her into his chest, wet clothes and all. He wanted to rip those wet clothes off of her, actually, but he was trying to be so good and do the right thing…which was getting harder by the minute. "It's not a problem."

He went up to Chase's room and found some gym shorts and a T-shirt in his dresser. He grabbed some socks in case her feet were cold. By the look of her chest, she could use some heating up. He hadn't meant to look, not really, but the way her nipples were poking through that shirt she was either freezing cold or really happy to see him, and he doubted it was the latter.

When he got back downstairs, he found her wiping her eyes and standing up straight. "Sorry, these allergies are killing me. I thought Nashville was bad." She pushed the mop back and forth, not looking at him.

His heart went out to her. She'd clearly been trying to do something on her own…who knew why, to save money? To prove something to herself? But whatever the reason, it was late at night, and it didn't appear she'd be done here anytime soon.

"Hey," he said, "go get changed. Better yet, take a shower. You can use the guest bathroom down the hall. I'll put that sink back together and go turn the water back on."

"No, I've got to get this all cleaned up." He touched her

arm, and she stopped mopping and met his gaze.

"Go," he said. "I've got this."

She nodded, trying desperately not to show emotion, like it wasn't written all over her face. He looked away from her, not wanting to make things worse. He went to the sink and reassembled it, and then headed outside.

He had the floor as dry as it could be when she appeared in the doorway, hair wet with Chase's clothes hanging off of her. He wanted those to be his clothes on her, not another man's.

"You're incredible," she said. "I don't know how to thank you."

He gauged the situation on the floor, trying not to look at her…figuring she didn't have on any underthings beneath that shirt and shorts, because all that was soaking wet. The thought of it wasn't helping the situation—the two of them alone in this dark house.

"I think the best thing to do is let it dry, and then you could probably use some commercial grade paint remover to take off the dull film in those spots over there." He waved a hand dismissively, realizing he sounded like a know-it-all, when really he was just trying to avoid looking at her. "But you know all that."

"I had to go with the dark grout, didn't I?" she said, looking at the spots where the white paint had stuck to the grout. "If I try to go back over it with more, it'll be too high." She narrowed her gaze at it. "Maybe if I took a nail file and sanded those parts down…"

He couldn't stop looking at her, knowing there was nothing between the two of them except a little cotton.

"Do you think?" she asked.

"Hmm? Oh, yeah. A nail file. That's smart thinking."

She ran her fingers through her hair, shaking it out, her waves falling around her face. "I think I need to just let it all dry and reassess it tomorrow."

"Sounds like a plan."

She blew air out her mouth, upward toward her hair. "What a nutty night."

He scratched his forehead, knowing he needed to back out of there as quickly as possible. "So, you say the shut-off valve is broken?" he asked, kneeling down by the sink. She joined him there, and he really wished she wouldn't have. He needed distance, not to be closer.

She pointed to the back of the cabinet. "I got the hot one off, but the cold one just spun around like a top."

"Mmm," he grunted, trying not to smell her. She probably smelled like Chase. That should turn him off. He took a whiff, but all he smelled was a clean scent, which didn't help matters. He stood. "If you don't need anything else, I guess I'll…" He pointed toward the door.

"No, of course not," she said. "I don't need—" she took a sharp inhale of breath, sort of like someone who had been crying and was trying to catch their breath, "anything else. I'm," she did it again, and he wondered now if it was a hiccup, "all set." She did it a third time, and now he knew it was the hiccups.

She smiled at him, raising her eyebrows, looking as if she was trying so hard to keep it together, but when the next hiccup came, she hit the table and shouted, "Damn it!" She wiped a tear from her eye. "I'm so sorry. I'm not usually this much of a total mess. This night has just been exponentially shitty."

He didn't have it in him to keep this wall up any longer. He pulled her into his chest and held her tightly, rubbing her back with one hand and holding her neck with the other. "It's all gonna be fine." He had no idea what "it all" was, but he wasn't sure what else to say.

She hiccupped into his shoulder, letting him hold her to him, surrendering to whatever was taking her down at this moment. There was no way he was walking out of there right then. He pulled away from her, holding her shoulders. "Would you like to talk about anything?"

She shook her head, wiping her eyes with the back of her hand. "No, thanks."

He grabbed a paper towel and handed it to her. She dabbed her eyes and wiped her nose. "Sorry, I know this sort of thing is a huge turn-on for guys. Please try to contain yourself."

She was clearly trying to make a joke, but she had no idea how true her words were. He opened up Chase's refrigerator and pulled out a couple of beers. "Do you like IPA?"

She gave the beer a longing look. "I can't drink my client's beer. It's unprofessional." A smile crept across her face, and she busted out in a laugh. He joined in and pulled her to him again. "It's not that bad. Tomorrow's a new day."

She pulled away. "Thank God." She surveyed the beer and then eyed Blake. "Do you think he's got anything stronger than this? I think I need an immediate buzz."

Blake looked around, trying to figure out where the liquor might be.

She cleared her throat, and when he met her gaze, she pointed at a cabinet. He found Chase's stash. "What's your drink?"

"Tequila," she whispered. "I swear I'll buy him a replacement bottle tomorrow."

Seanna got down shot glasses while Blake retrieved the bottle. "Do you want salt or a lime?" he asked.

She wiggled her fingers. "Just bring on the liquor... please."

He hadn't planned on drinking with her, but he didn't feel right walking away from her right now. She needed someone, and he was there. It wasn't like he could tell her to call Bo and walk away. That would just add to her already shitty evening. Where was Bo, anyway? He should have been the one she called. Had he still not asked her out?

They clinked glasses and downed the liquor. She set her glass down. "Hit me again." He did, and they went for round two. She closed her eyes and collapsed into a kitchen chair.

He looked at her side-eyed. "This is about more than a kitchen full of water, isn't it?"

She gauged him, and then twirled her shot glass with the tips of her fingers. "I'm not gonna drag you down with me again. You've done your time."

"Is this about your ex?"

She rolled her eyes. "I talked to him earlier. I hadn't in weeks, and I knew I needed to...mainly to make sure he was actively looking for another place to live. My worst nightmare is that I'm going to get there in December to move out, and he's going to be laid up on the couch not having moved a thing." She held up a hand. "Not my worst nightmare, but you get it."

Blake narrowed his gaze. "Suppose that's the case. He's laid up in his underwear eating potato chips with dirty socks and nudie magazines all over the floor."

Her eyes widened. "You know him so well."

He smiled. "So what happens next? You give notice to the leasing agent that you're not coming back, we move all your stuff out and leave him in there, and then they have to get the cops to make him leave. You may lose your deposit, but you probably weren't expecting to get that back anyway, were you?" She gazed at him, curiously. "What?" he asked.

"You said *we*."

He blinked, playing back his words in his head. *We move your stuff out.* He didn't know why he said that. In his head, he just imagined himself helping her with this. But he would be in Kansas in December.

"Sorry, I didn't mean to say that. Of course, I'd love to help, but I'll be…"

"In Kansas. Yes, I know." She gave him a tired smile. "Thank you. I know there would be little more thrilling for you than to get to meet my deadbeat ex and load up a moving truck." She patted his forearm. "You've done quite enough just being here tonight." She nodded at the tequila bottle. "Hit me one more time, baby. Is that how she sang it?" She gave him a lazy but mischievous smile, her hand around the shot glass.

"This liquor is doing you right tonight, isn't it?"

She held up her glass, resting her elbow on the table. "It's doing me just fine," she said, and then downed the third shot. She stood up, a little wobbly. "Whoops," she said, getting her balance. "I think I have my second wind." She pulled two beers out of the fridge, popped both tops off with her bare hands, and then handed him one. "What do you think about that wall? Does it need another coat of primer?" He turned to look at it, but when he turned back around, she was already out of the room. He followed her into the living room where he found her at Chase's stereo. "What is Chase, eighty-five? I've been looking at this old-school stereo equipment for the past two weeks. It looks like something out of an eighties breakdancing movie. Does he not know technology has gotten smaller through the decades?"

"Oh, but you haven't heard this thing. It's like walking into Club La Vela."

She tossed her hand into the air and then covered her mouth with it, eyebrows raised. She waved a wobbly finger at him. "You've been to Club La Vela?"

He looked her up and down. "Why's that so funny?"

"Because you're a hundred and eight. Club La Vela is for twenty-one-year-olds."

He raised an eyebrow and spoke very slowly. "I'm only a hundred and seven."

She grinned at him. "Old man. Trying to rub up on jailbait." She looked him up and down. "You're disgusting."

"When were you in there? Aren't you turning thirty in a couple of days?"

She peered at him, and he knew he was busted. "How did you know that?"

Sebastian was going to kill him if he ruined the surprise. He'd been on his case all week about RSVPing to the party on Friday. There was no need for Blake to go to that. He didn't need people asking him about when he was leaving and, moreover, why he was leaving. But the night was about her and not about him, so he hadn't figured out what he was going to do yet.

"You told me." She'd mentioned that night on the beach that she was turning thirty, she just hadn't said exactly when, he didn't think.

"When?" she asked.

"That first night I met you."

She squinted at him. "On the beach?"

"Yeah."

"That was not the first time we met."

"I know," he said.

A grin infiltrated her face. "I thought you were Cassidy's boy toy that first day I met you. I was all like, 'Damn, Cassidy. You're doing yourself right.' Then she was all like, 'He's just my friend. I'm way too old for him.' Mmm hmm. Right."

Seanna usually seemed to say whatever was on her mind, but he got the feeling that he was getting a special show of her uncensored this evening.

"I don't know what you're talking about. I'm just friends with your aunt."

She leaned in toward the stereo punching buttons, seemingly at random. "You're telling me you don't think she's attractive?"

"I didn't say that."

She pointed at him. "See! I knew it." She put her attention back on the stereo.

"I'm not the one who's got it for her." As soon as the words left his mouth, he regretted them. Three shots of tequila should not loosen his lips like this. What proof was that bottle he'd pulled from Chase's stash?

She turned to him wild-eyed. "Who? Who's got it for Cassidy?" He shrugged, taking a drink of his beer. She grabbed his shoulders and shook him, holding the beer bottle against his arm. "Who's got it for Cassidy? Is it Chase?" He shrugged again, giving a noncommittal shake of his head. She pointed at him, one eye squinted. "Who? Tell me."

"Why don't you ask her? She knows."

She did a snap point thing. "It's Bo, isn't it?"

"I didn't say that."

"That's awesome! Oh, my God. She should totally hit that. He's hot."

Blake could feel his lip curling up. "He's not that hot."

"Says the straight guy. Here, let's call up Sebastian and see what he says." She patted down her shorts and then swatted her hand in the air when she came up empty.

Blake cleared his throat. "Speaking of Bo, have you seen him this week?"

She furrowed her brow. "Me?"

"Yeah, over here or whatever."

"No. I'd remember if I'd seen him."

Blake knew he'd asked Bo to take her out, but now that he was sensing she'd love nothing more, he was second-guessing himself…like he hadn't been for the past week and a half.

He needed to figure out an exit strategy, but he wasn't sure he needed to be driving at the moment and he still wouldn't feel right walking out on her now. He could call Bo. Tell him what happened and that they started drinking…wanted him to join in the fun. Then when he arrived, Blake could take his exit and leave Bo there to make sure Seanna got home or at least to Chase's guest room.

But the idea of setting the two of them up together in an empty house made his chest sizzle with jealousy. Not that Bo would try to have sex with her…not like this. He was way too good a guy. But at the least, they might kiss. Or worse…snuggle.

He hit a couple of buttons on Chase's stereo, and the first few notes of Boston's "More Than a Feeling" came through the speakers. Chase was such an old soul. Leave it to him to have his stereo stocked with classic rock.

She fisted a wad of her T-shirt and turned to Blake, eyes wide. "Oh, I love this song. My family would listen to music on Saturday nights when I was little, and my mom and dad would dance to this, and he'd sing it to her." She sang the first verse, spinning around the room and sort of doing the airplane or something. There she went, making him smile again. "Oh, he was such a bad singer, too. Kind of like me." She kept dancing, sort of high-stepping like she was walking through a cow pasture. She may have been a worse dancer than he was. The chorus came on, and she started singing it while looking directly at him. She took his hand, pulling him out to the middle of the room, still high-stepping. He set his beer down on the coffee table and just went with it.

She finished the chorus by winding herself into his chest, and then sort of dipping herself backward into his arms, making him feel like he'd won the lottery. She unwound herself from him and started in on the second verse. He remembered Chase had a karaoke machine in his massive stereo setup, and he found the wireless mic and handed it to her. Her eyes and smile widened, and she was on stage now, arms shooting up in the air with the long, high notes and head banging to the beat during the guitar riffs.

When the song was over, she ran to the stereo. "Is this that one CD of theirs? I want to hear the last song." She found the remote and skipped through to the final song. She closed her eyes and waited, and as soon as the first licks of "Let Me Take You Home Tonight" came on, a smile crossed her face that sent goose bumps popping up all over his arms.

She sang the first couple of lines with her eyes closed, and then opened them just in time to sing a line to him that made his legs turn to jelly. She'd sounded horrific on the other song, but on this one, her voice took on a sweet, soft tone that wasn't bad.

For the chorus, she pulled him back to the dance floor they'd created and eased her hands onto his shoulders, his making their way to her hips like it was the most natural thing in the world. They swayed together there, her singing sweetly, eyes closing and then opening just enough to catch a glimpse of him and smile.

If he could freeze any moment of his entire life to relive over and over, it'd be this one.

She lay her head on his shoulder, and they finished off the song, wordlessly, her arms snaked around him, grasping his shoulders from behind. Even through the part where the song sped up, they still stayed just like they were, swaying like it was a power ballad. The CD finished, silence sitting between them, and he cursed Boston for writing such a short song.

She pulled away from him, wiping her hair back out of her face. "Sorry, I got caught up…thinking about my mom and dad."

"No, it's fine." Now was the time to leave…walk out the door. He should ask her if she needed anything else, and go. It was that simple.

Her expression turned grave. "I'm so sorry. That was so insensitive of me."

He blinked, not sure what she meant.

"I wish you had memories of a family to share with me. I'm sorry you don't."

She was sorry that he didn't have a family. That was the first time in his life someone had apologized for his being an orphan. He wasn't sure what response he needed to have.

She narrowed her gaze. "Can I tell you something?"

"Sure," he said, a little uneasy.

"I hate this work."

He exhaled relief. "Plumbing?"

"Yeah, no more plumbing for sure. But I don't want to rebuild kitchens or bathrooms or redesign houses or anything like that. In fact," she leaned in, "I'm secretly hoping Chase won't pick me to remodel that house." She put a finger to her lips. "Shh." Her expression changed. "I hope you don't think all this was some sort of self-sabotage. You don't think that, do you?"

"No, of course not."

"I really hope you don't think that."

"What do you want to be doing?"

She shrugged. "I don't know. Is that not stupid? I'm thirty in a matter of days, and I don't know what I want to do with my life."

"You don't have to know yet. You've got plenty of time to figure it out."

"I loved what I did at my old job, managing things from the office level, generating business, going on sales calls, convincing people that our firm was the way to go. I think I'm good at that, you know? Working with people. Sales, I guess. Does that make me prissy…the fact that I don't like getting my hands dirty?"

He huffed a laugh. "On a night that left you soaking wet, I don't think that's an unreasonable way to feel."

She walked over to the stereo and flipped through a

handful of CD's. She held up one. "Oh, my gosh. FRAMPTON COMES ALIVE. You are kidding me, Chase. My parents had half of these." She held one up. "Oh, this one is actually really good. Do you like The Who?"

He scratched his head. "Yeah. I like that Led Zeppelin one even better."

She showed it to him and then held it to her chest. "You could put 'Over the Hills and Far Away' on repeat for the rest of the night, and I would be just fine."

That was one of his favorite Zeppelin songs. Figured. "Me, too," he said, working to regain his footing and not doing a very good job of it. With everything she said and did, he was falling deeper for her, which was not in his plan. He cleared his throat. "I'm starting to wonder who's the old curmudgeon, you or Chase."

She put the CD in the stereo and waited for the music to start, her eyes closed. The first few bars of "The Song Remains the Same" came on, and she closed her eyes. "God, why haven't I listened to this music in so long?" She turned it down a little where the volume was just slightly higher than background music. "I haven't listened to any music in so long." She took her beer off the mantel and plopped down on the couch, tucking her feet underneath her.

He wanted to join her, but he was supposed to be walking out the front door. "Why not?"

She shrugged. "I haven't made the time, I guess. I listened to a podcast on my drive down here from Nashville...not that I was really listening to it. I guess my mind isn't satisfied unless it's stressing out over something."

"You've had a lot to be stressed over." He got his beer from the coffee table, intent on taking it to the sink and pouring it out…leaving. "Do you want me to forward it to your song?"

"Oh, no. Fast-forwarding is a cheat. You have to work a little to get to what you want. Let the desire build so the payoff is even better." She glanced at him, her gaze telling a story, and then closed her eyes. She rested her head against the wall behind her, stretching out her neck. He could so easily walk over to her and trail kisses all over it, and down farther…

He woke himself up. "I'm gonna head out…if you don't need anything else."

She opened her eyes and met his gaze. "You're gonna miss out." Oh, he had no doubt about that. She nodded, indicating the stereo. "Our song's up after this one."

He stepped forward with every intention of walking to the kitchen, but somehow found himself on the couch with her. He settled in on the opposite side, beer in hand.

They sat in silence without the chatter of small talk, just listening to the song and breathing. She repositioned her body to face him, knees falling against the back of the couch. He wouldn't look at her, but he could feel her gaze on him causing his chest to warm, contributing further to the heady buzz he had going from the liquor.

The opening guitar licks of "Over the Hills and Far Away" started, and he couldn't help a glance at her. She smiled and inched closer to him on the couch…or had he been the one to move? Robert Plant's easy voice came over the speakers, and he found that it was definitely him moving closer to her. She didn't move, just kept grinning at him like she knew what he wanted. His hand reached up to her neck without his permission, his fingers sliding through her damp hair. "I'm moving," he said, idiotically, inches from her mouth now.

"Not tonight," she replied.

Just one kiss. Could he have that? Could he allow himself that?

Her lips were on his before he could do anything else about it. She slid her hand down to his leg and rested it under his knee, squeezing as they opened their mouths and took their kiss to the next level. He lost himself in the moment, his mind fuzzy and free, focused only on Seanna and what she did to him. He couldn't remember life before her, and he damn sure didn't want to know it after her.

The reasons he should walk away from her right now were stacked so high in his brain he could barely see straight, but the most important reason to back off was that she wasn't sober. If anything was going to happen between the two of them, it wasn't going to be in a tequila haze.

He pulled away and realized she was winding a lock of his hair around her finger. He really needed a cut. "Was that real or a dream?" she whispered, and then rested her arm on the back of the couch, laying her head on top of it. Her eyes got heavy, finally closing.

He let out a sigh, not believing he'd just allowed himself to kiss her. He stood and positioned a pillow on the end of the couch, and then eased her down to it. Covering her with a blanket, he watched her breathing steady.

He settled into the recliner and turned the television on low. He should leave, but he needed to make sure she was okay. He didn't think she was that drunk, but if something happened to her, he'd never forgive himself if he left now. He knew that better than anyone.

He exhaled a deep breath and let his head drop back behind him. Fuck. If he was going to get through this, he'd have to be stronger than he was tonight.

Chapter Fourteen

Blake opened the bag of ice he'd brought and poured it over the craft beer in the cooler. He really didn't want to be there. He liked these two guys too much. The last thing he needed was to grow closer to them when he was trying to get further away. But they'd both insisted and said this one last boat trip, just the three of them, would be in lieu of any going-away party. That was a fair enough trade. The last thing he needed was half the town gathered around him asking questions about his new job.

Besides, he was going to take this opportunity to confront Bo about why he hadn't asked Seanna out yet and convince him that he had to do it quickly…before Blake got further involved.

Chase patted his pockets. "Goddammit."

"What?" Blake asked.

"I left the damn keys to the boat at home. Can you believe that shit?"

"Give me your car keys, and I'll run get them."

"Nah, I'll do it. Just sit here and try not to drink all the beer. Bo will be here in a minute."

"All right," Blake said and took a seat on the cushions facing the sea.

Watching the waves crest and break, he thought about how much he'd miss the ocean when he got to Kansas. A wave of panic washed over his chest. He'd gotten used to that by now. The idea of going back to medicine gave him minor panic attacks, complete with a dizzy head. He wasn't sure he was ready for this. Not sure at all. He closed his eyes, trying to relax, but the flood of stress that had given him permanent lines between his eyebrows clouded his brain.

The crunch of gravel signaling Bo's arrival perked him up. This was perfect timing. They could talk freely before Chase got back. If Blake couldn't convince Bo to ask Seanna out, then he'd consider wrapping up his business early and getting out of town as soon as he could.

When he heard Bo getting close, Blake shouted, "Around the front deck. Chase forgot the keys."

Bo's footfalls were quicker than usual…lighter. Blake peered in the direction of the steps.

Seanna's chest sizzled as she rounded the corner and found Blake sitting by himself. She'd busted a move on him Wednesday night, and it'd gone all wrong. She'd thought their kiss was magical and was ready for more, but he'd graciously pulled away, putting the brakes on everything. She'd faked sleep just to save face, and then he'd lain her down and covered her up like a perfect damn gentleman.

"I…didn't think you were coming," she said.

He blinked, his eyebrows lifting sky-high. "I didn't know *you* were coming."

Oh, fantastic. Yet another situation he was forced into with her. Lovely. She glanced around the open deck. "I thought this was a professional mixer for Chase's colleagues."

Blake stood, peering around her. "Why's Bo's truck headed up the road?"

"He was just dropping me off. My car wouldn't start, and I was going to take Cassidy's, but he just happened to be at the shop when I went to get the keys from her, so he said he'd bring me. He was headed this direction anyway."

He frowned. "Cassidy doesn't take her car to the shop. She rides her bike."

What, was he calling her a liar now? And what business was it of his how she got there? "Well, she did today. I guess she had something to transport from the house to the shop that was too big for the basket."

The motor on the boat started at the same time someone said, "Hello."

They both jerked their heads to the cabin door. A petite woman with her hair French braided neatly wearing all black—pants, button-down shirt and tie—held up both hands. "I'm sorry, I didn't mean to startle you. I'm Natasha. I'll be handling the service for the two of you this evening." She pointed at the beer in Blake's hand. "I see you're set for a drink. Ma'am, would you like a cocktail? My signature cocktail is a lightly sweetened Mai Tai. We'll have white wine with dinner, so you're welcome to start with that. Or if you prefer beer, just let me know your favorite brew, and if we don't have it I'll recommend a similar, just as fantastic one."

Seanna narrowed her gaze, searching between the girl and Blake, who seemed to understand what was going on now, and looked super pissed about it. This was not Seanna's week. The boat rocked, and she steadied herself, grabbing onto the side of the hot tub.

"Are we taking off?" Blake asked.

"Setting sail. Yes, sir. Would you like a frosty glass for that beer?"

Seanna looked out at the parking lot. "I'm sorry, but aren't more people coming? Are we on the right boat? Chase O'Neil? Is this his boat?" The boat powered into the sound.

The woman inhaled a deep breath, as if the jig was finally up. "Actually, it's just going to be the two of you this evening…and myself and the chef, of course. She'll be doubling as your captain. Our deepest apologies that she couldn't introduce herself beforehand given the situation, but you'll meet her at dinnertime. Other than that and as few instances as possible, I assure you we'll be invisible. Now, let's make a decision on that cocktail."

Blake rubbed his knuckles against his forehead, which did not make Seanna feel any better about this situation. "There's been a mistake," he said. "Please kindly ask the chef or captain or whatever she is to turn this boat around and take us back to shore."

She squinted. "See, I'd be happy to do that, but my employer asked that I keep the evening on track and that includes cocktails." She clapped her hands together and held them there in front of her. "How about that Mai Tai, Ms. Perry?"

"So Chase is paying you to kidnap us," Blake said, his face lighting up fire-engine red. Seanna had been starting to talk herself into going along with this charade, whatever it was about, but with as pissed off and irritated as Blake was looking, she was about ready to jump ship and swim back to shore.

"Kidnap?" Natasha asked, looking overly confused and guilty as sin. "I'm not sure I understand. Didn't each of you come here of your own accord for an afternoon cruise?"

Blake's brow furrowed, his mouth shut tight, giving her the stare-down, but the girl was standing her ground.

"I'm barely 5'1 and weigh a hundred pounds soaking wet. Would you like to call the police?" Blake rolled his eyes, running his hand through his hair. "Okay look," she said, hands on hips, "Chase is paying me tonight whether or not the two of you agree to go on this rendezvous. But he's paying me double if you do decide to cruise, and I could really use the money. So…" She looked between Seanna and Blake, her eyes pleading. She scrunched up her face. "It's for my mother's operation."

Seanna had to give her props for her effort. She glared at Blake, and then looked back at Natasha. "We just have to ride on the boat, right? You get your money as long as we're gone from the dock for, what, an hour?"

"Three-hour tour," Natasha said with a wink.

Seanna shrugged. "That's fine with me." She dug in her bag and came up with a paperback, glaring at Blake. "I brought a book. I'll take the back deck, and you can have this front deck. Deal?"

He just looked at her wordlessly, his expression impassive.

"Deal," Seanna said. "And I'd love a Mai Tai. Thank you." She teetered down the narrow decking to the other side of the large vessel. Plopping down on a chaise lounge, she fished her baseball hat out of her bag and adjusted it on her head, pulling her ponytail through. There were worse things than spending the day on a luxury boat with a wait staff and a personal chef. She'd make the most of it, even if the asshole of the century was just steps away.

Natasha appeared with the Mai Tai, and Seanna took it from her. "Thank you. And thanks for putting up with us today."

"It's my pleasure."

"If you make him one of these, give him an extra shot of rum. He needs something to get the stick loose from his butt."

"No problem. But I think he's sticking to beer." She smiled and made her exit.

After a bit of traveling across the inlet, reading the same page about ten times, the footfalls coming her way indicated she was going to have to face him. She pushed her sunglasses up farther on her nose and stared intently at the page. And yes, the book was right-side-up. She checked.

"Hey," he said, standing ten feet from her like an idiot.

She flipped a page. "Hey."

"I'm sorry about that back there. I hope you know that had nothing to do with you."

Oh, the nerve. She shrugged with a little dismissive noise for effect.

He approached her. "I wasn't upset to be with you on this boat alone. I was pissed at Chase and Bo...am pissed. Aren't you?"

She glanced around at the open sea and up at the clear afternoon sky. "Furious."

"You know, Bo messed with your car. Try to start it when you get home tonight. I guarantee you it will be all fixed."

"He said he was good with cars and would take a look at it when he finished his errand on this side of town."

"Of course he's going to fix it. He's the one who broke it."

She narrowed her gaze at him, for the first time realizing just how furious Blake was to be on this boat with her. She wasn't sure how much more of this her ego could take.

He rubbed his hand through his hair. "They just…they don't have the right."

She let her book drop to her belly. "To what? Put two of their friends on a luxury boat ride for the afternoon? Those bastards."

"You know that's not what this is."

The boat slowed as they moved toward some sand dunes. She motioned at the chaise lounge beside her. "You can sit, you know. I don't bite…much."

He let a small smile slip, and then sat, facing her, his knees up around his chest in the low chair. Why couldn't he just relax back into the chair like a sane person?

"They could have just told us rather than tricking us," he said.

"Would you have come?" she asked. He looked down at his beer, and her stomach soured. "You know, we can enjoy this day if we want. We can let the sun warm our skin. We can eat what I'm sure is going to be a lovely, gourmet dinner." She leaned in toward him conspiratorially. "We can even enjoy each other's company. It's actually allowed."

The boat squeezed through a pair of sand dunes into a private cove with a small beach peppered with palm trees. She swung her legs around to the side of her chair and then stood. "What is this magical little piece of heaven?" She teetered over to the side and steadied herself with the handrail as the scene came into focus for her. Something resembling a long couch…or possibly a bed…with a white canopy covering it sat in the sand thirty or so feet from the breaking waves.

Her stomach flew up into her chest. This was getting ridiculous. She appreciated that their friends had good intentions, but she wasn't sure how much more humiliation she could stand. She wasn't someone who was a stranger to feeling embarrassed. The comments and teasing that had come with the development of a massive pair of golden globes at the ripe old age of eleven had taught her early on how to own the situation and brush off the degradation. But being nudged together by well-meaning friends into a romance with a man who would clearly rather be receiving dental work was testing her social graces.

She turned to find Blake's cheeks a nice shade of strawberry. "Have you seen this cove before?" she asked.

"Yeah."

She pointed at the bed. "Is that always there?"

He shook his head, massaging his forehead.

She clapped her hands together. "Fantastic." Her choices were limited. She could remain on the boat in what was quickly becoming one of the more painstakingly awkward situations she'd had the displeasure of being a part of in a long time; she could go down to that beach and lay on that *come hither* couch thingy, effectively signaling Blake that she was ready for advances he clearly would not be making; or she could jump into the ocean with the sharks, jellyfish, and other sea creatures who may want to sting or sink their teeth into her welcoming flesh.

She pointed at the open sea. "I'm getting in."

Since she'd thought she was going to be spending the day

on the boat, she'd worn the only two-piece she owned for easier access to things like the bathroom, thinking she'd be covered by her shirt and shorts the whole time. But since desperate times called for desperate measures, she had no choice but to strip down to her two-piece, which was probably on the verge of being too small now thanks to Cassidy and her shop of calories. Without giving Blake another look, she rid herself of her flip-flops and headed over to the ladder.

The next little bit didn't go quite as planned. When she imagined herself jumping off the ladder, she pictured herself bobbing happily in the water, and then going under when and if she chose, but what happened instead was a full-on submersion into a particularly rocky wave, which took hold of her tie-on top and wrenched it from her like a ten-time bridesmaid grabbing for a tossed bouquet.

She gasped for breath as she broke through to the surface of the waves which were decidedly not working in her favor, rising and falling in a dramatic fashion, her bobbing breasts on display for God and all humanity.

She could tuck her tail between her legs and cover her breasts with one hand as she made it up the ladder and over to her chair and her discarded shirt. Or, she could go another route.

As an orphan dredging his way through the foster care system, Blake had been faced with a childhood full of difficult challenges that had prepared him for life's hard edges. As a student making his way through college and medical school completely alone and without the financial or emotional support of a loving family, he had been faced with a variety of problems and issues that had taught him how to persevere through whatever life threw at him. But nothing in his world had begun to ready him for standing on this boat watching a woman he wanted more than anyone or anything he'd ever dreamed of do the backstroke in the open ocean topless.

He ran his hand through his hair, grasping it until the pain shot through his follicles. He glanced inside the boat at the galley to see if anyone was watching. A tall, thin woman in a black chef's shirt took a pan out of the cabinet while Natasha pulled the blinds shut on the one window in the area, giving the chef a triumphant grin. Natasha picked up a knife and went to work chopping a vegetable on a cutting board in front of her. Of course Chase hired women for this little caper. He knew Blake had to be civil around women and couldn't threaten bodily harm.

He walked back out to the deck and surveyed the beach area, even though he knew it well. There were no houses built on this particular land because it was wildlife protected. Additionally, the chef had positioned the boat ass end out to sea to warn others the inlet was taken. Knowing Chase he'd probably paid off the Coast Guard to keep the area clear for them. There wasn't much Chase wanted that he didn't get, and he had Bo pulling his strings on this deal...no doubt about that.

He stood at the railing, watching Seanna, who now had her back to him as she bobbed up and down in the water, having found her footing in a more serene spot before the breaking of the waves. Her wet hair brushed her shoulders as a wave dipped down, exposing her bare back.

He let out a deep breath, not sure how much longer he

could fight his urges where she was concerned. He'd been battling so hard with himself, coming up with every rationalization and justification as to how he could even kiss her and get away with it, and here she was swimming topless in the ocean without a soul around who was watching.

Her bathing suit top floated by. The panicked look on her face when she'd come up for air had told him it likely had been an accident. He'd been about to jump in after her until he saw her expression change and then she started doing the backstroke.

Taking off his shirt and tossing it on the chair, his mind raced with impure thoughts of what he wanted to do when he jumped into that water. He had to stop those thoughts quickly though before his mid-section told tales on him.

He jumped into the water and retrieved the top. Balling it up in his hand, he swam toward her, his chest tightening with every stroke. He found his footing on the ocean floor near her. "Did you lose something?"

She glanced over her shoulder, her arm covering her chest, her hand cupping her breast. Jesus Christ. She shrugged as if it was of no consequence to her, but then she held out her hand for it. She tried to put it back on, but she kept getting knocked down with the crashing waves.

"Can I help you with that?" he asked, the idea of touching her wet, salty skin heating up his body in the otherwise chilling ocean.

She looked over her shoulder with a self-deprecating expression. "If you can contain yourself."

Her words were meant as a joke, but he damn sure wasn't laughing. The waves calmed as he moved toward her and took the top, swallowing hard as she positioned herself in front of him. He reached around her with the top, his body coming closer to hers by default. When her ass bumped against his cock, he closed his eyes as sheer want flooded his midsection.

"Sorry," she said.

He wasn't.

He brushed the side of her breast with his wrist as he pulled the strap behind her. Connecting these two pieces of material was one of the saddest tasks he'd ever performed. She gave him the two strings, and then held up her hair with both hands while he took his time tying them together, wanting to lick her neck like a vampire thirsty for blood. He brushed his fingers along her shoulders as he finished, his libido so fired up he thought it might shoot out of the ocean like a rocket.

She twisted around to face him, her green eyes bearing into his. "Thanks."

"Mmm hmm," was all he could mutter.

She pointed over her shoulder, not taking her eyes off his. "The sun's setting."

He floated closer to her as he was vaguely aware of a Jet Ski zooming by behind them. "Mmm hmm."

His hands moved to her waist, his desire for her stomping down any momentary guilt or logical thinking. A series of waves flowed through, bumping her up against him.

"Whoops," she said, her gaze trained on his lips. The ocean took hold of them, pushing them toward the shore and breaking his hand from her. She grinned in the direction of the Jet Ski. "It's a good thing you came along when you did. Otherwise I'd have given that guy an eyeful."

The idea of another man looking at her bare chest made

his own light up like a stick of dynamite. But she wasn't his to be jealous of.

Another wave pushed through, separating them farther as if the ocean was doing the thinking for him. He blinked awake from the situation, like he'd been in a trance for the past five minutes. Goose bumps sprouted up on Seanna's neckline as a cool breeze passed over them, reminding him of how chilly the water was despite the heat that had generated inside of him.

"Do you want to go to the shore and dry off?" He glanced at the big bed on the small beach, the only thing missing from it a neon sign. He wanted to skin Bo and Chase alive. "I mean, it looks like there's a couple of towels over there."

"Sure," she said, and they both let the ocean nudge them toward land.

He made it to the bed first and handed her a towel from the foot of it. She wrapped it around her back, and then smoothed it up and down her legs and arms, ending with running her hair between the folds of the towel. He was trying so hard not to watch her, but all that exposed skin was holding him in some sort of trance, and her breasts shook with the motion of the towel. Jesus Christ he was horny.

She spread the towel down on her side of the bed and lay face down on it, resting her chin on her folded arms in front of her. He followed suit, mimicking her position.

Turning her head away from him, she let out a satisfied sigh like she was settling in…leaving him a full unabashed view. That body of hers was the culprit in all of this. He couldn't think straight around her as it was. Toss in her body in a bikini, and he was toast.

Her ass needed to be in a hall of fame somewhere,

rounded and firm and attached to those legs that looked strong enough to hike a mountain or hold her up when she wrapped them around his waist while he drove into her against the shower wall. God, if she was his, the things he'd do to her. He'd take the time to worship every curve of her body from her thighs, to her stomach, to her shoulders, and all the places in between.

He dreamed for a moment of a world where he was allowed to let himself fall in love…where he'd lived in this area forever like Bo, and she'd just stumbled into his life one day, and they were lying here now as unapologetic lovers. If she was his, this was when he would cup the back of her thigh and run his hand up toward her sweet ass. He'd let his fingertips graze between her legs with just enough contact to make her want him to go deeper with his touch, but he wouldn't. He'd move up farther and slide his hand over the curve of her ass and to the side so he'd have access to the inside of those bikini bottoms. He'd run his hand over her cheek and let it dip down between for enough of a tease to make her give him a playful look, warning him not to go there. Or maybe she wouldn't. Maybe she'd wiggle just a little, inviting him in. Nobody was looking after all.

She turned toward him, and he hoped he closed his eyes in time so she didn't catch him staring. "So," she said, "what's your theory?"

He blinked his eyes open, pretending she'd woken him from a snooze. "Hmm?"

"The private cruise…this couch/bed thing…our own personal staff. What's all this about? And don't tell me you can't find a date on your own."

He shrugged. "I'm guessing they're trying to hook me up

so I'll stay here instead of taking the job in Kansas City."

She snorted. "If I'm their final Hail Mary, they're screwed, bless their hearts."

She had no idea what a liar she was…or maybe she did. She had to know how he felt, even if he couldn't convey it to her. He'd never been a good liar.

"Besides, I never said I was staying here." She nudged him with her toe. "Hey, I know. We'll make them think it was a home run, and now I'm taking you back to Nashville with me."

There was a thought. Scoop her up and take her somewhere else…anywhere in the world where they would never have to speak with anyone else they knew again. Nobody would have to know about his past, and he'd have her all to himself. Watching her smile at him, he could see all the people who were important to her in her life and how she could never be someone who would cut ties with them. He could. He had. But part of why he liked her so much was because he knew she was a better person than he was.

"What's so great about this job anyway? How could it beat this?" She pointed over her shoulder at the ocean, but he couldn't take his eyes off of her. Color invaded her cheeks, and she smiled in that way that made her look half her age for the moment. She put her chin on her arms, and then glanced back at him. "Why do you look at me like that?" she asked, her voice soft and gentle.

It was his turn to feel the heat in his face. He furrowed his brow, inspecting his thumb. "Sorry."

She rolled over on her side, facing him. "You confuse me, you know?"

He did know…exactly. He was the biggest tease this side

of the Florida state line. "I don't mean to confuse you."

She narrowed her gaze in that way that told him she was getting ready to call him out. He loved and feared that quality of hers. "What were you like in high school?"

He'd prepared himself for a few possibilities of what she might say, but not that. He shrugged. "I played football. Studied a lot."

"Did you date a lot?"

He frowned, focusing on a broken shell behind the bed. "Dating in high school was…a challenge." She sat silent, waiting for him to say more. "I didn't have a car, so I couldn't really take a girl out on a date."

"Would your house parents not let you borrow theirs?"

"I never asked. I didn't want to stir anything up."

She smiled. "I'm guessing there were a lot of disappointed girls at your school."

He cut a look at her and then rolled over onto his side to face her. "What about you? Were you the prom queen?"

"You're hilarious."

"What were you like?" he asked, suddenly really wanting to know.

"I don't know. I wouldn't necessarily call it popular."

"Were you a late bloomer?" She'd definitely bloomed at some point.

"No, I wouldn't call it that. I was more of an early bloomer." She glanced at her chest. "These came along when I was eleven, which was way too early if you're wondering. The girls thought I was a slut because I had a slutty body, I guess, and the boys did me no favors in helping them think otherwise."

"How so?" he asked, but he guessed at what she was

hinting at and suddenly felt like shit for ogling her a minute ago.

She swatted the air. "Stupid high school stuff. In the past."

"Did anyone hurt you?" He hoped like hell that wasn't the case.

"I got asked out a lot. Lots of first dates. Lots of disappointment when they found out I wasn't an easy lay. I had this one guy get really pissed off when I told him no. He wanted to know what Scott Banks had that he didn't. I told him Scott Banks didn't have anything I was interested in either." She shook her head, looking off at the boat, her mind in the past. "He wouldn't believe me. He was so sure his buddy would never lie to him about screwing some girl."

He frowned, not sure what to say. She went on. "Lots of girls were pissed that their boyfriends turned their heads when I walked by at the pool. I hated these things so much I tried to get my mom to let me get a breast reduction."

Blake couldn't think of anything sadder than Seanna altering her body to try to fit in. "What'd she say?"

She pointed at her breasts. "What do you think she said?"

He couldn't help smiling around her. He'd never been much of a smiler his whole life...until now.

"That's why it doesn't bother me when Marigold or anyone else body shames me. It's not anything I haven't heard before and won't hear again. A lot of people have worse lots in life than a big butt and boobs."

The smile left his face as he stared at this woman he was falling harder for by the minute. This woman who made him want to laugh and jump into the ocean after her...this woman who wasn't afraid to be honest about herself...this woman who was so different from him, but rounded him out in ways he couldn't have dreamed of.

"I'm glad you never changed your body. It's beautiful."

Her brow slightly creased as she considered him, but she must have given up because she finally turned back over on her stomach and laid her cheek on her hands, facing him. She huffed a laugh. "I was just about to say that the whole thing made me into a good judge of character, but I missed the mark on Jason, didn't I?"

He turned over on his stomach, too. "You didn't misjudge him in that way, though. He wasn't just in it for your body."

"No, he wasn't. I'll give him that. I mean…he was into it, for a while at least. But when he got so focused on the gambling, he lost interest in sex. I was starting to think he was sleeping with someone else." She huffed a laugh. "What a simple solution that would have been. I could have just pawned him off on the new girl and been done with him."

She dug her forehead into her hands and gave a frustrated grunt into the cushion. "Every once in a while in this gorgeous place, with these new friends I love, I forget that whole part of my life…just for a minute." She turned back to face him. "Those little moments are like specs of gold. You're all so simple here, at least to me. So uncomplicated. Nobody here wants anything from me," she said with a chuckle, "except to send me on cruises with a handsome handyman." She held his gaze tightly. "You don't want anything from me, do you?"

He wanted way more from her than he'd ever ask her to give. That was the problem. He shook his head.

"You don't need to lie to me about anything either," she said.

He swallowed hard, feeling the weight of her gaze. He didn't respond.

"Tell me a lie," she said, her voice softer.

He gnawed on the inside of his cheek. "Nothing to lie about," he said, his gut churning.

"I didn't think so. That's the problem with you, Blake Evans. There's nothing complicated about you." He couldn't look away from her now. He'd give too much away. So he held her gaze, his chest on fire. "You deserve an uncomplicated girl. Is that what you want? A simple girl without baggage and ties to other men?" She wasn't teasing or smiling. She just locked her gaze onto his.

"I don't want that," he said, his voice coming out husky, like he'd spent the night in a cigar bar.

She grinned. "Maybe you don't want a girl at all. You and Bo are awful tight."

He licked his lips, focusing on hers, barely even hearing what she was saying. His hand was itching to make its way across her ass…his hand *was* making its way to just that spot.

She glanced over her shoulder when he made contact with her, a curious expression of bemusement sneaking across her smiling lips.

"I'm leaving for Kansas soon," he said, focused on his hand moving over the small of her back.

"I know," she said.

"I can't get into a relationship," he said, his hand easing back over her cheek and down to her thigh. He wasn't bold enough to tickle between her legs like he'd dreamed of earlier, but the fact that she wasn't stopping him from touching her now was fuel for his fire.

"Who said I wanted one?" she said.

She rolled over on her back, letting his hand smooth over the back of her thigh to the front of it. Focusing on something behind him, she blinked, and then sat up. "We have company."

He followed her gaze to a speedboat powering toward their boat. Chase's black hair came into focus as he waved. The engine cut off and Blake could make out Bo grabbing for the ladder and steadying the boat against the big boat.

"What are they doing?" Seanna asked.

Bo held out his hand for Natasha, who made her way down the ladder and hopped onto the speedboat. The tall woman was right behind her. Chase gave a salute to Blake and Seanna, and then the boat headed back into the sound.

Seanna pointed. "They just left us here." She stared at him, wide-eyed and incredulous.

Suddenly, Blake was no longer pissed at his friends. He could kiss both of them, but he'd rather kiss the woman beside him. "That's a damn shame."

She smiled and relaxed back on the bed, her hand behind her neck. "All alone out here, huh? What should we do?"

He touched her stomach, easing his hand around her waist. "I can think of so many things I want to do right now."

"What's stopping you?"

He wasn't sure there was a force on earth that could stop him from kissing her right now.

Running his hand up her arm, his lips met hers, and his eyes closed as he drank in her salty taste. She ran her hand through his hair as she opened up for him…her mouth and her body. Her hips rose to him, welcoming him to lower himself onto her. She ran her hands down his back to his ass where she squeezed as she drew her hips up to him again. He wasn't sure how much more of this he could take.

"You're killing me with that," he moaned.

"I've worked for this. I deserve this prize," she said, squeezing his ass again.

He planted his face in her neck, cursing himself for not bringing a condom out here with him.

She nudged him off of her. "Come on. Let's get back to the boat. What I want to do to you can't be viewed by Mother Nature."

Chapter Fifteen

When Seanna reached the top of the ladder, she really wished she exercised more, because she needed to regain her strength pronto. Not that it'd been a tough swim, but she'd already been breathless to start. To finally have Blake to herself to explore, she would rally.

When he made it to the top of the ladder, she tossed him a towel, and they dried off. Blake wrapped his towel around the two of them, bringing her in to him, their bodies pressed up against one another. "You're a fast swimmer."

She gazed up at him. "I had something to swim for."

He let the towel fall behind her, and his hands went to her ass as his mouth met hers again. He walked her backward a few steps before pulling away and taking her hand. "There's a bed down below."

"How nice for us."

He led them down the stairs to a tiny bedroom where rose petals were sprinkled on the bed. "You've got to be kidding me."

She grinned. "I love your friends so much."

"That's just damn cheesy," he said, pointing at the bed.

She collapsed onto it, tossing some rose petals on top of her. "I've never made love on a bed of roses."

"I'm happy to be your first." He dove onto her, making her giggle like a teenager. She practically felt like one right then. He reached behind her and untied her bikini top. "I never wanted you to put this back on to begin with."

"You should have busted a move sooner then."

Her top fell loosely around her, and he quickly rid her of it, admiring her bare breasts. It was times like this that made all the juvenile jokes about her big boobs worth it. He cupped them both, running his thumbs over her nipples. "Your body is so beautiful." He said it like he meant it wholeheartedly, and his words unleashed a proud femininity inside her.

She lay back and lifted her arms over her head, giving him free reign. Closing her eyes, she bit her lip as his mouth covered her breast, his tongue exploring and warming her. Her back arched instinctively, pushing her breast farther into his mouth. If she wasn't careful she'd choke him.

He pulled away, his face flushed. "You have no idea how badly I've been wanting to do that." She nudged her other breast toward him, and he gave it equal treatment, his erection brushing her inner thigh as he worked. He moved down her body, slipping his fingers into the sides of her bikini bottoms. "These are in the way."

She lifted up so he could pull them down. "Off they go. And get those off while you're at it," she said, motioning to his trunks.

He slid her bikini bottoms down her legs and let them drop onto the floor. Staring at her exposed bikini area like he was a starving man looking at a filet mignon, he shuffled out of his wet bathing suit, his cock springing free, saluting her.

He started to go for it, but she closed up shop. "Not this time. But I promise I'll let you next time, when I've not just come in from the ocean." Would there be a next time? She had just assumed, but now she wasn't sure that was the best assumption to make.

He looked up at her like she'd just given news that his dog died. "I don't care about that. I just want to—"

"Next time. Just get inside me before I explode, okay?" She glanced around. "Surely there are condoms somewhere. They've thought of every detail. If they missed the condoms I'll shoot them." Blake pulled open a drawer under the bed and came up with one.

She narrowed her gaze. "Do I even need to ask how you knew that was there?"

"Lucky guess. I swear to God."

"Mmm hmm. Just get the damn thing on." While he fooled with the wrapper, she took hold of him, wanting to get the feel of him in her hand. He was going to be just the right size. He wasn't humungous, but he was plenty big for her and growing bigger by the stroke. "This might be the most perfect cock I've ever seen. It looks like it was made to fit me."

He grinned at her. "Let's find out if that's true." He slid the condom on, and she opened up for him, rubbing her inner leg against his ass while she waited. She couldn't believe she was finally going to get him inside of her. She'd been dreaming of this moment since she first darkened Cassidy's doorstep. He touched her, feeling his way around a little, making her squirm. "I didn't expect you to be that wet."

"It was the boob stuff. My nipples are super sensitive." She wouldn't dare mention that she hadn't been wet like that so quickly for Jason or any other guy ever. It was simply the idea of being with him making her that way.

"Good to know." As he guided himself into her, she closed her eyes, taking him in, her body filling to capacity. Damn, either he was bigger than she thought, or she'd been way too long without sex. She let out a grunt as he pushed deep inside of her. "Are you okay?" he asked.

"Yes, I'm perfect. Please keep going."

He did as told, and she moved with him, the two of them finding their rhythm together. She let out deep huffs of air as he lowered himself down on her, their bodies plastered together, the weight of him crushing her in the most delicious way. Her breaths came out stilted.

"Am I too heavy?" he asked.

She pressed on his back, holding him down. "No. Stay here."

The closeness to him filled her heart as much as his cock filled her core. She never wanted him off of her. Jason had liked her on top. He had this thing where he'd hold her boobs while she rode him, which was fine sometimes. But every once in a while she wanted to be screwed rather than do the screwing. She guessed he'd figured out other ways to fuck her over.

Blake kissed and then bit her shoulder lightly, which made her smile as he kept pumping inside her over and over. "I can't make it much longer," he breathed. "It feels too damn good."

"Come on, baby," she whispered in his ear, grabbing his ass cheeks, pushing him even closer to her. He followed orders well, emptying himself inside of her, or inside of the condom, thankfully. As much as she liked him—and to be honest, *like* wasn't a strong enough word—she damn sure wasn't ready to have a little one of him running around.

He breathed into her neck, his damp hair brushing her cheek. "Fuck," he whispered.

She grinned. "Was it good for you, too?"

He lifted up, eyeing her. "You didn't…did you?"

"Not yet," she said, lifting an eyebrow.

He nodded, his cheeks flushed red. "Stay still. I'll be back in a flash." He headed for the bathroom, giving her a beautiful view of his perfectly rounded ass on the way there. She loved a guy with some ass on him. So many were lacking in that department. When one had a good one, she just wanted to squeeze it on an ongoing basis.

She cozied under the covers while he was gone, the removal of his body heat against hers leaving her cold and desperately wanting him to return.

He walked back in and got in the bed with her. "Are you cold?"

She hiked her thigh over his hips. "Not anymore."

"You keep that up, and I'll be ready for round two in just a minute."

"I can handle as many rounds as you can last."

"Mmm," was his reply as he clasped his hand over her ass. They seemed to have a mutual love for each other's asses. "Are you sure you won't let me down there?" He slid his finger between her cheeks and down to her sweet spot, passing her other spot, thankfully. She wasn't saying no to that, but she'd need a few more vanilla nights before she'd give that spot any more consideration.

"Not tonight. But if Chase and Bo trap us on a boat again, I'll stay out of the ocean so you can."

"I don't care about that."

"I do. I like to put my best foot forward."

Still reaching between her cheeks, he slid his finger inside of her. "I love how wet I make you."

"Mmm," she replied, not wanting to give anything away.

"What do you like, Seanna?" he asked. The sound of her name coming from his low, husky voice gave her nerve endings a shot of adrenaline.

She hiked her leg up farther, opening herself to him. "You seem to be finding your way just fine." She let out a groan as he hit a really good spot. Wrapping her arm around his back, she gripped his shoulder, pressing her body against his. He moved his fingers up and down, and she found another rhythm with him, this time all about her satisfaction. Heat filled her as she pushed her body into his, wanting even closer to him than they were now, which was impossible. His fingers slid up and down, in and out, wetting the spot between her cheeks, and then making their way back to her core. His teasing maddened her to the brink of insanity. She hadn't been sure about her ass earlier, but she had no complaints at the moment. He was being coy, barely teasing her, nothing intrusive, but enough of a flirtation with the idea to make her squirm with anticipation.

She pressed down on his shoulders, pushing herself upward as the sensations roared through her body like a freight train, culminating in release that had her screaming out like a freaking porn star. She'd spent plenty of nights this past year with her hand down her shorts, but she realized now those had been sad substitutes for this.

She collapsed down onto him, breathing into his chest. He rubbed her back. "You're so fucking sexy." She bit his nipple in response, and he smacked her ass.

She giggled.

"I'm sorry I didn't last longer. It'd been...a while. I was out of practice."

"You lasted plenty long, seriously. I don't usually have one during sex...intercourse, I mean. I have them many other ways so feel free to knock yourself out trying."

"Challenge accepted. I'd love to make you come in as many ways as possible."

She smiled. "You're not how I pictured you'd be."

"How did you picture me?"

"Something more...conservative, I guess."

"You want conservative?"

"I didn't say that. I just said I thought you'd be like that."

"Why?"

"I don't know. Maybe because you're so reserved. You don't like to talk about yourself. You seem to always be holding back from me." He searched her gaze, not answering the unasked question. She smiled. "I'll never get you to talk, will I?"

He ran his knuckles over her back. "I've told you more than I've told any woman, actually."

"Really?"

"Yeah, I really have."

"Did you leave someone in Atlanta? Is that why you came here?"

He bit his bottom lip, his breathing coming a little faster. "I left...something in Atlanta. A different life."

"Is that what you're doing now? Leaving another life for

Kansas City?" She kissed him on the lips so he wouldn't have to answer that. "Sorry. That was out of line. I didn't mean to put you on the spot. Sounds like you've got a great opportunity in KC. I'm happy for you."

He furrowed his brow, searching her eyes again.

"You're always doing that," she said.

"Doing what?"

"Looking like you want to tell me something. What do you want to tell me, Blake?" He stared at her, and she stayed quiet for as long as she could, which wasn't long. She shook her head. "Whatever it is, don't force it. There's lots of time." She tossed back the covers. "There's food up there. We should go eat it if we're gonna go in for round two here in a bit." She stood up off the bed, and he chuckled. She turned around. "What?"

"You have a rose petal on your ass."

She wiggled it for him. "It's my new look. I call it artistic ass."

He followed her to the stairs and stopped her just before she started up them. "I hear you. And I'm getting there, okay?"

A warmth filled her heart like she'd never known. "That's fine. Take your time. We're in no rush."

Chapter Sixteen

Blake stood in the corner of Sebastian's living room, his heart beating in an irregular pattern. It'd been doing that since he dropped Seanna off at Cassidy's house late last night. He couldn't believe it had been less than twenty-four hours since he'd seen her…since he'd been inside of her. He could have spent the night and all day today in bed with her, and it wouldn't have been long enough.

He'd come so close to revealing everything to her, but he'd chickened out like a huge coward. Having free reign to touch her body—to drive himself inside of her again and again, three times if they were keeping count—was enough to keep his mouth shut, at least for the evening. He just wanted one untainted night with her, one night where she knew him as Blake the handyman and not Blake the murderer.

Tonight was her birthday. He wasn't going to sully her thirtieth birthday by informing her she'd been sleeping with a liar…and worse. But he would tell her everything soon. He'd be prepared to walk away from her immediately. Bo had offered up his crew to help with anything that needed wrapping up with his business between now and the time he was planning to leave. He'd take Bo up on that if he needed to. Get out of town. Get out of her face forever, if that was what she wanted. Not tonight though.

Bo handed him a beer and they tapped the necks together. "Seanna's turning thirty, huh?" Bo asked.

"That's why we're here." Blake pursed his lips at Bo. "I take it you got her car fixed."

"Oh, yeah. One of the battery cables had come loose."

"Just came loose, huh? All by itself."

Bo grinned. "Something like that. You can thank me anytime you like."

"For stranding me?"

"Alone with the woman of your dreams. You're welcome." Bo cut his eyes at him. "Chase said a few of his condoms were missing."

"That's just creepy," Blake said. "He counted his condoms?"

"Hell no, but you just told me you used some."

Blake rolled his eyes, leaning against the back of the couch. He hated it when Bo got him. "Fuck you."

"So you had a good time?" he asked.

Blake met Bo's gaze and couldn't help the stupid grin he'd had all day. "Pretty damn good."

"Good enough to convince you to stay?"

Blake took a long drink of his beer, thinking about that. He wanted to stay now more than ever. The idea of leaving Seanna made him sick at his stomach, but he couldn't keep up the lie with her. That was no way to live for him or her. "We've been over this."

"How long do you think it would take for everyone to

get over the fact that you're a doctor? Six months? A year, tops? There's so much gossip in these communities, these people will have forgotten about you and your shit before Christmas." Blake glared at him. "All right, Easter. July Fourth tops. Point is you're not special. The world doesn't revolve around you, contrary to popular belief."

"I don't think it does."

"Then get on with it. Out yourself. We could do it tonight." Bo cupped his mouth, one hand still holding his beer bottle, and whispered where only Blake could hear, "Blake's a doctor. He's gonna get a job at a hospital, so don't ask him to fix your toilet while he's resetting the bone in your broken leg."

Blake stared at his friend, wishing there was some way he could reconcile all of this in his brain as easily as Bo seemed to think it could be. "What about Seanna? Does she deserve to be stuck with another guy who lies to her?"

"I don't know. Does she deserve to get dumped by the guy she's falling in love with?"

Blake rolled his eyes. "You don't know that she feels that way."

"I drove her to the boat yesterday. You should have seen the way she looked at me when I brought up your name. You'd have thought I was Santa Claus on Christmas morning."

The lights went out, and Ashe's voice sounded through the house. "They're pulling up!"

Blake's heart sped up like a buzz saw just at the idea of her coming near the house. He had to figure a way to put his head back on straight.

Sebastian was talking so loud Blake could hear him

through the door. The plan was for Sebastian to tell Seanna he was taking her and Cassidy to dinner for her birthday, and then pretend he forgot his wallet. Then Cassidy was going to suggest they all come inside so Seanna could see his house. So Sebastian was carrying on about how dirty it was and how they should ignore the dishes in the sink.

The lights flew on and, "Surprise!"

Seanna blinked, either truly shocked or playing the part very well. "You are kidding me!" She shoved Sebastian, and then brought him in for a huge hug. She turned to Cassidy. "Did you know about this?" Cassidy shrugged and smiled, and then she got hugged as well.

Seanna scanned the room, and when her gaze locked on Blake's, her smile grew even bigger, her face glowing with color and warmth.

Bo leaned in to Blake's ear. "Yeah, she's not falling for you one bit."

Ashe and Desiree appeared with champagne flutes for Sebastian, Cassidy, and Seanna, and then a server appeared next to Blake and Bo with a tray. "Champagne?" she asked with a smile, her eyebrow rising.

Bo held up his bottle. "I think I'm all set with this, darlin', but feel free to check back with me later."

The girl's face widened in a smile. "I'm here to serve." She bit her lip, looking him up and down, and then headed to another group.

"You're all talk," Blake said.

Bo narrowed his gaze at Blake. "I'm some talk."

Blake huffed a laugh as Marigold appeared, pointing at the server. "I am prettier than her." She took another look. "Maybe not prettier, but I'm thinner."

"What makes you think that makes you better?" Bo asked.

"Skinnier wins every time," Marigold said.

Bo relaxed against the back of the couch. "Says you. Why don't you quit worrying about who's the skinniest and eat something? There's enough food over there to serve all four armed forces."

"I don't eat. The point is, why are you being all flirty with her, but I could stand naked on the coffee table and the two of you wouldn't bat an eyelash?"

"You want me to bat my eyelashes at you?" Bo said, and then started doing it, moving closer to her, which she seemed to love.

She pushed him back to his spot. "Don't touch me."

"I didn't. You're the one who just touched me."

Chase came up to them, champagne glass in hand. "Will you two quit bickering?"

"You too good for beer?" Bo asked.

Chase admired the glass. "I like the finer things in life when they're served to me at somebody else's house."

Marigold put her hands on her hips and looked Chase up and down. "You, too."

"Me? What'd I do?"

"I'm sick of the three of you flirting with everything with boobs except for me."

"Baby," Chase said, laying a southern accent on thick. "You're the finest woman in this room, and we three heathens are way below your standards."

She smiled, turning to walk away. "And don't you forget it." Her exit would have been perfect if she wouldn't have bumped into the server, knocking over the two champagne glasses, which the woman caught sideways on the tray. Another server appeared almost instantly with a roll of paper towels and began wiping up the floor. Marigold winced. "Sorry."

Seanna came up holding out her hands. "How are you all such good liars?" She pointed at Blake. "Especially you."

He swallowed down a big ball of cotton in his throat.

"That's right," Bo said. "You two were together a while yesterday, and nothing came up about your birthday, huh? You must have been busy doing something other than talking."

Seanna bumped Bo in the hip. "You're a big ole liar, too. I asked you yesterday in the car what you were up to this weekend, and you said you were busy working all weekend."

"Well, I had to take a break to come to your party now, didn't I?"

"Yes you did. And thank you," Seanna said.

Marigold strolled over to them. "Seanna." She pointed at her. "I got it right this time."

Seanna pointed back. "Marigold, so glad you came."

She shrugged. "It's my circle of friends. You can count on me being wherever they are."

"By the way, I never did ask you, how did your friend's daughter like that turtle brownie?"

"Oh, she liked it...a lot. She said she'd like some more sometime...soon."

"Well, you tell her to come back to the shop and get another one anytime she likes."

"I will." Marigold looked Seanna up and down, and then glanced at her own dress. "Not too many people can pull off this color, you know."

Seanna put her arm around Marigold, their royal blue

outfits similar, but looking a hundred percent different on each woman's body. "I think we both wore it best."

Marigold eyed her, but Blake could see her softening to Seanna. She had that effect on people.

"So," Seanna said, "would anyone like to introduce me to all my friends?" She glanced around. "Who are all these people?"

Sebastian swooped in. "You will love them all and they you before the night is over. Come on, and we'll mingle."

Seanna gave the guys a look. "Fabulous."

Sebastian gave her ass a little spank, and they walked off. Blake would be an idiot to be jealous of a gay man, but he wanted his hand on her ass so badly he thought he might just be.

An hour and a half had gone by since Sebastian had stolen Seanna away from Blake, and he'd had about all he could take. She'd sneaked glances at him while she was talking to other people, winking at him, raising her eyebrow, and once wiggling her ass at him. He typically enjoyed hanging out with Chase, Bo, Marigold, Desiree, and Ashe, but with Seanna teasing him across the room, he was ready to ditch these jokers.

Marigold slid her arm inside his. "Okay, so I sort of see her fabulousness."

He grunted in return.

"God, Blake, quit trying to be so coy. It's cute for a while till it gets old, then it's really tired."

"I didn't say anything."

"Well say something…do something, please," Marigold said. "You're exhausting to watch."

"You don't have to look."

"You know that's impossible for me." She let go of his arm and pushed him a little. "So what's up with Kansas City?"

"Just a job."

She put her hands on her hips. "Well, it better be a damn good one to leave all of us. Seriously, why Kansas when you live in one of the most desirable locations in the country, arguably?"

"Who's doing the arguing?"

"I am. Seriously, Blake, we love you. We hate this...all of us do." She pointed to all their friends scattered around the room. He'd spent a lot of fun evenings with those people, but none of them knew him—not really—except Bo, and Blake had told him too much. Marigold nudged him. "They're all too kind and respectful to say anything to you, but you know I'm not. Are you sure this is the right thing? Leaving this special place? Leaving all of us?"

He wasn't sure, not by a long shot. But he did know that he could never reveal his true self to these people. He couldn't handle them being a part of that dark person he left behind...the guy who haunted him when he was alone.

"Just promise me you'll reconsider. Can you do that?" she asked, looking up at him with such sincerity. She hardly ever showed this side of her, so when she did, he didn't know what to do with it.

"Okay," he said.

Her face widened in a grin, and then her expression dropped as she looked behind him. "Well, look who's coming to say hello, now that I've finally got you to myself. But of course she is."

He turned to find Seanna inching toward him, a mischievous look in her hazel eyes.

Marigold shoved him lightly. "Go on. Take him," she said to Seanna. "He clearly doesn't belong to me anymore." Marigold gave just enough of a smile to let them know she was kidding...sort of...and then walked away.

"Did you ever belong to her?" Seanna asked.

Not like he belonged to Seanna. "Nah...unless you count as an employee. She's a good customer."

"Oh yeah? And what exactly do you do for her?"

He brushed her arm with his thumb. "Not nearly as much as I've done for you, and I haven't even gotten started yet." She gave him a closed-mouthed grin, and he tugged on her shirt where it fell over her hip. "How much longer do you need to stay at your own party?"

She glanced around. "Oh, I think I need to stay the duration. But I've put in an hour and a half and made my way around to most everyone. I think that earns me a quick break. What do you think?"

He glanced around the room to make sure no one was paying attention, and then took her hand. "Come with me."

Seanna took two steps to Blake's one as he hurried them across the highway toward the public beach access stairs. As their feet hit the planks of the wooden stairs, the booming noise echoed through the dark evening. They reached the other side of the bridge which dumped them out on the beach, the ocean roaring as it licked up to the shore.

"Wait!" She giggled, hopping as she pulled her strappy sandals off.

He pulled her to a line of cabanas and went straight to

the third one in the row, letting go of her hand. "Wait right there." He headed behind the green and white striped structure, and then emerged with a key.

She grinned a mile wide. "You are kidding me. What if the owner shows up?"

"He's occupied right now, hosting your birthday party."

Her hand flew to her mouth. "Oh, my God. Get in there."

He opened the cabana and let her into the cramped space, but it was more than enough room for their needs. He grabbed a towel down from a shelf, spread it over the white-cushioned couch, and then turned back toward her. "Is this okay? I mean…we can always go back to my house."

She collapsed down on it. "This is more than perfect." She pulled him toward her by the waistband of his pants, unbuckling his belt. She undid the button to his jeans and tugged them down along with his boxers, his cock springing free.

He grabbed her shoulders, inhaling a sharp breath as she took him in her mouth. His expression contorted as his hand worked its way to the back of her head, lightly cupping it as she moved up and down on him, taking him in as far as she could. She eased up to the tip and focused her efforts there, her own core lighting up at the groan of pleasure he let out.

"You've got to stop," he breathed, but she knew that was the last thing he wanted her to do. "I'm going to…" He trailed off as she squeezed his thighs, letting him know it was fine to let himself go…of course it was. He held her head, letting out a primal sound.

Dropping down to his knees, he closed his eyes and covered his face. "Fuck," he breathed.

She wiped her mouth with the back of her hand, watching him curiously. His head fell into her lap as he pushed against her stomach, almost as if he was begging for something. He was facedown right at her core, and his breathing heated her up, making her nuts.

He finally lifted up to meet her gaze, his face beet red and damp. For a minute, she thought he was upset with her about something, until he tugged at the bottom of her shirt. She held up her arms, and he pulled it off of her.

He ran his hands over her silk bra, staring at her breasts like they were an unearthed treasure. She reached behind her back and undid her bra, letting the straps fall down her arms. He moved in close, taking one nipple into his mouth, gentle at first as he tongued it, and then finally covering it with his mouth and sucking hard. She wrapped her legs around his back in response, the sensations heating up her core. When had foreplay been this magnificent? Had it ever been?

He gave the other breast equal time, his hand on the outside of her thigh squeezing like he meant it. He worked his way down to her stomach, his hands moving up to the waistband of her pants. He undid her button and zipper, and she lifted for him to pull the pants off of her. Luckily for her, he took her underwear down with them.

He ran his hands over her knees and up her thighs appreciatively, spreading them wide as he inched closer to her core. He nibbled at her inner thighs, kissing and biting as he moved toward her. She eased down to the edge of the couch, relaxing back on the puffy cushion, getting nice and comfortable.

He spread her apart, and when his tongue made contact with her, she closed her eyes, taking in the warmth on the most sensitive part of her body. It'd been so long she'd practically forgotten what it felt like, and now that she knew again, she vowed never to let her life get so fucked up again. This…a talented tongue…was entirely too precious a treasure not to experience often.

He found the sweet spot inside of her with his fingers that hadn't been activated in years, and the sensations roared from more places in her body than she could count. As the heat built inside of her, she squeezed him with her thighs until the final wave of release settled inside of her.

He pulled away, resting his forehead against her thigh. She brushed the hair back from his face, catching her breath and bringing herself back down to earth.

"That was worth the wait," he said.

As awesome as the orgasm had been, she wasn't finished. She needed more. She needed him inside of her yesterday. "Any chance you have a condom on you?" she asked.

He exhaled a deep breath and gave her a look that clearly indicated he did not.

"Fuck," she said, because no other word would suffice. What kind of guy didn't have a condom on him? The kind who didn't sleep around, she guessed. Now she just wanted him more.

He stood and walked around the cabana searching, still wearing his button-down shirt, but that was all. He opened the drawer of an end table, pushing the contents around until he finally closed it empty-handed. He looked in every crack and crevice of the place, including inside the small refrigerator and at the bottom of a basket of towels. She did her part by checking in the couch cushions, but no luck was to be had.

She finally turned to face him, and with his expression as hopeless as she imagined hers was, all she could do was break out with a smile. He dove for her, lining her out on the couch, burying his head in her neck. "Fuck!" came his muffled cry.

She giggled. "I think we'll live."

He pulled the couch cushions from behind him and tossed them onto the floor, and then fell off of her onto the couch.

"I can't believe you didn't have one in your wallet or whatever. I thought all guys did that."

"Mmm," he grunted.

She pinched him in the stomach. "You're a man of few words, aren't you Blake Evans?"

"Some things are more fun than talking," he said, rounding his hand over her waist and cupping her breast.

She undid the buttons on his shirt and tugged it away so she could run her hand over his chest. "Do you think they've noticed we're gone yet?"

"Definitely," he said, his voice low and sexy as hell.

"Re-entry is not going to be pleasant."

He toyed with her nipple. "Then let's not go."

"And stay here all night condom-less?"

"That'd be fine with me."

She smiled, closing her eyes and letting him play with her breast.

"Your body is so beautiful." His words were so matter of fact...not at all like he was saying them to get into her pants, but like he meant them with all his heart. She fought the urge to make a self-deprecating joke about her big butt and thighs.

"Thanks," she whispered as he ran his hand over the curve of her hip and around to her ass. He cupped a cheek lightly and worked his way up the middle, grazing a finger down the center. "Are you a butt guy?" she asked.

He rolled her on top of him, cupping both of her ass cheeks and then pushing her upward on him, her center pressing against his erection. "I'm definitely into your ass."

"We're entering dangerous territory here, don't you think?"

He closed his eyes as he ran his hands over the small of her back and then down to her ass again. "I know. I'm just not ready to leave here yet."

"I'm not either."

"You're not on the pill?" he asked.

She'd gotten off it last January, more as a precautionary measure so she wouldn't slip and give in to Jason. "Nope. I've not had a reason to be." He gripped her thighs, pushing her against his erection. She closed her eyes and let out a little grunt of frustration. "You've got to stop doing that."

To her disappointment, he rolled her off of him, depositing her on the couch next to him. "Yes, ma'am."

She ran her hand down his side and around to his back, thinking of all the questions she had for him, but knowing not to ask a single one...not right now. She had him in a vulnerable position, and as much as she wanted to take advantage of that, she was afraid to lose this side of him she'd been begging to see for weeks now.

She kissed his chest with soft, light motions, running her hand down to his ass. His body was lean with just enough muscle and tone for her taste. She eased her hand down to his thigh and around to his front, taking hold of him. He closed his eyes and inhaled a sharp breath. Moving her hand up and down on him, she watched his brow furrow and his features tighten. God, she loved that she could do that to him.

She inched down his body, positioning herself on his thighs. She took him in, loving the sensation of him filling up her mouth. She went up and down on him, taking him as far back as she could at first, and then putting all her focus on the sensitive side of him. She glanced up at him and caught him watching her, which gave her a funny sense of empowerment and sexual goddess-ness. She went to work on him, hard, and it wasn't long before he was coming apart, his whole body quaking with the sensations she gave him.

When he finished, he grabbed for her, summoning her back up to him. He drew her in close to him, flattening her chest against his. He rested into the back of the couch, pulling her against him. "It's hard for me to believe you're real sometimes."

She huffed a laugh, making a figure eight on his shoulder with her finger. "You're just in a post-blowjob haze."

He stared at the ceiling, seeming a million miles away from her.

"What do you think about all the time?"

He looked down at her. "What do you mean?"

Resting her head on his chest, she said, "We should get back."

"I know. We will." But neither of them moved.

"I've never had anyone throw me a party before...well, except my mom, of course." She winced after she said that. "I'm sorry."

"Seanna, don't say you're sorry for having a mom who threw you parties."

"I know. Okay." She kissed his shoulder, and then said, "So I know you didn't date much in high school, but what about after that? Who have been the great loves of your life?"

"Well, I've got one living at my house right now."

She sat up, gauging him, knowing she was being set up, but still unable to not be a sucker.

"She's a beautiful blonde. Loyal. Eats like a horse but she works out a lot. She's a runner."

She pinched his nipple. "You better be talking about an animal."

He smiled. "Sadie. I got her when I first came here. I don't know what I'd do without her."

"What kind of dog?"

"Mutt, I guess. I imagine she's got some golden retriever in her."

"You rescued her?"

He huffed a laugh. "I didn't rescue her. Some good folks at the Humane Society did that. I just paid for her and brought her home."

She smiled against his chest. Of course he did. "You're avoiding the question."

"What question?"

She bit his shoulder in response.

"Oww!"

"That didn't hurt you."

"It did, too. You better kiss it." She did, and he let out a satisfied moan. He rubbed her lower back. "I guess Jason was a big love of your life at some point, huh?"

"I thought so, but I can see now that what I felt for him wasn't the real thing. He was marriage material. I know that sounds crazy now, but at the time I met him, he really was.

He was great at his job, kicked ass, actually. He was so tenacious. I believe he cared about me. It's easy now though to see all the places where he was really selfish. But when you want something to work so badly, you rationalize a lot."

He frowned, staring at the ceiling with great intent.

"Have you done that, Blake? Rationalized your way through a bad relationship?"

He looked at her, his eyes searching hers like they so often did. "Yeah. I've done that."

Just a few words, but they told her so much about him. She had to admit, hearing confirmation that Blake had loved in some way before wasn't fun for her. The silence and mystery surrounding him had its benefits. But she knew whatever he didn't want to talk about in his past didn't matter anymore anyway. They were here now. He was hers for this moment. He never showed interest in any other women. He seemed laser-focused on her...even though he made clear he was leaving for Kansas City soon.

That idea gave her a minor panic attack that she couldn't handle. She sat up off him. "We should head back." She stood up off the couch, and he took her hand. She turned around to him, forcing a smile. "What? You know we do. It's a party for me."

He stood and faced her, holding her in front of him with his hands cupped around her shoulders. "I was in a bad relationship, too, once. It was hard, and I failed her...a lot. I thought I loved her, but I didn't understand love then." He pushed her hair back from her face, and studied her features intently, as if he was memorizing them for a test.

His intensity struck chords inside of her that she never knew existed before. When he was like this with her, all she wanted to do was press herself close to him, fill all the gaps and holes inside of him with her warmth. She wanted to be the one to make everything in his life that'd been bad leave him so she could bring in the good, the positive…the love.

All of the sudden, all she wanted to do was shake sense into him. Why was he talking about leaving and going to Kansas City when she was right here in front of him, ready to love him? Ready to keep him smiling all the time and cook for him, she'd figure out how, and write silly little notes that she'd leave for him when she left for work, and take him down to the beach and go skinny dipping with him in the evenings and make love to him constantly. She'd never tire of making love to him as long as she lived. She was sure of that.

She grabbed him by the shoulders. "Don't you see me? I'm right here."

He blinked like he was waking up from an insane dream…or maybe a nightmare. The white parts of his eyes cracked red, like he was straining to hold back his emotions. "I see you," he whispered. "My God, do I see you."

Her stupid phone buzzed, breaking the moment. She grabbed her pants and pulled it out of the pocket. "It's Sebastian. We need to go."

They dressed, and she checked herself in the mirror above the little sink, fixing her makeup the best she could. He waited on the couch, head in his hands. She turned to him and plastered on a smile. "Ready?"

He nodded and grabbed their towel. He motioned with it. "I'll wash it and return it."

She loved him for that…and so much more.

Chapter Seventeen

Sebastian looked up from his spot on the couch. "I was about to call the police."

Ashe shook his head, swirling his finger around his ear and mouthing, "Drama queen."

Desiree sat flipping through a magazine while Marigold and Chase played a game of slapjack on the coffee table. Bo and the server he had flirted with earlier stood by the dining room table seeming to be getting along just fine, and a handful of other party guests Blake didn't know headed toward the door.

"Where's Cassidy?" Seanna asked.

"She left about five minutes ago," Ashe said. "Rob and Gwendolen were leaving, so she hitched a ride."

Sebastian closed the door and turned to them. "That just leaves us."

Seanna checked her phone. "Gosh, were we gone that long."

"Where were you, anyway?" Marigold asked.

Desiree glanced up from her magazine, giving Blake a look that made his cheeks heat up. She flipped a page. "Stroll down the beach?"

"Yeah," Blake said, pocketing his hands.

Sebastian put his hands on his hips. "Well, are the two of you staying or what? Have a seat." He headed for the dining room chairs.

"Let's go swimming," Chase said.

"Nobody has their suits," Desiree said.

Chase waggled his eyebrows. "Even better."

"I have suits," Sebastian said. "Follow me upstairs, ladies, and I'll find your perfect fit. I keep new suits in the guest rooms."

Ashe jerked a thumb over his shoulder at Sebastian. "Of course he does."

Blake looked over at Seanna, and she shrugged. "Guess I'm getting suited up." He watched her walk up the stairs behind Desiree and Marigold, wondering what the hell he was doing. Every minute he spent with her made him doubt everything. He ran scenarios through his head constantly. Could he keep going just like this? Swear Bo to secrecy and live life as a handyman with her here in South Walton forever? He could hold the lie about who he was and vow to spend his life making hers comfortable and safe, no matter how much he wanted to practice medicine…or how much she deserved to know the truth about who she chose to spend her life with.

"Catch!" Sebastian shouted. Blake looked up just in time to catch a pair of swim trunks. He held them up. "I think these are mine."

"I know they are. I've had them here since you left them Fourth of July."

"Thanks."

He got changed in the hall bathroom and met Bo, who

was coming out of Sebastian's room. "You have a good walk down the beach?" Bo asked, grinning like an idiot.

"It's not like you missed me." Blake nodded toward the kitchen where the catering crew was cleaning up.

"It's not happening," Bo said. "She's moving back to Knoxville where she's from after Christmas. Going back to school to be a nurse."

"Christmas is a long time from now."

She came out of the kitchen and grabbed a plate off a buffet, giving Bo a big grin before she headed back in. "I've had enough of the short-term. It's not worth it...getting involved, getting right to that point where you think this might be the one you're meant to be with, and then having your heart ripped out, leaving you depressed and lonely. I'd rather sit at home with Jake watching reruns of *Family Guy*."

Bo walked toward the pool, and Blake followed him, Bo's words rattling around in his head and pinching his gut.

Bo jumped in the pool and picked up a volleyball, hitting to Ashe who hit it back to him. Bo hit it to Blake, and he set up Chase a few feet away from him for a spike that Bo had to duck away from. "You son of a bitch," Bo yelled.

The girls filed out looking good in their bikinis, and Seanna did a running cannonball into the water. She came up holding her hands out to the side. "What's my score?"

"Ten!" several of them shouted.

"Best birthday ever," she said, giving Blake a smile, and then she turned to Sebastian. "Get your skinny butt in here with me."

"Well, I'm not going to top that jump, but I will show off my diving team skills circa seventh grade."

He stepped to the end of the diving board and turned

around, balancing on the end with the tips of his toes. He jumped up in the air and did an inverted dive to rival Greg Louganis. He emerged from the water to applause and whistles all around. "Why, thank you," he said, batting his eyelashes.

"I'm next," Marigold said, shuffling over to the board. "How did you do that?"

"I'll show you tomorrow when we're all sober," Sebastian said.

"I haven't even had that much." She walked to the end of the board and started jumping. "This is fun. It's like a—"

She slipped on the board and fell awkwardly to the side, her head bouncing off the board and leaving a smear of blood, her body dropping into the pool like a sack of potatoes. Bo, who was already in the water, dove for Marigold's limp body, bringing her up to the surface through a red cloud of water.

Instincts Blake hadn't felt in three years kicked in like he'd been practicing medicine yesterday. He looked directly at Chase, who wasn't in the water, and pointed for emphasis. "Call 911." Blake turned to Sebastian. "Go get a stack of towels. Hand towels and full size." He grabbed a beach towel from a chaise lounge and spread it out while Bo met him at the shallow end of the pool with Marigold coughing up water. He helped Bo lift her out of the water, carefully, stretching her out on the beach towel, aligning her head and spine.

He looked up at Bo. "Place both of your hands on either side of her head to keep her still in case of spinal injury." Bo pulled himself out of the water and did as Blake instructed.

Once her coughing slowed enough, Blake cradled her head, Bo backing off, and checked for damage to the skull, noting a deep cut on the right side.

Sebastian appeared with the towels.

Blake looked back at Bo. "Take over holding her head in place again." He turned to Sebastian. "Give me the hand towel." Sebastian did so without a word, and Blake held the towel against the wound. "What time is it?"

Sebastian glanced over his shoulder. "Um, 10:34."

Blake nodded confirmation, and then smiled for Marigold. "You're doing good. It's a minor wound, it just bleeds a lot because there's a lot of blood vessels close to your scalp. It looks worse than it really is." He wouldn't mention his concerns about an underlying skull fracture or intracranial injury.

"Who are you, my doctor?" she said, her voice scratchy from the choking.

He took it as a joke and not her being out of it, but he couldn't be certain of that. "Don't speak, and try not to move. The paramedics will be here soon." He looked up at Chase. "Go out the front door and wait for them at the end of the drive. Wave them to you as soon as you see them coming down the street." Chase nodded and headed back inside.

Blake could feel the towel soaking through, and he looked at Sebastian. "I'll take another." He stacked the towel on top of the soaked one, holding it in place, applying steady pressure to stem the bleeding, careful not to push too hard in case she had an underlying skull fracture.

Marigold's eyes shot up to the towel, and she opened her mouth, but Blake cut her off. "Shh, it's nothing to worry about. Don't talk, don't move. Just be still, okay? Can you do that for me?" He smiled. "Blink once for yes." She blinked, and he nodded. "Good. You're doing really good." He looked back at Sebastian. "Go get a couple more towels just in case, and take everyone else inside. I think this is one time Marigold probably doesn't care to be the center of attention." Sebastian gathered their crew and emptied the area of everyone except Bo, who was watching him without a word.

Marigold frowned. "I know it hurts," Blake said, "but you're okay." She closed her eyes. "Do you feel dizzy or lightheaded? Blink once for yes, twice for no." She blinked once, slowly. "Think about the time we all drove to Pensacola for that monster truck thing for Bo's nephews. Remember that? They had more fun with you than they did with him." She blinked, trying to smile, and Bo gave Blake part of a smile. "Or think about that time we all went paddleboarding, and Chase squealed like a two-year-old when he thought he saw a shark."

"Yeah, think about that for sure," Bo said. She smiled as the hint of a siren sounded in the distant.

"See, there's your ride," Blake said. "Just a few more minutes now till the paramedics come. Can you hang in there for me?"

He kept talking to her until the paramedics made their way to them, flanked by Sebastian. Blake passed his patient off to one of them.

"Did you call as soon as it happened?" she asked.

"Yes, ma'am," Blake said.

"How long have you been applying pressure?"

Blake looked at Sebastian, and he said, "Twelve minutes." The paramedic inspected the towel and then put a neck brace on to stabilize her spine. She discarded the additional bloody towels, leaving the bottom one in place to preserve any clot, and quickly wrapped sterile gauze around it for the transport ride.

Blake stepped away, allowing them to do their job. He had to look away. He didn't want to be tempted to instruct them on anything. They knew what they were doing. He was the rusty one.

It wasn't long before they had her on a back board and stretcher heading through the house. Blake collapsed onto a chair, rubbing his forehead. Bo stood next to him and clasped him on the shoulder wordlessly.

Seanna came outside with a towel wrapped around her, closing the doors behind her, and Bo made his leave.

"Are you okay?" she asked.

He blinked, bringing himself back into this world. "Yes, of course."

"You're really good in a crisis. How'd you know all that stuff?"

He considered her. The question was simple, but the answer seemed to hinge on so much. He could tell her right now, and he'd be free of the lie. Or he could keep up the charade. As she stared into his eyes so matter-of-fact...so naïve of him, he knew what to do.

He stood. "I'm going to head home. Can I drop you home on my way?"

She blinked, trying to hide the hurt in her eyes, which made his stomach sick. "Um, no, thanks. I'm going to hang a little while, maybe wait for Sebastian to get back with Marigold."

"He went with her?"

"Yeah."

"Good." He held out his hand to her, and she took it, giving a small smile. "Happy birthday."

She huffed a laugh. "It really was a great one."

He nodded. "I'll talk to you tomorrow."

"Yeah."

As he let go of her hand, a tide shifted in him, a darkness settling into his chest as he walked away from her.

Chapter Eighteen

Seanna wiped down the countertops, and then took a moment to inspect her work. She'd spent the week repainting the walls, getting them the color she originally wanted; retiling the backsplash; making some tweaks to the readymade cabinets to give them a custom feel; and touching up the kitchen in a way she could be proud to present the final product to her client. Her work had helped keep her mind off the bigger problem taking up entirely too much of her head space.

Blake had dutifully called her on Sunday as he said he would, but the conversation lacked heart. He was slipping away from her as the days dropped away, and she was powerless to change his heart. Something had shifted in him on Saturday night when Marigold hit her head. The whole incident had been truly frightening, there was no question about that—the blood in the water and on the towels that had been discarded by the pool when the ambulance left, uniformed paramedics stomping through what was previously an elegant, champagne-filled party with equipment and a stretcher, Marigold's still body being taken out on that stretcher.

Blake had taken charge of the situation like he'd done it a thousand times before. That was the part she couldn't understand. Did something about that incident make him change his mind about her? The idea that he realized he had feelings for Marigold crossed her mind, but she couldn't reconcile that as a truth, and she didn't think that was wishful thinking on her part.

She caught Chase's image in the corner of her eye and picked up a few tools quickly before he came inside, getting the kitchen as perfect as she could make it for presentation.

He tossed his keys down on the kitchen table and looked around. "Man, this looks like a real kitchen now and not something out of an old house I'd have lived in when I was in college with six other guys."

"I'm glad you like it."

"I do. You get the icemaker fixed in the fridge yet?"

"Yep. They replaced it this morning."

"I guess I owe you a check." He pulled out his wallet and handed her a folded-up check.

She shoved it in her pocket without checking the amount. "Thank you. If you have any problems with anything, please call me. I want the opportunity to fix whatever arises."

"You have any interest in quoting out that gut-job? I closed on it today. I could run you over there and let you eyeball it if you like."

Something clenched at her gut, the idea of starting on this house sounding miserable. She needed to keep working though, and this was what her training was in. Outside of being able to find a job like her old one where she could use her knowledge of building to sale services, she was stuck, at least until she could get herself on her feet. She could work on that while she worked on this gut job. "I'd love to."

He looked around. "This place looks fantastic."

All she could think of was holding that platter up to the spewing faucet like Wonder Woman, waiting for Blake to come rescue her. "I would love to go see it tonight, but I'm supposed to be at Sebastian's right now checking on Marigold. I can call her and tell her I'm going to be a minute."

"Ah, hell no. It's the weekend. I'll take you over there Monday or Tuesday. You go. Give her a hug from me."

She smiled. "I will." She grabbed her purse from the kitchen chair and shouldered it. "I can't thank you enough for these opportunities."

He glanced around his kitchen. "Looks like I'm the one who got the benefit."

"I know it's inappropriate, but can I hug you?"

He huffed a laugh. "Sure. I'll take off my client hat and put on my friend one."

She walked over to him and wrapped her arms around him. He pulled away. "So are you thinking of staying here permanently?"

The idea sounded fantastic...settling into this town with all these wonderful people so far away from the mess she'd been dealing with back home for a year. If only she could convince Blake to stay here with her, she'd never leave.

"If you all will have me."

He grinned. "I feel confident rendering a huge yes on behalf of the group."

She smiled back. "Thank you. I'll text you Monday about the quote on the gut-job."

"Sounds like a plan."

She held up her hand in a wave and headed for her car. Exhaling a deep breath behind her steering wheel, she checked her phone. No texts. She was used to the disappointment by now. She checked her email, which was stupid because Blake didn't even have her email. One email stood out to her over the junk. One of the companies she'd applied to weeks ago. She clicked on it, expecting a rejection letter but was shocked to see it was a personalized email, familiar even.

It was from Isabelle Pointer. She'd worked in HR at the firm up until about a year ago when she had her baby. Seanna thought she was staying home, but she was working for this company Seanna had applied to, apparently.

She'd found Seanna's resume when cleaning out her junk folder. The job she had applied for was too far down the line to start from scratch with interview one, but there was another opening for a junior project manager, and did Seanna want to interview for it?

She huffed a laugh. Didn't that figure. She'd have jumped on this offer weeks ago, but she was ready to stay here now…quote out the job for Chase. She was fairly certain she could get it. He was into helping people, the big ole sweetie he was, and she imagined he'd be no different with this job than he'd been with the first one, especially if he was offering to take her to see the property next week. Project management wasn't her favorite work, but it paid well, and it would keep her here and enable her to make that last payment on her apartment.

She thought about Blake and his distance from her. He was leaving and she was staying. That was the way this could go. But he wasn't gone yet. She just had to figure out how to change his mind.

Sebastian answered the door wearing a navy blue apron. "I hope you like million dollar chicken."

"Oh, I didn't know we were having dinner."

"Of course we are, sweetie. I can't have a guest over at six o'clock and not offer food. Come on in."

She stepped inside the foyer. "I hope you didn't go to trouble for me."

Marigold repositioned herself on the couch. "Let him go to all the trouble he wants. He loves it." Seanna imagined that he did.

"How are you feeling?" Seanna asked, focusing on the bandage on the top left corner of her forehead.

"Much better. Nurse Sebastian has done a very good job." She smiled over at the kitchen.

"You're welcome!" he shouted.

"So," Marigold said, "have you convinced Blake to stay yet?"

Seanna sat on the couch with her. "No. I haven't really talked to him much this week."

"Seriously? What's up with that?"

Seanna shrugged. "I really don't know, to be honest. Something changed…right after the accident."

"My accident?"

"Yeah. I don't know. We were okay, and then we weren't." Seanna narrowed her gaze at Marigold. "Are the two of you…"

Marigold's eyebrows shot up. "Dating? Blake and me?" She busted out in laughter and then put her hand to her head. "Oh, don't do that. It makes my head hurt."

"So…no?"

"God no. Not for lack of trying on my part though. None of these guys are ever going to date me. I'm too much for them. I tease, and I try like hell with them, but truthfully, I like it how it is right now. I can flirt with the three of them all day long, and we can still hang out. All my romantic relationships have ended explosively. I like having three great, positive, straight guy relationships in my life that I know will continue. Blake can fix anything. Chase can buy anything. And Bo's the most fabulous date on the planet to take to your ex's sister's wedding."

Seanna chuckled. "I'll bet he is."

"So, I take it Blake's in retreat mode."

"He's full-on undercover."

Marigold sat back on the couch, shaking her head. "That guy. He's so tough. But if anyone can pull him over this threshold, it's you, Seanna. I've known him three years, and I've never seen him date anyone. I thought he might be gay, but Sebastian's gaydar ran cold on him from the start."

"Yeah, I can confirm he's not gay."

"Bragger. You're going to have to pull him through this, Seanna, whatever it is."

"How? I can't stalk him. If he's not interested—"

Marigold held up a hand. "He's interested. If you're anything like me, you want him to make the first big emotional move. But he's set to leave in about a month. Time is ticking. Put it on the line. Tell him what you want from him. Ask him to stay."

Seanna exhaled a deep breath, staring back at Marigold. "If you'd have told me six weeks ago that I'd be having this conversation about any man, I'd have thought you were a nut job."

"A lot of people think that about me as it stands."

Seanna laughed, finally getting why they all were so close with her. "I'm so glad you're doing better."

Marigold's cat eyes widened as she got a conspiratorial expression on her face. "That was hot, how Blake was all take charge when I hit my head. I'd love to be with a guy like that. You're a lucky girl."

"We'll see about that."

The doorbell rang. "Sooner rather than later. That's him," Marigold said.

Seanna stilled. "Are you serious?"

Sebastian peeked out from the kitchen. "Seanna, will you please get that." He gave her a little smile, then went back to the stove.

She turned to Marigold. "You two are awful."

"He stopped by earlier in the week. We could tell something was off. Sebastian could at least. He's nothing if not intuitive." The bell rang again.

Seanna narrowed her gaze. "I'm not sure if I should thank the two of you or hurt you."

Marigold pointed at her forehead. "I've got that part covered."

Seanna smiled and then headed for the door. She opened it to find Blake standing there holding a bottle of wine. His eyes went wide. "Oh, hey."

"I see they warned you about dinner. I thought I was just stopping by to see Marigold."

He furrowed his brow, gripping the wine bottle with two hands. "I'm sorry I haven't called or texted much this week."

"It's no problem. In fact I think I owe you one from Thursday. I've been super busy with Chase's kitchen. I finished this afternoon."

"Oh, cool. I'll have to go see the finished product."

"Yeah, it's in better repair than the last time you saw it. Come on in," she said. He turned his attention to Marigold on the couch, so Seanna took the wine from him and brought it to Sebastian in the kitchen. "Blake brought you this lovely bottle of wine, and I'm bringing you a bottle of whoop ass."

"Oh, please. You know you're happy to see him."

"But does he want to see me is the question."

Sebastian tapped a wooden spoon against a pot. "Of course he does, sweetie. He just needs some nudging. You know how straight men are. They all need a little guidance. This friend of mine from high school tells this story about her current husband all the time. They'd dated briefly in high school, and then she sees him when they're like twenty-five coming out of the grocery store. She says hello, and he pretends he doesn't hear her when she's sure he did. She's so pissed off that she marches across the parking lot, tracking him to his car, and then confronts him while he's loading in his groceries. They got married three months later. Now what if she had let that boy go? Those two little brats of theirs wouldn't even exist right now."

"So you think I need to confront him?"

"The word confront is so harsh. How about a nudge?"

She smiled. "Where's your corkscrew?"

He opened a drawer and handed it to her. "Use the crystal glasses in the buffet in the dining room."

"Yes, sir."

She filled four glasses, and then headed out with two of them. Marigold held up her hand. "None for me…ever again. Well, not ever, just not yet." She peered at the kitchen. "You coming along in there, Bastian?"

"Yep. Plating now."

Marigold headed that way, leaving Seanna standing there with two glasses of wine. She handed one to Blake, who was sitting in the chair.

"Thanks."

She held up her glass to him. "Thank you. I came empty-handed."

"Have you seen the wine wall in the dining room? There's about a hundred bottles in there. I think we could have managed."

She sat on the couch. "Just." She forced a smile, but she really wasn't feeling it. What the hell was wrong with him? He looked at her like he wanted to devour her half the time, yet he'd practically ignored her all week.

"So, are you getting your business wrapped up here?"

"Yeah, I've been working on it all week." He frowned. "I think I may actually head to KC a few weeks early…get settled before I have to start my new job."

She nodded, her heart dull from the words, but they weren't a shock. They sat in silence for a few moments, watching the muted television, which had been left on HGTV. Seanna was vaguely aware of the back door opening and closing, but it wasn't until she heard a car starting in the drive out front that she perked up. "Where are Sebastian and Marigold?"

Blake peered into the kitchen, and then went to the front door, Seanna on his heels. Sebastian's car zoomed up the cul-de-sac toward the main street. "You've got to be kidding me."

She headed to the dining room where she found two plates of million dollar chicken with green bean almondine and new potatoes. "Well, your friends are nothing if not persistent."

He met her in the dining room, running his hand through his hair, his face colored. She looked up at him and started laughing. That was all she knew to do. He smiled, though it didn't seem to come as easy to him as it did to her.

She tossed up her hands. "Well, at least they didn't take your truck."

He glanced at the front door and then back down at the table.

"Just go, Blake. There's nothing stopping you this time."

He stared at her, his brow furrowed, looking like a mountain laid on both of his shoulders.

She took his hand and pulled it up between them, threading her fingers with his. "I don't know what's in Kansas City that's not here, but if you stay, we can find it…together."

Chapter Nineteen

Blake stared at their clasped hands, a vice grip squeezing his heart. Keeping his distance from her this week had made his heart sick with pain, but standing here in front of her, he realized his pain hadn't even scratched the surface yet. The sincerity in her eyes was so real and true that he had no choice but to bring her hand to his mouth and kiss the tips of her fingers. "You can't imagine how much I want to stay."

She moved closer to him, wrapping his arm around her waist. "You can have it, Blake. You can have all of me."

He slid his hand down her ass, pressing her up against him. Her mouth met his, and he lost himself in the intensity of her touch awakening him from a week of separating himself from her. She walked him backward toward the stairs, and then took his hand and led him up them to the first room they came to.

She slid open the bedside drawer, peered inside, and then closed it back. As she pulled the comforter down and tossed away the excess pillows, he had a vision of her doing this very same thing in their own home. They'd both come home from a day at work. He'd fix dinner for them, and they'd cuddle on the couch watching some brainless television, and then head back to their bedroom to make love and fall asleep, her naked body pressed to his. How did the dream of such a simple, perfect life become so intangible for him?

She turned around and took her time undoing the buttons on his shirt. A shiver traveled through his body as she rounded her hands over his shoulders, and tugged his shirt off of him. She unbuckled his belt and undid his pants, letting them drop to his knees. He stepped out of them, naked there before her, but with still so much about him he wouldn't let her see.

She ran her hand over his balls, letting the weight of them fall into her palm, making his cock stand at attention. He'd never known a woman's touch could make him lose control of his senses and his brain function. When she dropped to her knees and took them into her mouth, he breathed so heavy he thought he might steam up the windows as the sensation of her mouth on the most sensitive part of his body lit a fire inside of him.

She lifted herself onto the bed, pulling her shirt and bra off of her in one big motion and tossing them away. She pulled her shorts off and scooted back on the bed. "Come here, Blake."

Something about the way she said his name so matter of fact, almost like she was calling him out, caused a wave through his stomach, and it also tightened his erection. He lay beside her, and she moved her hand up his arm. "I was with Jason for two years, and I'm fairly positive he never cheated on me, not with another person, that is. Have you slept around much these past few years?"

He stared into her eyes, wanting to tell her one truth, one

fact about himself that he typically wouldn't admit to. "I haven't been with anyone in over three years before you."

She smiled, moving her hand up to his forehead, and ran the tips of her fingers through his hair. "I want to feel you inside of me. It's a safe time of the month if you'd like that, too. If not, there're condoms in the bedside drawer."

He didn't answer, just climbed on top of her and guided himself inside. Her wet warmth surrounding him sent a surge of heat through his stomach and up through his chest...the most natural thing he'd ever felt in his life, primal and simple, yet thrilling in a way that made him never want to be outside of her body again.

Her eyes closed, her brow furrowing as she gripped his biceps. He pushed inside of her over and over, wanting to last till midnight if he could, but with how good her bare flesh felt against his, he'd be lucky to last the rest of the minute.

The sensations soared inside of him, fueled by both the physical act of pumping inside of a beautiful woman and the emotions he was feeling for her. He lost himself as the heat built within him, but the grip on his arms woke him up to the expression on her face which he understood now was the one she got when she was getting ready to come apart for him.

He pumped harder, willing himself not to ruin this for her. He wanted to be the one to give this to her...to make her come for him, because of him, all around him.

She let out a sound like she'd been holding her breath and then gasped for air again, holding her breath one more time until she let everything out, releasing her grip from his arms. All it took was one more push into her wet warmth, and he let himself go inside of her.

He collapsed onto her, holding his weight in his elbows and knees so it wouldn't crush her, but he needed the feel of his bare body against hers as he steadied his breathing.

She pulled his head up off of her and smoothed his damp hair out of his eyes. "I love you, Blake Evans. I want to be with you."

He searched her eyes, wanting to tell her he loved her back. He did, Jesus Christ, he did. He'd never understood love until her. But everything was so crystal clear now, that he could write books about it…libraries.

He could tell her everything right now. He'd ask her to get dressed, and they'd go sit on the couch downstairs so he could tell her the entire story. If she hated him, she could get up and leave and never have to see him again. He'd leave for KC tomorrow. He was just stalling at this point anyway.

The downstairs door opened, and Sebastian's voice filled the house. "Seanna!"

They both sat up, and she shouted back. "Upstairs!"

Footsteps sounded, and Blake jumped off the bed and shut the door. "Just a minute." He tossed Seanna her clothes.

"I'm so sorry to interrupt," he said from the hallway. "It's Jason. He's here, at the shop with Cassidy."

Seanna stared at Blake motionless, her face turning white. "I'm not ready for this."

Blake slid onto the bed with her. "You don't have to go. I'll go handle the whole thing."

"No, I need to."

"I'm going with you."

"No, I'll just…" She trailed off, glancing around.

He pulled her attention back to him. "I'm going with you. I'm not arguing about it."

She smiled. "Is this our first fight?'

He huffed a laugh. "Yeah. Wanna make up?"

They dressed and headed down the stairs where Sebastian was waiting in the living room. He stood up off the chair. "I am so sorry, you two. We had this whole night planned. We were just picking up Cassidy at the shop for dinner, and he was there. I tried to text you, but I figured you didn't have your phone." He gave a significant look in the direction of the bedroom they'd just left.

"How long has he been there?" Seanna asked.

"I don't know. It didn't seem like long based on the content of their conversation. He was asking where to find you and getting a little belligerent."

"Let's go," Blake said.

"He's fine," Seanna said. "He's never hurt me, not physically. And Cassidy is badass. She can totally handle herself."

"I left Marigold there with her, so between the two of them, the poor guy will probably wish he'd never shown up," Sebastian said. "I'll follow you all over there."

He and Seanna jumped in his truck and made the quick drive to the shop, which felt like it took a lot longer than it usually did. Blake wheeled into a front parking place next to a red Lexus. "Is this his car?" Blake asked.

"I don't know that car. He probably finally got his repossessed."

Through the glass, Blake could see a guy sitting at one of the tables near the counter digging his thumb into his forehead. He and Seanna got out of the truck and Blake opened the door for her, Sebastian bringing up the rear. The guy looked up at them, and Blake connected him with the picture he'd seen in that article he'd read about him weeks ago, except in that picture, he wore a shirt and tie with a conservative haircut, looking like he belonged in a Gordon Gekko movie. Today he looked like he'd crawled out of a meth lab. Not quite, but just about.

When the guy saw Seanna, his whole body visibly relaxed, like finding her was the answer to the universe's biggest questions. "Oh, shit, Seanna." He walked toward her, feet away from hugging her, wrapping his filthy body around the woman Blake loved, expecting her to be some sort of problem-solver past what she was already doing for him...maybe even putting her in danger, giving some debt collector wielding a baseball bat ideas about how he could make Jason pay by threatening those close to him. Alarm shot through Blake's chest, and he instinctively took a step in front of her. "Who the fuck are you?" the guy asked.

Seanna took Blake's arm. "It's fine. What is it, Jason? Why are you here?"

Jason looked between Seanna and Blake, an irritable frown on his ugly face. "I need to talk to my fiancée."

"Fuck you." The words were out before Blake could stop them.

"Who the fuck are you?" Jason asked, sizing Blake up. That's right. He better think twice.

Cassidy appeared between them. "Let's just dial this down a notch. Jason came here to talk to Seanna. Sweetie, is that something you are okay with?"

Seanna turned to Marigold and Sebastian. "Why don't you all go back home? Cassidy and Blake are here. It's fine." They nodded dutifully and headed to the parking lot.

Jason glared at Blake and then turned to Seanna. "I need to talk to you alone."

"I really don't care what you think you need. I don't want to be alone with you. Not now, and not ever again."

"Why? Because you know you love me?"

"No, because I've had enough of you," she said in a rush. "You drag me down. You're like a current pulling me to the bottom of the ocean. I can't breathe right around you anymore." She put her fingertips to her throat, and Blake wanted to kill this son of a bitch.

"I'm here to tell you I'm paying you back for everything, paying us back."

"Right now?"

"Yes."

She blinked with a moment's hesitation, and then said, "That's great. Just leave the money or the check or whatever and go."

He looked around like he was confused. "I drove all the way down here to talk to you."

"You really shouldn't have."

"This is our business, Seanna, not anyone else's."

"We don't have any business anymore, not after I make that last payment."

He met Blake's glare for a moment, and then looked back at Seanna. "Are you with him now?"

"Yes," Blake answered without hesitation.

He jerked his head back and bore his gaze into Blake's, but this time with interest. "Who are you? Do I know you?"

Blake froze for a split second, his blood running frigid. "Why don't you leave? She doesn't want you here."

Jason stared at Blake a minute longer, and he swallowed down some bile. Jason might not figure it out now, but he would soon enough. He pulled open his wallet, slapped a check down on a table, and then looked up at Seanna. "I'm going to text you the name and address where I'm staying. I'll be there tonight. I want you to think about us, about how we were before. That's how I'm ready to be again. And I'll never let a day go by where I don't work like hell to make all this up to you."

He gave Blake one last murderous stare before shoving his way past him and to the door. It took everything Blake had in him to be the bigger man and let it go, but as much disdain as he had for that piece of shit, he had more love for Seanna. And he knew a throw-down between him and her ex was not the way to go here, not unless absolutely necessary.

Seanna picked up the check with a shaky hand and then set it back down.

Cassidy looked at it and then huffed a laugh. "Where do you think he got that kind of money?" Seanna frowned at her aunt, and Cassidy rubbed her back. "I'm sorry, sweetie."

"Why don't we sit a minute," Blake said.

"I have a bottle of wine in the fridge. I'll be back in a second," Cassidy said.

Seanna sat down and rubbed her forehead with the tips of her fingers. "I don't even want that money. God only knows how he got it or if the check would even clear."

The bell on the door dinged and Bo and Chase came in. "What's going on?" Bo asked.

"What are you doing here?" Blake asked. Marigold and Sebastian came through the doorway next with Ashe and Desiree on their heels.

Bo scanned the room. "We were at the bar at Whiskey Bravo when Marigold texted us to get over here."

Ashe pointed between himself and Desiree. "We weren't missing out on any drama."

"I just wasn't sure how dangerous he was," Marigold said. "I knew they were close by. We were meeting there for dinner."

"Who was it?" Chase asked.

Seanna shook her head. "It was my ex. It's fine. He's fine. He's gone."

Marigold pointed to the parking lot. "He's actually not gone."

Blake stood up, adrenaline shooting through his veins. Jason slammed the door to the car.

"What the fuck?" Chase asked.

The door to Seaside Sweets flew open, and Jason stood scanning their group. His gaze landed on Chase, who looked scarier than the rest of them but was more likely to buy the house a round of beers than kick anyone's ass. He needed to be worried about the guy standing next to him. Bo would take down the Atlanta Falcons if he thought they were messing with one of his people.

Jason shifted his gaze to Blake, pointing. "I know who you are."

As Blake stared down this sorry piece of shit, all he could think about was how stupid he had been. He'd had weeks to tell Seanna, years to tell the rest of them. But he'd moronically thought he could pull this lie off, keep all these people he loved in the dark about him. And now in one single performance, this asshole would be the one to take him down.

Bo stepped closer to him. "You don't fucking know him. Get out."

"Yes I fucking do. He's—"

Bo got right up in his face. "You say one more goddamned word, and I'll beat your ass so hard your mama won't be able to identify you."

"Bo," Blake said. "It's over."

Bo looked Jason up and down. "You bet your ass it's over. Get the fuck out."

Blake put his hand on Bo's shoulder. "I'm serious. It's done. I can't do this anymore." Bo stared at Blake hard, asking him if he was sure without opening his mouth. Blake nodded, and then turned back to Jason. "Go ahead."

Jason glanced at Bo and back at Blake like he wasn't sure.

"Go ahead with what?" Seanna asked.

"Tell them how you know me," Blake said.

Jason met Seanna's bewildered gaze, and then stabbed his finger at Blake. "He fucking killed his fiancée."

Blake didn't deny it, just held Jason's deadly stare until he dared to meet Seanna's gaze.

"What?" she asked.

"He didn't fucking kill anyone," Bo said.

"Let him tell it," Blake said.

Jason glanced around again, wary, but he had no problem plowing forward. "He killed her. She said so in her note. It was fucked up. She cut her own wrists, but he was the reason. And when she showed up at the ER, he finished the job. She should have lived. Everyone knew it, but he wouldn't let anyone else near her. Is this who you want to be with? A murdering son of a bitch?"

Bo stepped up to him again. "Call him that one more time and see what happens."

The look on Seanna's face was enough to bury him. "What is he talking about?"

"It's true," Blake said, his voice coming out quieter than he meant for it to, so he cleared his throat and stood up straight. "I was a doctor before I came here."

"What?" Marigold said, and Sebastian nudged her, biting his thumbnail.

"You're a doctor?" Seanna asked.

Jason glanced between the two of them. "You didn't know that?"

His stomach churned like a vat of vomit. "I was working when she came into the ER, bleeding out. I'd just broken it off with her, and we thought we had her settled. I was going to leave town. Her parents thought it would be best that way. I had no ties to Atlanta, anyway. But she didn't want that, and she let me know in the most emphatic way she could." He stared at a crumb of cake on the floor, the whole night playing out right there on top of it. "She cut herself just enough to make a statement, to tell me I wasn't going anywhere, not without her." He balled up his fist. "If I could go back and make it right, I would have stayed. I would have married her. I would shut up about it and suck it up. I could have figured it out, how to live with her." He looked up at the ceiling. "I swear to God, I would have stayed with her."

He stared at a spot on the ceiling, visions of their tumultuous relationship playing out right there like a movie—the times she would hit him so hard he'd have to tell stories about being in a bar fight, the time they ran into a woman he'd been on a date with before she'd ever come along, and Tara calling her a whore, the time she went a week without showering and locked herself in the bathroom for the night, leaning against the door, her feet locked against the bathtub so he couldn't open it without hurting her, him sitting on the other side begging her to come out, blinking himself awake all night so he could make sure she was still alive. He'd begged her parents to place her somewhere she could be monitored all the time. They'd thought Blake had been sent to them from heaven to save their daughter. They'd finally taken her into their custody, and he'd thought the nightmare was over after years of madness, but it'd just started.

The silence surrounding him woke him up, and he met the gazes of all the people around him. Cassidy, who'd been his first friend when he came to town. Chase, who he'd met when he first started his business and had thrown more referrals his way than he had time to handle. Sebastian, who took care of all of them like a doting father. Marigold, Ashe, and Desiree, who colored their get-togethers with their humor, their individual styles, and their love for this friend group. Bo, who'd been the brother he'd never had, and who had the kindest heart of anyone on the planet. And Seanna, who'd shown him what a real relationship with love and heart looked like.

"I'm sorry," he said to all of them. "I'm so sorry."

He turned and headed for his truck.

Chapter Twenty

Seanna stood dumbfounded as Blake backed out of his parking place in front of Seaside Sweets. What had just happened? She couldn't even start to process through it. Doctor? Fiancée? Murder? Blake? All her mind could do was flash words out in front of her like a neon sign.

Bo gave Jason a look that would have put the fear of God into Charles Manson. "Let's get something clear. You get in your car right now, and you leave this town. If I ever spot you anywhere near him or her again, I'll fucking kill you." Seanna believed every word out of Bo's mouth, and by the look on Jason's face, he did, too.

Jason looked at Seanna one last time, and then walked out the front door. Something told her she'd never lay eyes on him again.

Bo put both his hands on his hips, the muscles in his biceps protruding out of his T-shirt sleeve like they'd been agitated. "Sebastian, why don't you take everybody to the restaurant. I'm gonna stay here with Seanna for a minute. Don't wait on me."

Sebastian nodded, and then came over to Seanna and

wrapped his skinny arms around her. "I love you, sweetie." He kissed her on the cheek and then herded his friends out the door.

Chase looked down at Bo, his brow furrowed with concern. Seanna didn't think she'd ever seen him look serious. "Call or text me if you need me. I'll get wherever I need to be fast."

"I know you will," Bo said. "Go on. Keep a lid on the gossip as much as you can, at least until I can clear everything up for everyone."

"Will do." Chase turned to Seanna. "I'm a text away for anything you need. You hear me?"

She nodded. "Thanks, Chase."

Bo rubbed his hand over his head, his face losing some of its bright red color. "Goddamn, that lit me up. Are you okay?"

"Yeah," Seanna said, looking down at her hands, which were shaking like crazy.

"Come here," Bo said, and pulled her into his chest. Cassidy stepped closer and rubbed on her back. A tear streamed down Seanna's face, but she held back from bawling like she wanted to.

She pulled away and met Cassidy's gaze. "Did you know about any of this?"

Cassidy shook her head. "I didn't."

They both looked at Bo, and he held up a hand. "I did but only for a few weeks now. He didn't kill her. You both understand that, right?"

Seanna swallowed, and Cassidy blinked with a moment's hesitation. "Yes, of course," she said.

"She was sick," Bo said. "Bipolar disorder. I read about it out of curiosity after he told me the story. It's no fucking joke."

"No, it's not," Cassidy said. She nudged Seanna. "You remember our cousin Bethany? Her daughter has it."

Seanna nodded, but she didn't.

"I'm telling you," Bo said, "he's beat himself up about her for three years now. He doesn't feel like he deserves any kind of normal life. I think meeting you has had a profound effect on him though."

She wasn't sure how much her chest could take the strain of this. She was going to die of a heart attack at thirty years old. "He's been lying to me," she said, her voice coming out softer than she intended.

"It's been killing him, too. He's been scared shitless of telling you. He didn't want you to see him like this."

She moved a shaky hand up to cover her stomach. "I can't do this again. I can't get involved in all this lying and deception."

Bo furrowed his brow, staring at her wordlessly.

"Don't look at me like that," she snapped.

He held up both hands. "I don't mean to. I'm not judging you or telling you what to do. I just think you need to know that he's been in goddamn turmoil for three years now…hell, for a lot longer than that, I'm assuming. He's not lived the same life as you and I have." He pointed at Cassidy. "Family who loves you and would do anything for you. He doesn't know what that is. He's only known survival. Hell, the first year I brought him home with me for Christmas dinner, you should have seen the look on his face the whole time. It was like he was watching a movie the way he studied all of us. He'd never seen a family like mine who cut up and loved on one another. Talking to him about it afterward I damn near broke down in tears, learning about how he grew up."

"In a children's home, right?" Seanna said.

"When he was in high school. Has he told you how he lived before that?"

Seanna shook her head, her chest tightening, a tear running down her face. Cassidy handed her some napkins from a dispenser on a table.

"He was shuffled around from group homes and foster homes. He won't say a lot about it, but you can draw your own conclusions."

When Blake had talked to her about growing up as an orphan, he'd made it seem so positive—living on a farm, talking about how he and the other kids were like rock stars. But now that she thought about it, he'd only talked about his teen years. She'd been so naïve to think he was giving her the full picture, and she'd been so careful with pulling information out of him that she hadn't thought to ask about his childhood.

"Whatever he went through back then must have sent him on a path of wanting to help people," Bo said. "You should have heard the way he described his relationship with that woman. I couldn't tell where being a doctor ended and any kind of romantic relationship started. I don't think there was a difference."

Seanna knew Blake had a life before her, before moving to this town, but he'd been so quiet about any romantic past that it'd been easy for her not to think about it. Having all this dumped on her chest felt like being trapped under a boulder.

She ran a shaky hand over her forehead thinking about him and Jason standing there facing off in front of her, two men who had lied to her in epic ways. "I can't deal with this right now."

Bo held up his hand. "I know. I realize this is a lot to throw at you. I've got to go talk to him anyway." He pulled his phone out of his pocket, taking a step toward the door.

"Why?" she asked dumbly.

"Because if I don't none of us are liable to ever see him again."

Her heartbeat sped up. "What do you mean?"

"I mean I can see him packing a bag, grabbing that dog, and hauling ass out of here. What just happened here was his worst fear realized. I can guaran-damn-tee you he's not sticking around for the fallout." He pushed open the door. "I've got to go." Hesitating, he turned back to her. "I'm sorry, darlin', about all of this." The door closed behind him, and he was gone.

She turned to Cassidy, speechless, and Cassidy held open her arms. "Come here, sweetie." Cassidy held her there while she attempted to process all that had just happened.

She pulled away. "Jason knew him," was all she could think to say.

"I know, sweetie. Let's just take all of this one step at a time. You want to go back to my house?" Seanna nodded, and Cassidy forced a smile. "I've just got to grab my purse."

As Seanna waited for Cassidy to come back, a fist closed around her heart. It was happening all over again…that tug at her conscience, at her will…wanting to forgive Blake for lying to her, wanting to hold him and work through all this with him and help him heal. But she'd just spent the last year doing that for Jason, and her help did nothing but come back to haunt her.

How had she let this happen? She'd opened her heart wide for a man she barely knew, and she was right back in that same goddamn spot she'd been in when she first arrived here, trying to separate herself from the lying and the deceit, and instead, she'd caught herself up in a brand new web.

"You ready to go home?" Cassidy asked.

Seanna blinked, staring at her aunt. "Yeah. I am."

Chapter Twenty-One

Blake stood in his bathroom, thinking. His body wasn't moving as fast as his brain wanted it to. *Get out.* That was all his mind was saying. But his heart was stuck back at Seaside Sweets watching Seanna's face crumble at the revelations about him, like dealing with her piece of shit ex wasn't enough for one day.

Sadie stood there panting up at him full of frenetic energy. "Shaving kit," he said out loud. He had to keep reminding himself what he was doing. Leaving. Taking just what he needed, and going. The place had come furnished as a vacation rental. Blake had convinced his landlord to let him stay permanently in exchange for work on his other properties. It'd worked out to be a mutually beneficial relationship. Just one more good thing he was leaving behind.

As he headed to the bedroom, the front door opened and Sadie ran to the living room with a woof. Blake cursed himself for not locking it. As much as he wanted it to be Seanna, his body relaxed with relief to see it was Bo, if it had to anybody.

Blake pretended to ignore him as he opened the top

drawer of his chest and gathered his underwear and socks in one fell swoop.

"You missed one," Bo said, pointing at a lone sock.

Blake grunted, shoving crap into his suitcase.

"Can we just have a conversation?" Bo said. "That's all I'm asking for."

"You can talk all you want." Sadie jumped up on the bed and lay down.

Bo shoved Blake's suitcase away with his foot and then looked at Blake, eyebrows raised in challenge. Blake closed his eyes, his mind reeling. He needed to leave. That was all he could think about. Going to his truck.

Blake tossed up his hands. "What's there to say that hasn't already been said today?"

Bo leaned in like he was going to whisper a secret. "Are you telling me that you're going to let that slimy little prick have the last word here?"

"Why the fuck not? He didn't lie."

"He fucking did so. You didn't murder anyone."

Blake tossed up his arms. "I might as well have. I left her. Do you get that? I pawned her off on her parents and left her to die."

"She wasn't dead or dying. Just sick."

"And I'm a doctor. I could have stuck it out, saved her."

"Oh really? You're a psychiatrist? Man, you're busy."

Blake stabbed a finger at him. "You know what I mean."

"No I don't. I know you met this girl and liked her. Somewhere along the way, you found out she was sick and you stuck it out with her."

"I left her. Where did I think she was going to go from there? Who else was going to be with her?"

Bo blinked, letting the words float between them like a barge. They stood there in silence while the weight of Tara's death suffocated Blake.

Bo was the first one to speak. "She wasn't a kid at your group home, Blake. She was a grown woman. Sure, she deserved to have a partner who loved her and took care of her, but so did you...so *do* you."

Blake's breathing came harder, quicker, and he closed his eyes while he took control of his body, calming himself like he did when he seemed to be losing his grip in the ER, reminding himself that what was in front of him was important and deserved his focused attention.

He met Bo's gaze. "I can't stay. You know that, right?"

"Why?" Bo asked, his voice calm and steady.

"I can't come back from this. Looking at all their faces tonight...the confusion, the disappointment, the fear. I can't face them again."

Bo didn't say a word, just walked out of the room, Sadie on his heels. The front door shut, and they were both gone.

Blake blinked. That wasn't like Bo. He was the most stubborn motherfucker Blake had ever known. When Bo came into the house, Blake had been ready for a showdown, not a bow out. Who did Bo think he was walking away from him like that? And what was he doing with his dog?

"Hey!" Blake shouted, kicking the suitcase out of his way. He shoved open the screen door and came to an abrupt halt on his front porch when he saw the display in his front yard. The friends he'd left at Seaside Sweets stood there, arms locked into one another's, Bo on the end.

"If you're going to leave," Chase said, "you're going to have to get through us."

A lump crawled up Blake's throat so big he wondered where his next breath would come from. Desiree broke off the end and walked over to him, putting her slim hands on his cheeks. "It's going to take a whole lot more than this to make me doubt my friendship with you." She kissed him on the cheek, and then walked away.

Ashe came up behind her, looking him up and down. "You know I've always thought straight people were crazy. This ain't no big thing." He threw his arms around Blake and gave him two quick squeezes before heading over to stand with Desiree.

Sebastian jerked a thumb at Ashe. "The gays love the drama. Not me, of course." He gave Blake a sincere smile. "You are my friend. Friends don't walk away from one another. You wouldn't let me do that. And I won't let you." He winked at Blake and then leaned in to his ear. "You're the only one who understands about my family. I need you. Please don't leave." Sebastian gave Blake a sweet kiss on his cheek, squeezed his arm, and then walked away.

Marigold stood in front of him, a big smile on her face. She raised her eyebrows, crossing her arms over her chest. "A doctor? If you thought I pursued you before when I thought you were a handyman, you just wait." She wrapped her arms around him. "Don't even try to be more fucked up than me. I won't be shown up." She pressed herself against his chest, and then joined the others.

Chase stood in front of him, his long arms out to his sides, palms up. "If you leave town, who's gonna keep the spare key to my car? You've unlocked me like ten times now."

Blake looked over at Bo, and he said, "Don't look at me. PCB's a half hour from here."

Blake turned his gaze back to Chase, his heart bursting with the emotion of the past couple of hours that felt like a year.

Chase smiled. "I know Bo's your BFF, but I love you too, man. I'd do anything for any of you bastards. I don't want you to go, brother." He pointed at Blake as he swiped his eye with the back of his finger. "You're going to ruin my reputation with all this serious talk. The girls think I'm hot 'cause I'm funny."

"Nah, we really don't," Marigold chimed in.

Bo stepped in front of Blake and shrugged. "Looks like we got through the initial fallout. Think you can stick around for the rest?"

Blake hadn't cried his whole life until the day at Bo's house, and here the tears were again, falling from his face without a damn bit of permission from him. His friends surrounded him, mowing him down, their huge group teetering back and forth as everyone tried to hug harder. Sadie barked and ran toward them at rocket speed, circling them and then running to the back of the house.

As they separated, Sebastian handed Blake the handkerchief out of his shirt pocket. "I always thought I'd have to give this up to a lady someday, but if it's got to be a hot guy, oh well."

Blake cleaned up, composing himself. "I don't deserve you all."

"Well, none of us deserves each other, so we're all even," Ashe said.

Blake let out a deep breath, noting with intense sorrow the absence of the most important person in his bunch of friends.

"Let's go to my house and order pizza," Chase said.

"I thought Seanna finished your kitchen," Sebastian said. "You should be cooking us dinner." He met Blake's gaze and his expression dropped. "Oh shit, honey. I'm sorry. We'll figure out how to get her back. We just need to keep you here right now."

Marigold steepled her hands in front of her chest. "Will you stay?"

Blake glanced around at this oddball crew of his…two pristine gay guys, a hippie woman, a debutante, a redneck, and the funny guy who owned half the town. How they all came together as a perfect circle of friends was beyond him, but it worked better than anything in his life ever had.

He nodded. "Yeah, I'll stay."

They all applauded like he'd given a performance of some kind and pushed into him for one last hug. He'd never been hugged so much in his life, literally.

"Dinner's on me," Chase said.

"In that case, let's go to Café Thirty-A," Ashe said.

"Be fine with me," Chase said.

"Pizza at Chase's sounds perfect," Sebastian said. "I want to see the new kitchen anyway."

Chase pulled his keys out of his pocket. "I've got a boatload of beer there, too."

"No swimming," Marigold said, and they all laughed their way to the cars.

Blake called Sadie, and she came running. He let her back inside, Bo staying behind while he locked up. "We'll work the other out, okay?" Bo said.

Blake forced a smile and nodded. "Yeah."

Bo was doing his best to put on a brave face for Blake, but Blake was no dummy. Seanna was hurt the most with what happened, and Blake didn't know how to fix that.

"I think this needs some time to breathe," Bo said. "She needs a minute to understand everything. I talked to her, but I could tell I wasn't helping. She's got Cassidy with her, so that's good."

Blake's stomach rolled imagining what Cassidy must be thinking about him right now, how much he'd hurt her niece. "I've messed so much up," Blake said.

"I know. I'm not arguing it. But it's time to start fixing things. Come with me over to Chase's. Let's eat pizza and let this group be around you now that they know. Let them see you're the same person they've always known. Get this initial bit under your belt. You won't believe how easy it will be the next time you see them."

Blake gave him a look. "Have you done this before?"

Bo chuckled. "Fuck no. I'm winging it as I go, like I handle everything else. Come on. Let's go eat."

Blake followed Bo to his truck, trusting him with his entire life, knowing full well he could.

Chapter Twenty-Two

Cassidy handed Seanna the canvas grocery bag she'd packed for her, and Seanna peeked inside. She looked up at her. "I'm never going to be able to eat all this."

Cassidy shrugged. "It's a long drive."

Seanna dropped the tension in her shoulders and ran her key ring in a circle around her finger. "You don't think I'm doing the right thing, do you?"

"I never said or thought that."

Seanna narrowed her gaze. "You're a terrible liar."

Cassidy smiled. "I just want you to be happy, sweetie. If taking that job back in Nashville will do that for you, then that's all I care about."

"I don't have the job yet," Seanna said.

Cassidy gave her a look. "That first phone interview seemed to go pretty well Saturday. And just the fact that he took the time to talk to you on a Saturday says a lot."

"Yeah, probably that I'm going to have to work Saturdays."

Cassidy shrugged. "We're off Sundays and Mondays at Seaside Sweets if you ever change your mind." She pointed at her. "That's a standing offer."

Seanna gave her a smile. "You have no idea how comforting that is, and how tempting."

Cassidy wrapped her arms around Seanna. "I love you, sweetie. Come back soon…for a visit, okay? Fly down, and I'll pick you up from the PCB airport."

"I'll do it. Love you, too."

She kissed her aunt on the cheek, and then got behind the wheel. She kept it together until she got to the end of Seagull Lane, and then tears started flowing. She pulled over in the Seaside horseshoe parking lot until she could get herself together. A gray truck that looked like Blake's across the lot had her frozen solid from head to toe. She couldn't see him…not right now. Her mind was made up, her path clear. Fate had stepped in with the job opportunity, and with one of her friends helping the process along, she seemed poised to have everything fall into place back home.

Home. Nashville was home, not Seaside.

An older gentleman opened the door of the gray truck and hopped in, deepening the already bottomless void in Seanna's heart. She put the car in gear and backed out of the space, heading back where she belonged.

Chapter Twenty-Three

Blake had no idea how much was enough time to let pass, but with the days crawling by like slugs, he was about to lose his mind. He'd texted Seanna on Tuesday and gotten no response. He'd expected that, so he let another day go by and tried again. Nothing. He drove by Cassidy's house like a teenage boy stalking the girl he liked, but he hadn't seen Seanna's car for a few days, which made him wonder all sorts of horrible things.

Friday marked a week since he'd been outed, and something felt significant about that day. He pulled up to Seaside Sweets and walked through the front door. He didn't feel welcome to slip in and out of the back like he usually did and like Cassidy used to encourage him to do.

He got in line behind two other customers, waiting his turn. Cassidy caught his eye at one point and gave him a tight smile that made his stomach ache.

When the last customer left, Blake stood face-to-face with Cassidy, the counter a welcome barrier between them.

"Hey, Blake," she said, her voice steady and polite, not kind though. That was the best he could ask for.

"I wanted to give you both some time before I came by."

She wiped down the counter. "Well, you could have come by as early as Tuesday morning. Seanna's been gone since Monday."

His heart fell fifty stories. "She's back in Nashville?"

"Yep. Job offer, as of late yesterday. When she left, it wasn't in the bag yet, but it looked promising."

His brain throbbed at the idea of where she was living. "And is she back at her condo?"

Cassidy frowned. "I don't know, and I'm not interfering."

His stomach cramped at the idea of her back in that same situation with that weasel. He gripped the edge of the countertop, his fist balling up against the glass.

Cassidy put her hand over his, and the shock of it had him looking up at her quickly. "I'm glad you're staying. I value our friendship, and I'm here for you."

That now familiar pain formed behind his eyes. "Thank you. I feel the same."

She leaned over the countertop, still holding his hand. "Go. Get. Her." She let go and pulled her phone out of her back pocket, typing into it while his adrenaline started to kick in. She nodded at his phone as it dinged. "That's her address. She starts the job Monday, so get your ass up there this weekend."

He smiled, Cassidy's support meaning more to him than she could ever know, and then suddenly, a brick wall stopped him. "Any suggestions how I get her back?"

She shrugged. "You're gonna have to open your heart wide, Blake. Make sure you're giving her your real self, as much of it as you can afford to give and more. Can you do that?"

His knees went weak at the thought, but if it meant getting her back and getting her to stay in Seaside, the pain and humiliation was worth it.

"You bet your ass I can."

Cassidy grinned, and then shooed him away. "Go!"

Chapter Twenty-Four

The elevator dinged, and Blake stepped off, glancing around for a sign anywhere with numbers and arrows. He spotted one and headed down the hallway. Maybe he should have checked himself in a mirror somewhere to make sure he didn't look like an escaped convict. Elevators usually had mirrors, but the one he rode in was padded for movers.

He stood in front of the door to Seanna's condo…her place with Jason. Surely he wasn't there with her. What would Blake do if he was? How would he react if Jason opened the door? His hand instinctively balled up into a fist. He couldn't do that, not right away at least.

He'd rehearsed a million things to say to her in the truck on the eight-hour ride to Nashville. He was sorry was the first, second, and eightieth thing. Past that, he wasn't sure. All he knew was that he was going to be honest with her and speak from his heart. He was going to rip open wounds that had been sealed up for decades, whatever it took to help her understand and come back home with him.

He stood with his fist raised, ready to knock, when the

door flew open. A short, dark-haired guy stood there holding a set of car keys. "Who are you?"

Blake blinked, rechecking the number on the door. "I'm looking for Seanna. Is this the right apartment?"

The guy pursed his lips, his nostrils flaring. "Daryl!" he shouted over his shoulder. "Is this the asshole?" he asked in an out-of-place Jersey accent.

Another guy appeared, a little taller and rounder, holding a red plastic cup, brow furrowed. "No. If you're looking for Jason, you can fuck off. He's not around," the guy said, his southern accent making more sense to Blake.

"Where is he?" Blake asked out of curiosity.

The taller guy looked Blake up and down. "I look like his mama? I don't fucking know. And before you try to pull some stupid shit, you should know Rick here's an officer of the law, so take your bullshit out of here, understand?"

Blake was caught somewhere between wanting to kick this guy's ass and wanting to thank him for being protective of Seanna and her apartment. "I'm not here for Jason. I'm looking for Seanna."

The taller guy, Daryl, spit into the red cup, a bulge protruding under his lip. "Who the fuck are you?"

"Who the fuck are you?" Blake gave it back to him, starting to get pissed off with this cat-and-mouse game.

"I'm Daryl Goddamned Perry. Who the fuck are you?"

Blake relaxed at the name. Perry was Seanna's last name. "I'm Blake...Blake Evans."

Daryl just stared at him blank-faced.

"I'm a friend of Seanna's, from Seaside."

Seaside seemed to be the magic word. Daryl's hard expression softened. "You know Cassidy?"

"Yeah, she's a good friend. She sent me, sort of," he said under his breath.

"Sent you to do what?" There wasn't a piece of bullshit in the Greater Nashville Area that was going to get past this guy. Blake was starting to like him.

"I'm just...I'd like to talk to her, please. Is she here?" Blake tried to peer around these two, but they were holding the doorway solid.

"Daryl nudged the other guy. "Go on, Rick. And will you pick me up a bottle of Coke before you come back? All she's got is Diet Coke in here." Rick nodded with a wave and headed off. Daryl opened the door and let Blake in, but there was nowhere for them to sit down. The living room had been cleared of furniture.

Daryl shut the door behind them. "I take it you're the guy she's been seeing down there these past couple of months. Cassidy told me about you on the phone the other day."

Blake wondered how pissed off Cassidy was when she had that conversation. "You're Seanna's brother?"

"Yeah. Did you even know she had one?"

Blake remembered her mentioning a brother, but just in passing. "Yeah."

Daryl rolled his eyes. "It's fine. We're not too close. My fault. I'm pretty irritated with myself about that, too, you know. If I'd not been so goddamned wrapped up in my own life and work, I might have taken the time to see something was bad wrong with her this last year. We could have avoided all this." He glanced around her apartment. "I'm here now though, trying to make up for it. You here to get her to forgive you?"

Blake supposed he was, but wasn't sure that was the right answer. "I just want to talk to her."

Daryl narrowed his gaze. "Like Jason just wants to talk to her."

Blake's chest heated up. "Has he been here trying to see her?"

"Of course he fucking has been." He shook out his hand. "Busted up my knuckles punching him in his squirrely little mouth." Blake smiled, sorry he'd missed that. Daryl sized Blake up again, and he wondered if he was in for a punch himself. "She doesn't need to do any more talking."

The idea of Blake and Jason being in one equally shitty group in Daryl's head infuriated Blake. "No, this isn't that. I need to apologize."

"How many times you think Jason's apologized over the past year?"

Blake ran his hand through his hair. "No, I'm just…this isn't that."

"I heard you say that the first time. Look, man, you seem like a nice guy, probably even a decent one at heart." He looked him up and down again. "Doesn't look like you went into medicine for the money. But Seanna's been to hell and back with Jason this past year. The last thing she needs is more drama in her life. You got a sister?"

That always felt like a trick question to Blake. No, he didn't have a sister now, but he'd had fifty or sixty sisters at various points in his childhood. Usually, he'd just say yes or no to avoid having to explain, but he was done lying. He scratched his forehead. "Sort of. I'm an orphan, but I lived with girls all through my childhood."

Daryl lifted his eyebrows like Blake's words were unexpected. "All right then, imagine one of them had just been through what Seanna went through with Jason this past year, and here I come along, having put her through more lies and deception, knocking on your door, telling you I need to talk to her. Would you let me get to her?"

Blake imagined this scenario, except with Marigold or Desiree…or Cassidy. Tingles ran up his arms. "No fucking way."

Daryl gave him a smile like he was a school teacher delivering a bad grade. He patted Blake on the shoulder. "Let her be, will you? I know it's tough, man, but if you love her, you want what's best for her, don't you?"

Blake nodded, glancing around the apartment, thankful he'd come at a time she wasn't home, wondering if he would ever instinctively know right from wrong again.

Daryl gave him a little nudge, guiding him toward the door. "I appreciate your being a standup guy about this. It's the right thing to do."

Blake turned to Daryl just as he was about to shove him out the door. "Is she doing okay right now?"

Daryl gave a tight smile. "She's going to be all right. She just needs some time with her family. We've got this." Daryl winked at him, spit in his cup again, and then shut him out.

Blake stood in that hallway, staring at the closed door blankly. He couldn't believe how stupid he was. He'd garnered so much hope and possibility during the long drive, and now he was leaving, knowing for sure it was wrong for him to have come here. He got back on the elevator, his heart sinking with every floor he got away from her apartment, which clearly wasn't even where she was anymore. Her brother was seeing to that. As much as Blake hated him for what he was doing, he was thankful for him.

The door opened, and a dark-haired woman stood with two matching boys and…

"Blake?" Seanna said.

Blake stood there so long without moving that the elevator doors started to close again. He stopped them with his arm and scooted past to stand in the lobby with them. Seanna turned to face him, and so did the woman and the two boys.

"Umm," Seanna said, "Marie, this is Blake. And this is Josh and Joseph."

One kid shook Blake's hand dutifully, but the other turned his shoulder to Blake, his eyes on a spot on the floor. He reminded Blake so much of himself when he was that age and how he'd have that same reaction to strangers, which was often, considering the way he grew up. These days, he would see kids grab their mother's legs and stare with curiosity when they met a strange adult, but like this kid, when Blake was little, he just wanted the adult to go away.

"It's nice to meet you all," Blake said.

Seanna's face flushed. "Go on up, Marie. I'll be there in a minute."

"Okay," she said, staring at Blake warily.

"It's fine," Seanna said. "I promise."

It wasn't lost on Blake that she was reassuring people about him the same way she'd had to do for Jason when he'd confronted her in Seaside Sweets.

Marie tapped her son on the shoulder. "Go ahead and hit the button."

But he just stood frozen. The other one jumped in and hit it, and the elevator opened back up for them. Marie waved as the doors closed.

"Your nephews," Blake said.

"I'm sorry about Joseph. He's—"

"He's absolutely fine. I'm so sorry. I shouldn't be here." He turned to walk off, but his feet wouldn't move.

"Well, you are here."

He met her gaze. Her family had kicked into motion and were surrounding her with love and support at her time of need. They were the solution. He was the problem.

He shook his head, looking down at his hands, and then back up at her. "I'm really sorry. I've got to go."

He walked out, feeling like a huge rubber band was holding him back, digging into his chest with every step he took. But there was no question that he needed to leave this space…this family.

Chapter Twenty-Five

Seanna pushed the door open to her apartment, zoning in on her brother. "What just happened?"

He gave her that lazy, condescending look he did that told her he was the brilliant big brother, and she was the piss-ant little sister. "You don't need to be dealing with that shit right now."

"Daryl," Marie scolded.

"Run the kids down to the lobby for a minute and get them something from the snack machine." Marie lifted her eyebrows. "Please?" he asked. She gathered them and headed off, and he turned to Seanna. "Look, he seems like a decent guy, and I know you like him, but we've got to get you back into a stable life for a little while, and that's not gonna do it."

"What did he say to you?"

He waved her off. "He wanted to talk. But about what? Getting you back down to Florida? You came to me for help, and I'm thrilled that you did, but now you've got to let me help you. We're gonna get you out of this apartment and moved into Josh's room until this is all over, and once you're settled at your new job, and you've made your last payment for that piece of shit, and you've got a little cushion for deposits and all that, we'll find you an apartment, okay?"

She ran her hand through her hair. "I know, and I'm thankful, but you could have at least let me talk to him."

"Sweetheart, no offense, but talking is what got you into all this...letting Jason talk you into stupid shit like paying his goddamned rent."

"He didn't ask me to pay it."

"So you just offered?"

"No, it wasn't...look, next time, let me decide whether I can talk to my own boyfriend or not."

"You weren't here."

"You could have asked him to stay. You knew I was coming back."

"That's why I had him leave."

She beat her fist on the bar and then rested it against her forehead. Daryl was right. She had gone to him, and he'd instantly put his life on hold to help her. She obligated herself to follow his lead, as much as she wanted desperately to deviate from the plan right now.

Daryl patted her on the back. "That guy ain't going nowhere. Trust me. Settle into our plan. Start this new job. Get this lease terminated. Give Rick and me some time to figure out how we're going to get Jason out of your life permanently."

She met Daryl's gaze. "You're not allowed to do anything illegal."

"Rick's a cop. How are we gonna be illegal?" She gave him a look, and he smiled back. "Trust your big brother for once, will you?"

She exhaled a monster breath. "Once. And thank you."

He spit into his cup. "Mmm hmm. Now help me untangle these wires connected to the TV in your bedroom."

"I'll be there in a second. Let me text Marie to come back." She did, and then stood there at the bar that separated her kitchen from her living room. Blake was in Nashville, nearby. Even if he got in his car to drive home now, he couldn't have gone far. He was one text or phone call away. All she had to do was reach out to him, and he'd be back here in a flash, ready to talk to her about whatever it was he came here for…to apologize? To win her back?

"What are all these devices back here anyway?" Daryl shouted.

She let out an exhausted breath. He was right. They had a plan, and she was thankful for it, thankful for him. She just wished the utter emptiness from the void of Blake that capsized her insides would subside even a little.

Daryl appeared in the doorway. "Seanna?"

"I'm coming," she said.

"I know what you're doing."

She pursed her lips at him. "Why'd you have to choose now to be so involved in my choices?"

"Because now's when I'm needed."

She smiled at him and let him take her in for a hug.

Chapter Twenty-Six

Sebastian tossed a hand towel over his shoulder and glanced around Cassidy's kitchen. "Did we get it all?"

"Yep," Blake said. "Except the placemats and napkins. I didn't want to go nosing around in Cassidy's room for the dirty laundry basket."

Cassidy poured the rest of the wine in her glass. "Nose all you want. It's been so long since a man's been in there, it could use the masculine scent you'd leave behind." Sebastian rolled a bunch of R's on his tongue and Cassidy laughed. "Should I open another bottle?"

Blake scratched his chin, his chest going a little tight. "I'm gonna head home."

Cassidy pulled a bag out of the fridge. "Not without leftovers."

Blake took them. He knew he shouldn't, but he couldn't explain why he didn't want them without giving himself away. He smiled at her, his heart starting to empty. "Thanks, so much."

"Well don't look so sullen," Sebastian said. "It's turkey and dressing, not a kidney. I'll take more wine, but only if we can see if there's one of those fantastically cheesy Christmas romance movies on."

"You like those?" Cassidy asked.

"I know. I'm a sucker for a great love story. Toss in Christmas, and I'm a goner. Sure you won't stay?" he asked Blake.

"No, but you two enjoy it."

Sebastian shrugged and then gave Blake a hug. "Happy Thanksgiving." Blake held onto him for longer than he should have, and Sebastian finally wiggled a little. "Is that a turkey leg in your pocket or are you just happy to see me?"

Blake pulled away and then went in for Cassidy, closing his eyes and holding her against his chest. She patted him on the back. "Thanks for bringing the cranberries. I'm no good at making those."

Blake pulled away and gave them one last look, holding his hand up in a wave.

"Bye," they said, and then turned to the business of opening a new bottle of wine.

On the ride home, Blake couldn't help but run the past year over in his brain…really just the past few months. He didn't seem like the same person he was a few months ago. Some of the changes were good, and some of them scary as hell. All he knew though, was that there was no moving backward anymore, and no stalling out.

His stomach flew up into his chest as he pulled his truck into his driveway. At first he thought he was imagining things, conjuring up something in his screwed-up brain. But when Seanna stepped out of her Honda, he knew this was real. The universe was fucking him, one more good time.

He shut his truck door and made his way to her, his face

flushed with heat, even though the temps were somewhere in the fifties this evening. "Hey," he greeted her.

"Hi," she said, messing with her car keys, standing there in a pair of tight-fitting jeans and a pale pink sweater looking like a figment of his fantasies. "I'm sorry for just barging in on you like this. I wasn't sure...I just wasn't sure."

"It's no problem. Did you just get to town?"

"Yeah, I'm surprising Cassidy. I'm going to help her through the holiday weekend. I know she could have used it earlier this week getting the pies ready, but I couldn't get off work."

"How is work?"

"It's good. Well, it was good. I quit, actually."

His eyes went wide while his stomach somersaulted. "You quit your new job?"

"Yeah, I'm moving here."

His heart sank, the blood rushing down his face. Her expression turned sour, and he realized she must be reading his reaction. He forced a smile. "That's great. You're going to love it here. It's the best place I've ever lived. Of course, I'd never left Georgia before I moved here, so what do I know?"

She smiled, but it didn't quite reach her eyes. "Can we go somewhere to talk?" She pointed vaguely to his house.

He stared at it a minute, and then shook himself into action. "Yeah, sure." She followed him to the door, and Sadie came running out as soon as he got it open.

"Hello," Seanna said, bending down. "So this is the hot blonde. I can't believe we haven't met until now." Sadie took the attention with her typical indulgence, but she lost interest when she spotted a squirrel.

Blake let Seanna in, and she glanced around. "Wow, you really are a minimalist."

He pointed at the couch. "Have a seat. I'm sorry, I don't have anything to offer you to drink."

She waved him off. "Oh, I'm fine. I drank a Big Gulp on the way down today."

"Do you need to…?" He pointed at the hallway.

"Oh, no. I stopped before I came here. I actually went to Cassidy's first and saw your truck. I knew you'd be there. I didn't want to blow up your Thanksgiving by crashing. I've been waiting here for a little while. Not too long."

"I wish you would have joined us," he said, making the understatement of the year.

She wiggled a little, adjusting herself on his couch, looking down at her hands. "I had lunch a couple of weeks ago with someone you may know. Valerie White?"

He hadn't heard that name in years. "Yeah, I remember Valerie."

"I know her through Jason. She had worked with him in Atlanta. She moved up to Nashville a couple of years ago, and Jason and I had dinner with her and her husband a few times, welcoming them to town."

He thought about it a minute. "Aaron, right?"

"Yeah, good memory." She looked back down at her hands. "I reached out to her after…I got back home. I wondered if she knew you, or knew about you like Jason had." She met Blake's gaze. "She thought a lot of you— thinks a lot of you. She told me you had a reputation around that hospital as being a really good doctor."

He tried to keep his expression as impassive as possible, biting on his tongue.

"She told me nobody thinks you had any culpability in what happened. She said your ex-fiancée," she cleared her throat, "Tara, was really sick."

He nodded, trying to keep it together. Hearing Seanna struggle to say Tara's name—clearly grappling with this whole conversation—tore his heart to shreds.

She reached for his hand. "I'm sorry I left without us getting to talk about any of this, but I was so freaked out...not about what you said happened, but about the fact that you had this whole life you hid from me. It felt like I was hitting replay on the past year with Jason, and I couldn't go there again. But I see now that this is something completely different." She met his gaze. "I see that this is something we can work through together." She ran her thumb across the back of his hand, sending a shiver through his chest.

He squeezed her hand. "Thank you, for saying that."

She smiled at him. "I love you, Blake. I want to be the one you can talk to about all this stuff. Let's figure it out, all of it. Let's communicate and take this one step at a time, together. Can we do that?"

He stared down at their clasped hands, his whole body numb. He let go of her hand. "I'm leaving, Seanna, for Kansas City, tonight." Her chin dropped, her mouth wide open, but no words came out. He glanced around the house. "In fact, I've already moved out. What you see here comes with this place. My truck's already packed. I just came back here to grab Sadie."

She licked her lips, her expression searching his. "Nobody told me."

"Nobody knows. They were all so kind when I tried to leave the first time. I knew if I let anyone know, they'd try to get me to stay, and I really need to go." She just stared at him, her eyes wide. He took her hand again. "I'm so sorry you quit your new job."

She looked back down at their clasped hands. "What's the job?"

"I'm going to be a doctor again, working in an ED with a guy who I worked under in Atlanta. It's the perfect way for me ease back in. And I need to do it. I mean, people are counting on me. I've made a promise. And besides that, I need to practice again."

She nodded quickly, furrowing her brow. "Of course. Of course you do." She took her hand from his and dabbed the corner of her eyes with the back of her finger. "That's great, Blake. It's really fantastic."

"Seanna—"

"No, I'm serious. I don't mean to sound like I'm not. I'm really, truly happy for you."

His mind raced with options, possible solutions. Because losing her again wasn't something he was sure his heart could cope with and survive. "Come with me." She huffed a laugh. "No, I mean it. Come to Kansas City. We'll make a life there to start."

She smiled, shaking her head. "Oh, geez."

"I'm serious."

"I know. And that's sweet, and thanks for the offer. But I'm done following the penis." She held both hands out to her sides. "I followed it here and look what's happening. I've got an opportunity here working for Chase's company, directly. Learning more about the business, sales and beyond that. It's more than what I've been dreaming about doing. We're meeting tomorrow about it." She smiled again, and then looked down at her lap. "But thank you." She stood up.

He did the same. "Seanna—"

She let out a huge sigh and pressed her hand against his chest. "Oh, Blake. I think this is fate laughing its ass off at us. Sometimes you've just got to take the beating and move on." She walked toward the door.

He followed. "I can wait. I'll go tomorrow."

She held up her hand. "Oh, God, please no. Please do me the huge favor of a clean break. Will you? Because I can't sit around in la-la land for another minute."

She headed out the door and toward her car, and he followed, running his hand through his hair. He couldn't back out on Kevin, not days before he was supposed to start. Could he? She opened her car door and started to get in.

"Hang on," he said. "Just…hang on."

She stood there, hand on her hip, looking up at him. When he didn't say anything else, she reached up and pressed her lips against his. She pulled away, hands on his shoulders. "I love you, Blake. Goodbye."

She slid into the driver's seat and started her car. As she backed out of the driveway, he cursed himself for not parking behind her and blocking her in. Why hadn't he done that?

As her car disappeared down the street, a piece of his heart he wasn't sure he could live without went with it.

Chapter Twenty-Seven

Seanna gripped the napkin in her lap with her clammy hands. She should not be this nervous, but she'd been this way since the plane touched down in Kansas City.

Chase looked over at her. "You okay?"

"Yes," she answered quickly. "I'm just thinking about the presentation."

"Hey, it ain't all that. We're here to present an opportunity, not cure cancer."

"I know. It's just…it's important."

He smiled over at her. "I know it is. I want this to work out, too. I haven't had anybody to take poker money from."

"What about Bo?"

"Who do you think takes all my money?"

The door to the restaurant opened, and her blood pressure went up again. When a middle-aged couple walked in, she relaxed.

"Go to the bathroom," Chase said.

"Why?"

"Because you're making me nervous. Besides, you've got something in your teeth."

Her hand went up to her mouth. "I do?" He gave her a look, and she frowned at him and headed that way.

She let out a huge breath, checking herself in the mirror. She adjusted her boobs in her bra and checked her perfectly empty teeth, thank you very much, Chase. "It's just a presentation," she said to the mirror. "You've done like six of these in the past five months."

A commode flushed, and she straightened up and smiled at the woman who walked up to the sink beside her. "Hello," Seanna said.

The woman smiled back. "Nervous about something?"

"Yes," Seanna said. "I'm making a presentation to a potential...key player."

The woman took a cloth towel from the stack of them. "Aren't you supposed to imagine the person in their underwear?"

Seanna huffed a laugh. "Unfortunately, in this case, that would make this ten times harder."

The woman smiled. "Good luck."

"Thanks," Seanna said, and inhaled one last deep breath.

When she followed the woman out of the bathroom, she stopped in her tracks at the sight of Blake and Chase hugging it out at their table. He was just as yummy as she'd remembered, yummier, actually. He'd cut his hair to a respectable length. She'd loved his waves, but now she could see more of his face, which was a marvelous thing. He was paler than the last time she'd seen him...a consequence of working inside instead of out in the Florida sun. His nose was more prominent now that he didn't have so much hair down in his face. She wanted to kiss it...and his cheeks, and his neck, and his lips...

A thin, blonde woman came up behind him, putting her arm on his back. Seanna's stomach dropped as Blake returned the touch, reaching for her arm. He turned to Chase and made introductions, both of them beaming with smiles.

She wanted to crawl back into that restroom and stay there until they closed. Then she wanted to beat Bo Harrison upside the head for telling her Blake wasn't with anyone. How would Bo have known that for sure, anyway? It wasn't like Blake was a flowing river of information about himself, particularly his love life.

Blake's gaze met hers, and she swore her heart stopped beating for the moment. With Chase keeping the woman busy with chatter, Blake just stared at Seanna and lifted his hand in greeting.

She had to move, go over there and see him, meet his girlfriend...fiancée?...wife? With each step she took, the pain in her heart expanded until she wasn't sure she could carry it around in her chest anymore.

"Hi," she said, approaching their group.

"Hi," Blake echoed, and then silence hung between all of them.

The woman, her eyes so kind and oblivious to the awkwardness that consumed Seanna, smiled. "Hello." She looked at Blake for an introduction.

Blake blinked, waking up from staring at Seanna. "Kelly, this is Seanna Perry." He left it at that, no further explanation of who she was. What should he have referred to her as, his ex? A girl he almost had a relationship with? A woman who once professed her love for him, and then he left for a new life minutes later?

"So nice to meet you," Kelly said. "How do you know Blake?"

Seanna's mouth opened but no words spilled out. Thankfully, Chase had plenty of them. "We both knew Blake when he lived in the Florida panhandle. Do you know South Walton?"

She pointed. "30A, right? We stayed once in Rosemary with some friends."

We?

She waved at someone across the restaurant, and then took Seanna by the arm. "It is so nice to meet friends of Blake's. You have no idea how much he is adored and appreciated at the hospital. I feel like I left the staff and the patients in extremely capable hands." She turned back to Blake. "Please tell Kevin hello."

Blake nodded. "I will." She waved and headed off. Seanna met his gaze with so many wordless questions. "That was the doctor I replaced at the hospital."

The life flowed back into Seanna's bloodstream. "Oh. She seems really nice."

"Yeah, she's great. She must be taking a night away from the baby."

They glanced over to see her hugging a group of women about her age.

Chase clapped his hands. "So, I brought my associate with me. I hope that was okay."

Blake stared at Seanna. "Of course." He moved toward her and brought her into his arms for a hug. She inhaled the clean scent of his button-down shirt, wanting desperately to move over to his neck to get a good whiff there, but she'd have to save the mauling for later...if she ended up so lucky.

"Shall we sit?" Chase asked, offering Blake a seat across the table from them. The server appeared holding a bottle of wine. "I ordered wine, but if you want a beer, it won't hurt my feelings."

Blake nodded at the bottle. "Wine sounds great."

He met Seanna's gaze as the server went through the ritual of opening the bottle and pouring a taste for Chase. Seanna smiled at the server, and then messed with her napkin. She couldn't get over the fact that Blake was right there, inches away from her after all these months. He'd consumed her thoughts day and night. Even with her mind filled with the new job with Chase that had kept her busier than she'd ever been, there was no shaking him from her brain or her heart.

"So let's get the business stuff out of the way so we can focus on catching up," Chase said.

"There's business stuff?" Blake asked.

Chase winked. "You know me. Always working." He gave Seanna a significant look, and she went for her bag while he talked. "I've been working with a group of investors. We're looking to open an emergency care facility in South Walton, right there on 30A. Not a hospital, but one of those quick care places, somewhere tourists and locals both can drop in unannounced when they step on a piece of beach glass or wreck their bike on the path. We'll have nurse practitioners like they do at the clinics attached to the drugstores, but we're looking to staff one to two doctors during business hours. No on-call. When we're closed, we're closed, but we'll look at the hours—make sure we're open enough to meet the needs but not work our staff to death." Chase nodded at Seanna.

"Here's the plans if you'd like to take a look." She handed him the blueprints, and he glanced over them, his eyebrows going up.

"Looks nice."

"These are rough," Chase said. "We've got a medical consultant working with the architect, but all opinions from those who are in the business are welcome."

Blake looked up at Chase. "You want me to look over your plans?"

Chase cut his eyes at Seanna, and she took in a deep breath, her heartbeat galloping. "We want you to practice there."

Blake stared at her, and then shifted his gaze to Chase, his expression too hard for her to read. Confusion? Apathy? Contained excitement? He ran his hand through his shorter hair, leaving it tussled and sort of cute. "Wow. I wasn't expecting this."

"Look," Chase said, "I'd want you to oversee the staff. We'll hire someone to run the place—do the scheduling and all that mess, but I'd want you to be the head doctor there. I just need someone I trust to be in charge of the medical stuff. You can name your salary, you know I don't care about that."

Chase had been nothing but kind, supportive, and giving to Seanna, but when he said stuff like that she could slap him around for how rich he was.

Blake eyed Chase. "How can you know you trust me when you have no idea what kind of doctor I am?"

Chase jerked a thumb over his shoulder. "I got my first reference a minute ago from that woman we just met."

Blake rolled his eyes, shaking his head at Chase. Seanna

had done that approximately eight thousand times during the last five months she'd worked closely with him.

"Why the hell do you want to get into this business?" Blake asked.

"I see a need." He cut his eyes at Seanna, and her cheeks filled with heat.

"It was one of a few ideas Chase's financial team presented," Seanna said. She'd made sure Chase wasn't doing this as some sort of matchmaking scheme, and he'd sworn up and down he wasn't. He said he would move forward with or without Blake, and she believed him. Blake gave him a doubtful look.

"It's something to think about," Chase said. "I don't expect an answer tonight. First thing in the morning is fine." He grinned at Blake and stood. "Well, I hate to order wine and run, but I've got a date."

"A date?" Seanna said, her heartbeat racing. "When did you make a date?"

"Earlier today. Girl who works the front desk at the hotel. She's off at seven. She's gonna show me around KC," he said, waggling his eyebrows. He drove Seanna up the wall. She still couldn't tell the difference between a joke and the truth when it came to him. She found it infuriating and understood more about why he was single in his mid-thirties the more she got to know him. She also adored him like a brother.

He nodded at Seanna. "Pick up the tab on your company card. And make sure he orders something expensive." He clasped Blake on the shoulder and was off.

She watched him walk out, and then pointed at the door. "He was my ride."

"I'm pretty sure I can get you back to your hotel."

She huffed a laugh, shaking her head. "I'm sorry. I didn't mean to be dumped in your lap tonight. I had no idea he was going to do that."

He smiled at her. "I'm okay with it, trust me."

She exhaled a deep breath, her stomach knotted up like a hammock. "How have you been? Are you liking practicing again?" No matter how much she thought about it, she still had a hard time processing the fact that Blake was a doctor. She couldn't get the images out of her head of him working with his hands, his tool belt strapped around his waist, sweat on his brow from manual labor.

"I like it, a lot. It's what I'm supposed to be doing. What about you? What are you doing for Chase?"

"Everything. I'm sort of apprenticing under him. He's teaching me, constantly. I'm going to meetings with him. He's showing me the ropes of his business, putting me in charge of all sorts of projects. I'm having a hard time keeping up."

"Do you like it?"

She laughed. "I love it. It's a fun office, and I feel like I'm really valued there. He's investing in me. I think I've finally settled on what I'm supposed to be doing."

He gave her a closed-mouth smile. "I'm so glad." He scratched his ear, inspecting his wine glass. "So, you and him…"

She lifted her eyebrows. "Chase and me?"

He shrugged, his face flushing.

She huffed a laugh, rolling her eyes. "That's a big fat no. I love him to death, but I'd freaking kill him if we were a couple." She twirled her wine glass. "What about you? Have you been seeing anybody?"

"No. Nobody." He gnawed on his bottom lip, and then met her gaze. "What about you?"

She shook her head. "Nobody."

His features visibly relaxed. "I've missed you."

She swallowed hard. "I've missed you, too."

The world around them seemed to melt away as he stared into her eyes in this dark restaurant in Kansas City. She might as well be on another planet with him.

He pointed down at the blueprints in front of him. "Is he for real with this?"

"Oh he's dead real. And I swear this fell in his lap, or at least I think it did. He told me it did. But come to think of it, I wasn't actually there when the investors presented it to him."

"How would you feel about having me back in Seaside?"

She opened up in a smile for him. "Really good."

He took her hand across the table. "I haven't known a lot of love in my life. I've known caring and affection, lust even, and something dysfunctional that I don't even know how to name. But until I got to know you, I hadn't understood what people meant when they said, 'I love you.' Those used to be just words I heard. But I understand them now." He squeezed her hand. "I love you, Seanna."

Her heart filled to the brim, threatening to detonate in her chest. "I love you, too, Blake."

The server appeared in front of them. "Would you like to start with some smoked salmon crostini or a cheese and olive board?"

"Umm," Seanna said. "Can we have like two seconds?"

"Sure," the server said, but Blake must have read the question on her face, because he nodded confirmation before the server could even step away.

She reached for him. "Actually, we'll just take the check for the wine."

"Oh. Is there a problem?"

"No sir," Blake said, smiling at Seanna. "We just need to go."

A small smile of recognition came across the server's face. "I'll hurry."

The Next Chapter...

For Bo Harrison, watching Blake dance cheek to cheek with Seanna in the middle of Seaside Sweets like nobody else in the world existed was like eating a really good piece of bitter, dark chocolate. He couldn't be happier that Blake had found a woman who made him grin like a moron, but something about the way those two gazed into one another's eyes like a couple of teenagers getting ready to hop into a back seat made the void in his own life seem even deeper.

Marigold sidled up to him and pointed at Blake and Seanna with her beer bottle. "Let's try to do that."

"Dance?"

"No, be that way. Let's get all gaga and starry-eyed about one another and make all these people want to throw up."

"I don't think it works that way, darlin'."

"Oh, come on." She took his beer bottle and set it on one of the tables along with hers. "Press your cheek against mine and close your eyes and dream that I'm your fantasy girl, and we'll make it be so. Come on." She wiggled her fingers at him.

"Am I your fantasy guy?"

She pursed her lips at him and picked her beer back up. "Buzzkill."

Chase came up to the two of them. "Well, friends. I do believe we did good this time."

"Us?" Bo said. "You're the one who's spending millions of dollars to bring Blake back to 30A."

"What the hell else am I gonna do with it? Besides, it's a good investment."

Marigold pointed at Blake and Seanna. "Why can't you be like that over me? I could be your trophy wife."

Chase chuckled. "I'd be your trophy husband if anything."

Sebastian came over to them, happy as a lark. "Can I get anyone anything else? Something to drink? Barf bag?"

"I know, right?" Marigold said.

"I joke," Sebastian said. "They are a beautiful thing, those two. We should let them go home though. They've probably only had sex eighty-five times since he got back, poor babies." He grabbed for Marigold. "Come here."

He took her hand and twirled her around like Fred Astaire and Ginger Rogers. Only when he danced her in circles around Blake and Seanna did they notice.

"Are you making fun of us?" Seanna asked.

"Yes!" they all said in unison. The two broke apart, but still held one another's hands.

Ashe walked over. "You've done your time with us tonight. You may go home now and ravish each other."

Seanna's cheeks went pink. "No, we're having fun."

"Go, please," Cassidy said. "A room full of single people can only take so much torture."

Desiree walked up, pulling her hair around her shoulder. "Anyone up for a movie? There's a late showing of *Love by Spain*."

"Ooh, I want to see that," Marigold said.

"Me too," Ashe said.

"I'm out," Sebastian said. "I've got houseguests…friends from high school. They just got in today. I need to get home to them."

Blake put his arm around Seanna. "We're gonna get home, too."

"Of course you are," Sebastian said.

Blake said something into Seanna's ear, then they kissed and pulled apart. Blake nodded at Bo and they walked outside.

"Are you doing anything tomorrow?" Blake asked.

"Nothing I know of."

"Wanna watch a game?"

"What game?"

Blake shrugged. "I don't know. Any game."

Bo rested his ass against his truck. "Look man, don't sweat it. You're back for good. There's plenty of time for us to sit and stare at a television together. Go spend time with your woman. You'll be sick of one another here in a few years. We'll catch up then." Bo gave Blake a smile for reassurance.

Blake shook his head. "I hated leaving without telling you. I just couldn't run the risk of you trying to get me to stay."

"I know. I get it. And I would have tried, so that was wise."

"As much as I hated being away, I think I needed that distance to get back into it."

Bo nodded. "Makes sense."

Blake gave Bo one of those looks that made him

emotional. "I don't know what I would have done without you this past year," Blake said. "You helped pull me out of a hole."

Bo shrugged, that wire pulling around his chest again. "I didn't do anything. You're the one who did the work to climb out."

Blake's eye got a little watery. "Thank you."

Bo and his brother Dale had never been close. That was probably Bo's fault. It was hard for anyone to get between Bo and his sister Shayla. But Blake felt more like a brother to Bo than his own. Bo liked helping people, especially people he loved like family. Watching Blake go from a solemn, sullen guy to this person in front of him now whose personality was almost unrecognizable to him was serious heartwarming stuff, almost too much for him right now.

Bo backhanded him in the arm. "Go on home. Nobody can stand to look at the two of you anymore." Blake grinned like an idiot, and Bo pointed at his mouth. "What is that thing on your face, by the way?"

Blake's hand went to his face a second before recognition registered. He tossed up his hands. "I can't help it. I'm in love."

Bo rolled his eyes and shook his head. He shoved Blake. "Get out of my goddamned sight."

They went back inside where everyone was helping Cassidy clean up. Bo jumped in, moving the tables and chairs back into place. When it looked like everything had been done, they all started coordinating rides to the movie. He nudged Chase. "You up for *Love by Spain*?"

"I think I'll pass. What about a beer at Alligator Alley?"

Bo was always up for a beer at Alligator Alley. It was a mile from his house in Panama City Beach, where he belonged. He loved his friends over on 30A, but the redneck in him needed to keep his roots grounded every once in a while.

They headed that way, Bo dropping his truck off at home. He didn't like to drink and drive even a mile, and tonight he had a feeling he was going to have a few.

Chase pulled into a space in front. "You okay tonight?"

"Yeah, of course. Why?"

"I don't know. It's like you and Blake have switched personalities or something."

Bo pointed at Chase. "I was not a grinning idiot before."

Chase smiled. "Nah, that's me."

"Damn right."

"Seriously," Chase said. "You okay lately?"

"I'm fine. Just…I don't know. I'm envious, I guess."

"I think what those two have is rare." Chase nudged Bo with his big old fist. "It'll be your time soon. Hang on, is today your birthday?"

"Fuck no," Bo lied.

"It is, isn't it?"

"How would you know that?"

"'Cause I remember that now from last year. It's the same as my brother's."

"How come you're not out celebrating with him?" Bo asked.

"He's with his girlfriend. How old are you today, anyway? Eighty-nine?"

Bo didn't even have a good comeback. "Thirty-five."

"Ah, you're just a baby. I'm thirty-seven."

"I can tell by your gray hairs."

Chase put his hand to his head. "Hey, at least I've got a bunch of hair."

Bo stared at the bar in front of them. "Are we gonna be sitting here on my fortieth birthday, hopeless as we are tonight?"

"How are we hopeless?"

"Don't you want kids and all that?"

"If by all that, you mean a wife…no. What, do you?" Bo frowned, and Chase nudged him. "Let's get on inside. You never know. The women of our dreams could be right there on the other side of that door."

"If they are, fifty bucks says they're headed back home in a week."

Chase rested his hand on the bottom of the steering wheel. "Nah, you can keep that bet. Come on. I'll buy us a couple of beers to cry into." They got out of the truck and headed toward the door. Chase let Bo go ahead of him. "I've got a good feeling about this night."

"That and a quarter might get you a stick of gum," Bo said.

Chase stopped. "No, I mean it. Something good awaits us inside of here."

Bo rolled his eyes, but that little bit of hope that kept his wheels spinning lit a flicker in his heart…that or he had indigestion from the pizza earlier.

Chase held his arms out and looked up at the sky. "Universe, I urge ye to bring forth suitable women to us here tonight. Let them be beautiful, if not by the face, then by the heart. We now enter this fine establishment, where your blessings await us."

Bo eyeballed him. "You're about the goofiest bastard I've ever known. You realize that, don't you?"

"I'm good with that title. You ready, Casanova?"

Bo smiled at his friend, and pushed open the door.

To stay informed of all Melissa's new releases, bonus content, and giveaways, sign up for her newsletter at melissachambers.com.

If you enjoyed this story, please consider leaving a review on Amazon. Your words are so valuable to authors, and even a really short review is very much appreciated!

Find out whom Bo meets on the other side of that door...

Seacrest Sunsets now available at Amazon!

Acknowledgements

Most people who know me have been hearing the words *Seaside Sweets* ad nauseam over the course of the past eight years. This book is the second book I ever tried to write, and has served as a tool for me as I've honed my writing skills over the years. The name of this manuscript included a V10 by the time I finally finished it, so yes, it was rewritten (at least) ten times! I know Seanna, Blake, Bo, Sebastian, Ashe, Desiree, Marigold, Chase, and Cassidy better than my own family. The idea of abandoning them at this point was completely out of the question, so I hope you, the reader, will continue to enjoy these characters in more books in this series.

With a book stretching over the span of years this one did, you can bet there are a lot of people to thank including four different critique groups and probably more beta readers than I'll be able to remember at this point, but let me try...

My writing husband, Greg Howard, has for sure heard the words *Seaside Sweets* more than anyone on the planet. Thank you for being with me from the start and continuing to take this writing journey with me even though you are soaring higher than a seagull at Seaside Beach.

Thank you to Lindsey Anderson who invited me to my first critique group and probably has read more versions of this book than anyone. You have such wonderful insights and are a treasured colleague to me.

Victoria Austin, Jessica Calla, Ellen Hairr, Cate Hart, David Kovach, Anna Landry, Rae Ann Parker, Beth Pattillo, D.B. Sieders, and Charissa Weaks, thank you for plotting with me, broadening my perspective, and redirecting me when necessary.

Jessica Calla, I want to be you when I grow up! Your industry knowledge and knowhow are perpetually saving my behind! Thank you so much for your help and for always cheering me on!

Big thanks go to Camille Kirby for advising me on medical terminology and walking me through the steps to treating a head wound.

Monica McCabe and Shannon Brown, thank you for your help with blurb writing for books two and three. You both have a knack!

Kristen Kovach and Natalie Sexton, thank you both for your cover advice and expertise!

To my editor, Trish Milburn, thank you for your keen insights and excellent grammar skilz!

To my husband, Jody, who listened as I read him this entire book years ago in its sad little infant state and told me how much he enjoyed it. Every writer needs a champion like you. Thank you for all the writing time over all the years. There are always parts of you in my heroes. How could there not be? I love you like a romance heroine loves her hero.

About the Author

Melissa Chambers writes contemporary novels for young, new, and actual adults. A Nashville native, she spends her days working in the music industry and her nights tapping away at her keyboard. While she's slightly obsessed with alt rock, she leaves the guitar playing to her husband and kid. She never misses a chance to play a tennis match, listen to an audiobook, or eat a bowl of ice cream. (Rocky road, please!) She's a member of RWA and serves as the president for the Music City Romance Writers. In addition to the Love Along Hwy 30A series, she is the author of The Summer Before Forever and Falling for Forever (Entangled Teen).

CPSIA information can be obtained
at www.ICGtesting.com
Printed in the USA
LVHW111303200919
631714LV00001B/138/P

9 781732 415607